ALREADY DEAD

CHARLIE HUSTON

www.orbitbooks.co.uk

ORBIT

First published in the United States in 2005 by Del Rey Books,
an imprint of The Random House Publishing Group, a division of
Random House, Inc., New York
First published in Great Britain in 2006 by Orbit

A CIP catalogue record for this book
is available from the British Library.

ISBN: 978-1-84149-526-2

Papers used by Orbit are natural, recyclable products
made from wood grown in sustainable forests and certified in
accordance with the rules of the Forest Stewardship Council.

Typeset in Fairfield by Palimpsest Book Production Limited,
Grangemouth, Stirlingshire

Printed and bound in Great Britain by
Mackays of Chatham plc, Chatham, Kent
Paper supplied by Hellefoss AS, Norway

Orbit
An imprint of
Little, Brown Book Group
Brettenham House
Lancaster Place
London WC2E 7EN

A Member of the Hachette Livre Group of Companies

www.orbitbooks.co.uk

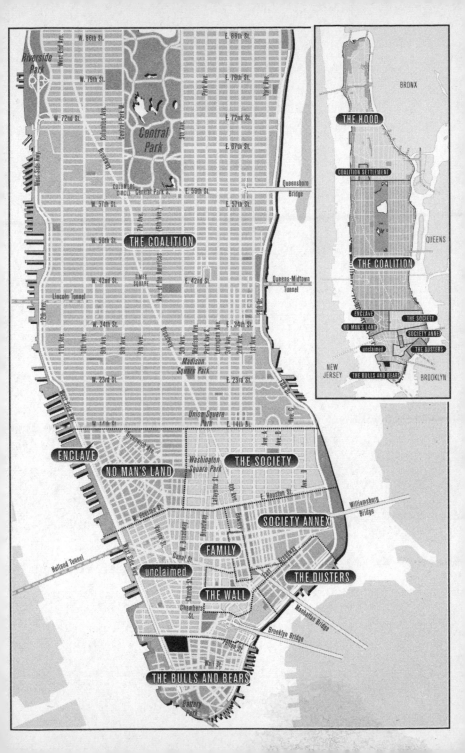

SMELL THEM BEFORE I SEE THEM. All the powders, perfumes and oils the half-smart ones smear on themselves. The stupid ones just stumble around reeking. The really smart ones take a Goddamn shower. The water doesn't help them in the long run, but the truth is, nothing is gonna help them in the long run. In the long run they're gonna die. Hell, in the long run they're already dead.

So this pack is half-smart. They've splashed themselves with Chanel No. 5, Old Spice, whatever. Most folks just think they have a heavy hand at the personal scent counter. I close my eyes and inhale deeper, because it could just be a group of bridge and tunnelers in from Jersey or Long Island. But it's not. I take that second breath and sure enough, there it is underneath: the sweet, subtle tang of something not quite dead. Something freshly rotting. I'm betting they're the ones I'm looking for. And why wouldn't they be? It's not like these things are thick on the ground. Not yet. I walk a little farther down Avenue A and stop at the sidewalk window of Nino's, the pizza joint on the corner of St. Marks.

I rap on the counter with the ring on my middle finger and one of the Neapolitans comes over.

—Yeah?

—What's fresh?

He looks blank.

—The pizza, what's just out of the oven?

—Tomato and garlic.

—No way, no fucking garlic. How 'bout the broccoli, it been out all day?

He shrugs.

—Fine, give me the broccoli. Not too hot, I don't want to burn the roof of my mouth.

He cuts a slice and slides it into the oven to warm up. I could eat the tomato and garlic if I wanted to. It's not like the garlic would hurt me or anything. I just don't like the shit.

While I wait I lean on the counter and watch the customers inside the joint. The usual crowd for a Friday night: couple drunk NYU kids, couple drunk greasers, a drunk squatter, two drunk yuppies on an East Village adventure, a couple drunk hip-hoppers, and the ones I'm looking for. There are three of them standing around the far corner table: an old-school goth chick, and two rail-thin guys, with impossibly high cheekbones, that have fashion junkie written all over them. The kind of guys who live in a squat but make the fashion-week scene by virtue of the skag they bring to the parties. Just my favorite brand of shitdogs all in all.

—Broccoli.

The Neapolitan is back with my slice. I hand him three bucks. The goth and the fashion junkies watch the two NYU kids stumble out the door. They push their slices around for another minute, then follow. I sprinkle red pepper flakes on my slice and take a big bite, and sure enough it's too hot and I burn the roof of my mouth. The pizza jockey comes back and tosses my fifty cents change on the counter. I swallow, the molten cheese scorching my throat.

—I told you not too hot.

He shrugs. All the guy has to do all day is throw slices in the oven and take them out when they're ready. Ask for one not too hot and you might as well be requesting coq au vin. I grab my change, toss the slice back on the counter and take off after the junkies and the goth chick. Fucking thing had garlic in the sauce anyway.

The NYU kids have crossed the street to cut through Tompkins Square before the cops shut it down at midnight. The trio lags behind about eight yards back, walking past the old water fountain with *Faith, Hope, Temperance, Charity* carved in the stone above it. The kids reach the opposite side of the park and keep heading east on Ninth Street, deeper into Alphabet City. Great.

This block of 9th between Avenues B and C is barren, as in empty of everyone except the NYU kids, their trailers and me.

The junkies and the goth pick up the pace. I stroll. They're not going anywhere without my seeing it. What they want to do takes a bit of privacy. Better for me if they get settled someplace where they feel safe, before I move in.

They're right on the kids now. They move into a dark patch under a busted streetlamp and spread out, one on either side of the kids and one behind. There's a scuffle, movement and noise, and they all disappear. Fuck.

I jog up the street and take a look. On my left is an abandoned building. It used to be a Puerto Rican community center and performance space, before that it was a P.S. Now it's just condemned.

I follow the scent up the steps and across the small courtyard to the graffiti-covered doors. They've been chained shut for a few years, but tonight the chain is hanging loose below the hack-sawed hasp of a giant Master lock. Looks like they prepped this place in advance of their ambush. Looks like they may be a little more than half-smart.

I ease the door open and take a look. Hallway goes straight for about twelve yards then hits a T intersection. Dark. That's OK. I don't mind the dark. The dark is just fine. I slip in, close the door behind me and take a whiff. They're here, smells like they've been hanging out for a couple days. I hear the first scream and know where to go. Up to the intersection, down the hall to the right, and straight to the open classroom door.

One of the NYU kids is facedown on the floor with the goth chick kneeling on his back. She's already shoved her knife through the back of his neck, killing him. Now she's trying to jam the blade into his skull so she can split it open. The junkie guys stand by, waiting for the piñata to bust.

The other kid has jammed himself in a corner in the obligatory pool of his own fear-piss. His eyes are rolling around and he's making the high-pitched noise that people make when they're so scared they might die from it. I hate that noise.

I hear something crunchy.

The chick has the knife in. She gives it a wrenching twist and the dead kid's skull cracks open. She claws her fingers into the crack, gets a good grip and pulls, tearing the kid's head open like a piece of rotted fruit. A pomegranate. The junkies edge closer as she starts scooping out clumps of brain. Too late for that kid, so I wait a couple seconds more, watching them as they start to eat, and listening to the other kid's moaning go up another octave. Then I do my job.

It takes me three silent steps to reach the first one. My right arm loops over his right shoulder. I grab his face with my right hand while my left hand grips the back of his head. I jerk sharply clockwise, pulling up at the same time. I feel his spinal cord tear and drop him, grabbing the second one's hair before the first one hits the ground. The chick is getting up off the kid's corpse, coming at me with the knife. I punch the second junkie in the throat and let him drop. It won't kill him, but he'll stay down for a second. The chick whips the knife in a high arc and the tip rakes my forehead. Blood oozes from the cut and into my eyes.

Whatever she was before she got bit, she knew a little about using a knife, and still remembers some of it. She's hanging back, waiting for her pal to get up so they can take me together. I measure the blank glaze in her eyes. Yeah, there's still a little of her at home. Enough to order pizza and pick out these kids as marks, enough to cut through a lock, but not enough to be dangerous. As long as I'm not stupid. I step in and she thrusts at me with the knife. I grab the blade.

She looks from me to the knife. I'm holding it tightly, blood spilling out between my clenched fingers. The dim light in her eyes gets minutely brighter as something gives her the word: she's fucked. I twist the knife out of her hand, toss it in the air and catch it by the handle. She turns to run. I grab the back of her leather jacket, step close and jam the knife into her neck at the base of her skull, chopping her medulla in half. I leave the knife there and let her drop to the floor. The second junkie is just getting back up. I kick him down, put my boot on his throat and stomp, twisting my foot back and forth until I hear his neck snap.

I kneel and wipe my hand on his shirt. My blood has already coagulated and the cuts in my hand have stopped bleeding, likewise the cut in my forehead. I check the bodies. One of the guys is missing a couple teeth and has some lacerations on his gums. Looks like he's been chewing someone's skull. Probably it belonged to the clown I took care of a couple days ago, the one with the hole in his head who tipped me off to this whole thing. Anyway, his teeth aren't what I'm interested in.

Both guys have small bites on the backs of their necks. The bite radius and size of the tooth marks make me take a look at the girl's mouth. Looks like a match. Figure she bit these two and infected them with the bacteria. Happens that way sometimes. Generally a person gets infected, the bacteria starts chewing on their brain and pretty soon they're reduced to the simple impulse to feed. But sometimes, before they reach that point, they infect a few others. They take a bite, but don't eat the whole meal if you get me. No one really knows why. Some sob sisters would tell you it's because they're lonely. But that's bullshit. It's the bacteria compelling them, spreading itself. It's fucking Darwin doing his thing.

I check the girl's neck. She infected the others, but something infected her first. The bite's been marred by the knife I stuck in her, but it's there. It's bigger than the others, more violent. In fact, there are little nips all over her neck. Fucking carrier that got her couldn't decide if it wanted to just infect her or eat her. Whatever, all the same to me. Except it means the job isn't done yet. Means there's a carrier still out there. I start to stand up. But something else; a smell on her. I kneel next to her and take a whiff. Something moves behind me.

The other NYU kid. Right, forgot about him. He's trying to dig his way through the wall. I walk over to him. I'm just about to pop him in the jaw when he does the job for me and passes out. I look him over. No bites. Now normally I wouldn't do this, but I lost a little blood and I never got to eat my pizza, so I'm pretty hungry. I take out my works and hook the kid up. I'll only take a pint. Maybe two.

The phone wakes me in the morning. Why the hell someone is calling me in the morning I don't know, so I let the machine get it.

—*This is Joe Pitt. Leave a message.*

—Joe, it's Philip.

I don't pick up the phone, not for Philip Sax. I close my eyes and try to find my way back to sleep.

—Joe, I think maybe I got something if ya can pick up the phone.

I roll over in bed and pull the covers up to my chin. I try to remember what I was dreaming about so I can get myself back there.

—I don't wanna bug ya, Joe, but I figure ya gotta be in. It's ten in the morning, where ya gonna be?

Sleep crawls off into a corner where I can't find it and I pick up the damn phone.

—What do you want?

—Hey, Joe, busy last night?

—I was on a job, yeah. So what?

—I think ya made the news, is all.

Shit.

—The papers?

—NY1.

Fucking NY1. Fucking cable. Can't do shit in this city without them poking a reporter into it.

—What'd they call it?

—Uh, *Gruesome quadruple homicide*.

—Shit.

—Looks pretty sloppy, Joe.

—Yeah, well, there weren't a lot of options.

—Uh-huh, sure, sure. What was it?

—This thing I'm working on, brain eaters.

—Zombies?

—Yeah, shamblers. I hate the Goddamn things.

—You get 'em all?

—There's a carrier.

—Carrier huh? Fucking shamblers, huh, Joe?

—Yeah.

I hang up.

It's not like I didn't know leaving the bodies over there could cause trouble, I just thought they'd sit till I could clean things up tonight. Now the neighborhood's gonna be crawling with cops. But that's the least of my worries just now, because the phone is ringing again, and I sure as shit know who it's gonna be this time.

Uptown. They want me to come uptown. Now. In broad daylight. I put on the gear.

In winter this is easy, just wrap up head to toe, pull on a ski mask and some sunglasses and go. I'm not saying it's comfortable, but it's easy and you stay inconspicuous. I'll be OK once I get to the subway, but it's four blocks from here to there, and once I get uptown it'll be another few blocks to their offices. It's those blocks between the subway stations and the front doors I worry about.

I know a guy wears a white delivery-boy outfit with white latex gloves, a big wide-brimmed white cowboy hat, and zinc oxide all over his face. It keeps him pretty well covered, but even in Manhattan he gets looks. Me, I use a burnoose.

I pull on the boots, baggy pants and shirt, then the robe. The headpiece always gives me fits and I have to relearn how it wraps every time I do this. Once it's on and feels like it won't unravel and fall off, I slip on white cotton gloves, draw the veil across my face, put on my shades and head out. Sure I get eyeballed a bit, but who gives a fuck, no one can see my face.

What I do care about is getting to First and 14th fast as I can. Even with all this cover, even with it being white and reflecting the sunlight, even though it's only four fucking blocks, I'm still getting the shit burned out of me by the short-wave UVs. And this isn't like the cuts I got last night that close right up and are gone in the morning. This hurts like hell and is gonna take days to heal. And if a patch of bare skin should happen to get hit by some direct rays? Well, I just need to be careful that doesn't happen. So I walk fast and think about aloe and ice-water baths while my skin gets roasted and my eyes tear up behind my shades and I make it to the station and rush down the steps to the sweltering, but dark platform.

The uptown guys are making a point. They could say what they need to say on the phone. They could wait for dark to rip me a new asshole, but they want to make me burn a little. They want to flex and teach me a lesson for getting sloppy. That's what's on the surface anyway. The real reason they're doing it this way is because I still haven't joined the Coalition. And the truth is, I haven't joined exactly because of shit like this. But I did get sloppy last night, and someone is gonna swing for it. So I'll fry a little to keep them happy and to keep myself alive. Because I don't want to die. Except, oh yeah, I'm already dead.

They have this building on 85th between Madison and Fifth. Nice piece of real estate. One of those anonymous brownstones that could be a consulate building or a discreet plastic surgeon's office. And, hey, right around the corner from the Guggenheim and the Met. Everything you want to know about these guys you can tell from the address: old, traditional, wealthy, powerful, and no fun at all.

I take the three steps up to the front door and press the button set in brass right next to the security camera.
—Yes?
—Pitt.

—Who?

—Joe Pitt. I have an appointment.

There's a pause and I slide into the sliver of shade available in the doorway.

—I'll need to see your face, Mr. Pitt.

—Are you kidding?

—I need to confirm your identity, Mr. Pitt.

This is choice. This is fucking brilliant. I hold the robe up over my head to shade my face and use my free hand to pull the veil quickly aside. I can feel the burn scorch my cheek and chin. I'll be bright red for a few days until it peels.

—Thank you, Mr. Pitt.

The door buzzes and I push it open and step into the foyer. It's a hardwood-and-muted-colors kind of a place. The weasel that made me strip is sitting at the security desk. I'd like to say that he's big, but that's just not the case. I'm big. This guy left big several workouts ago and has been living in huge ever since. He comes out from around the desk and looms at me.

—Sorry about the inconvenience, Mr. Pitt. May I take your things?

I pull off the robe and the headpiece and he takes them over to a coatrack while I check out my face in a mirror by the door. Yeah, I can see myself in the mirror, big deal. My face is a little pink just from being out, but there's a violent red streak across it from pulling open the veil. I can already see where the skin is turning white and flaking. It hurts like fuck. The steroid king comes back over and looks at my face.

—Hmm. I could get you something for that if you like. Some unguent or Bactine perhaps?

I stare at him.

—What happened to the guy used to be here?

—I'm sorry?

—What happened to the guy used to be here that knew who I was and didn't need to see my face?

—Oh, him.

The giant walks over to his desk and sits down so that he's back on eye level with me.

—He was executed.

No playful euphemisms around here, boy. No. *He was retired* or *dismissed*. Just get it out there. *He fucked up so we dragged him outside and staked his hands and feet to the ground and waited for the sun to come up and burn him dead from advanced skin cancer in about twenty minutes.* How do I know they did it that way? I said they were traditionalists. That's the way traditionalists do it.

—Too bad, he was alright.

Big boy just watches me.

—So any chance I can get in for my appointment? It's a really beautiful day out there and I want to make the most of it before it gets cloudy.

The giant picks up a phone and presses a button.

—He's here. I did. Thank you, sir.

He places the phone back in its cradle and points at the door across the foyer.

—Just up the stairs and to the right.

—Thanks.

I walk to the door and he presses a button on his desk to buzz it open. I stand there holding the door and turn back to him.

—Hey, who they got me seeing anyway?

—Mr. Predo will be meeting with you today, Mr. Pitt. Just up the stairs and to your right.

—Yeah, thanks.

I step through the door and let it swing shut behind me. Dexter Predo. Fuck. Predo is the head of the Coalition's secret police, and party chairman all rolled into one. He's the guy keeps everybody in line. He's the guy in charge of staking people out in the sun.

I take the stairs to the second floor. The stairwell walls are covered with portraits of great Coalition members from back a couple hundred years right up to the present. At the top of the stairs is a photo of the current Coalition Secretariat, the twelve members and the prime minister. But the truth is, most of the faces in this photo are the same as the ones in the first one down at the bottom of the stairs. Not a lot of turnover in the old Secretariat. Not pictured anywhere, Dexter Predo, a man who prefers to remain obscure.

The stairs reach up for three more flights, but I've never been asked beyond the second floor, and I'm not looking for an invitation. The upper floors are for Coalition members only. As it is I'm lucky my appointment isn't in the basement. I walk a short way down the hall to the first door on the right and knock.

—Come in.

Predo's office is modest as these things go. I mean, I'm sure all his little objets d'art are priceless, but it's not like he has a killer view of the park. Not that the shades would be up anyway. He's at an oak cabinet, pulling a file. Three guesses whose it is.

—Pitt.

—Mr. Predo.

—Please. Come in. Have a seat.

I couldn't tell you how old Predo really is, he looks about twenty-five, but he was around long before I was born. He looks up from the file, sees that I'm still standing and points to a chair in front of his desk.

—A seat, Pitt, have a seat. Be comfortable.

I sit, but I'm not comfortable, and it's not just because the chair is too small. Predo remains standing and flips through the pages of the file.

—Rough business last night, Pitt.

—Yes, it was.

—I don't suppose there was any way for you to reduce the damage?

—I don't suppose there was.

—You might have taken the time to destroy the evidence.

I look at my lap for a moment. He taps the edge of the file against the cabinet to get my attention back.

—The evidence, Pitt?

—That's a residential block, Mr. Predo. If I had torched the school the tenements next door would have gone as well. Bird and the Society would have been all over my back. Plus, there was the other kid still alive in there and all.

—I don't much care what Terry Bird and his ragtags have to say. And as for the kid? That was the evidence I was speaking of, Pitt.

I'm still wearing the white cotton gloves. I slip them off. The knife cuts on my left hand are just thin white traces now. By evening they'll be entirely gone. Predo gets tired of waiting for me to respond.

—Barring that, you might have rigged the scene. A murder-suicide perhaps.

—I'm curious, which one would have been the suicide? One of the shamblers with a broken neck? The chick with the knife in her brain? The kid with his head ripped open?

Predo pushes the drawer of the cabinet closed and walks behind the desk.

—The real question is how it got that bad in the first place.

What was it that kept you from destroying the filth more cleanly?

—They were eating the kid's brain. I wasn't gonna wait until they gobbled the second one and went to sleep. I had to go at the Goddamn things while they were feeding. They fought back. It got sloppy. Next time I'll let them have the kid.

—*Sloppy* is an apt word, Pitt. It did indeed get sloppy, and has potential to get sloppier. The police are involved. And worse, the press. Such a grisly murder with *Satanic* and *supernatural* overtones, how can they resist? It must be quelled, Pitt. It must be hushed before it draws too much attention and there are prying eyes. It is exactly the kind of business we avoid, Pitt. It is exactly the kind of business you are meant to take care of. It is why we tolerate your independence. And am I to understand that on top of this mess, there is a carrier involved? And that you failed to destroy that carrier?

Fucking Philip! I should have known. That prick never calls just to lend a hand.

—I'll take care of it tonight.

—How will you do that, Pitt, with your neighborhood crawling with police and newscasters and the curious?

—I'll take care of it tonight.

Predo stares at me. He drops the file on his desk and finally sits in his chair.

—You will need to. Tonight and no later.

I wait for it.

—We have found a patsy.

—There was a witness, you gonna change what he saw?

—No we are not, Pitt. We do not need to. The witness is our patsy.

I close my eyes.

—The child whose life you saved will now return the favor

by paying the price for this *horrid crime*. He, of course, has not volunteered to do so, but the evidence we have arranged will make his guilt a foregone conclusion by sundown. But for it to stick, you will need to see that there are no further incidents of this nature.

I open my eyes and look at him. He raises a finger.

—Be useful, Pitt. Your value to the Coalition lies in your usefulness. Be useful and inconspicuous. Destroy the carrier.

I get up from my chair.

—I'm more than useful. I take care of my neighborhood and clean up all the trash the Clans don't want to deal with. So unless you've found another slob to handle your business below Fourteenth, stay off my back.

I head for the door.

—Indeed we shall. But for now, be assured that the cleaning of last night's mess will come with a price, Pitt.

—Yeah, just like everything.

I pull the door open.

—One more thing, Pitt.

I stop and stand in the open doorway, my back to him.

—From what I understand, the boy's veins had been tapped. He had been bled. Unusual behavior for zombies, yes?

I stand there.

—Remember what your mother told you, *finish everything on your plate*.

I walk out and close the door behind me.

He's right, of course. Tap some kid's veins, take a couple pints and leave him breathing? You might as well put up a sign that says VAMPYRES FEEDING HERE, COME AND KILL US. Of course most people who heard about something like that would just think it was freaky, but there are folks out there who know. And those are exactly the ones we don't want around. Which is why my apartment is so hard to get into.

At my place on 10th between First and A, I have to punch a code into the street door to get into the vestibule, then open two locks to get into the building hallway. After that my door is the first on the left. It looks normal, but it's a factory door I salvaged. I had to rebuild the frame with steel bolsters so it could carry the weight, but it was worth it. If you want to bust into my place your best bet is to go through the walls.

I open the three-key lock, turning all the keys in the right order to keep the alarm from going off inside. I step in, close and lock the door and enter the five-digit code into the keypad that rearms the system. No one would hear the alarm if it did go off, not the neighbors or the police or even me. All that would happen is the lights inside would flash on and off to tell me someone was trying to get in, and a beeper I carry at all times would start to vibrate. And if I was at home, I would wait for whoever it was to get in, and then kill them and drink their blood. But that's just me.

I walk down the short hall to the living room, take off the burnoose and toss it on the couch. I want to get cleaned up, but I don't go into the bathroom on my right or through the kitchen to the bedroom. Instead I go to a spot in the living room, bend down, flip up a small square of hardwood and pull on the steel ring hidden underneath. A large panel set into the floor swings up, revealing a short spiral staircase. I go down, pulling the panel closed behind me.

This is the basement apartment that I rent under another name. This is where I live. I have a bed, a bathroom, a dorm fridge, a hot plate, my computer, my stereo and my TV and DVD player. The door down here isn't quite as fancy as the one upstairs. I just sealed it by driving nails directly through the door-frame and into the door. But first I installed a kick panel in the bottom half, I can boot it out from the inside and wriggle through if there's ever anyone upstairs I don't want to deal with. I also have a small window at sidewalk level, but I've dry-walled over it so no damn Van Helsing can sneak in here and pull the curtains away and burn me to death while I'm trying to sleep.

I run the tub. While I'm waiting I go to the mini-fridge and check my stash. This is the extra fridge, in the closet, the one with the padlock. I pop it open and take a look. With what I tapped last night I have a dozen pints stored up. That's not a bad stash, enough for a month or more. But like any good junkie I'm always looking to lay in a little extra for the dry times. I don't need it now, I drank one of the kid's pints last night, but it will help with the burns, and I can afford to bogart a little. I take one of the plastic pint bags and go sit in the cool tub.

My entire body is dark pink, just a half shade from red. The strip on my face is fire-engine and starting to peel. I sip from the pint. The taste of the blood uncoils things inside me. It oozes down my throat and I feel an instant tingling rush as the Vyrus that makes me what I am attacks the new blood and begins to colonize it. The burns ease up and I can almost see them lighten as I watch. I close my eyes, sip the blood and think about the zombies and how I'm gonna deal with this mess.

It's not like it's my job to kill zombies for Christ's sake. But the damn things are so sloppy until they fall apart that it's never a good idea to have them around attracting attention. Last week I caught the first sign that there might be a carrier down here.

It's just after sundown and I'm lounging in Tompkins, having a smoke, enjoying a sweltering summer evening. Normal shit, just like people do. I don't have a job at the moment, no money gigs, no errands for the Coalition or the Society, and no Good Samaritan crap. Just me on a bench puffing on a Lucky and thinking I might drift over to the Mister Softee truck and grab a cone. Then this squatter comes stumbling past me stinking to high heaven. Nothing unusual there, squatters all stink, and most of them are junkie freaks and expert stumblers as well. What tips me off on this guy is the bloody hole chewed in the back of his head.

I hop off the bench, wrap my arm around the squatter's shoulders and steer him toward a dark corner of the park. His head bobs around and he looks at me and gnashes his teeth a few times like he'd sure like to sink them into my noggin, but this guy is too far gone, just enough brain left to keep him on his feet for a couple days more. Once we get away from the dog run and basketball courts, I push him down on a bench and take a look at the back of his head. Whoever opened him up wasn't dainty about it. No tools on this job except maybe a rock. There's even a couple teeth lodged in the hole.

Zombies eat brains. It's their raison d'être. It's the thing that keeps them going. Rather, it's what keeps the bacteria that keeps them going, going.

They feed one of two ways. In the most popular scenario they eat the whole brain and whatever else looks yummy and they leave a corpse. That's not so bad. Zombies don't last long. They're too busy decomposing, their flesh being consumed by the bacteria. A straight-up feeder's gonna eat a couple people and fall apart soon, say a couple weeks at the outside. With a feeder, the worst case is they get distracted halfway through their meal and leave a guy with just enough brain to be able to walk around and cause some problems. Figure that's this guy here. He's leftovers. But sometimes you get a carrier, a zombie who bites their victim without feeding. Why? How the fuck should I know? To sow chaos and fear? To create confusion among zombie hunters everywhere? For fucking company? Figure mostly it's just to make more zombies. Who cares anyway? They're zombies for Christ's sake and when they pop up you got to rub 'em out quick. The alternative is to let them go around making messes and drawing attention. And the one thing we don't want is attention. And by *us*, I don't mean the undead or the damned. I mean the Vampyre, folks like me who are infected with the Vyrus. But that's a different can of worms.

So I had a shambler, not quite eaten. Might be a carrier out there, might just be a feeder that let his prey get loose. Regardless, this guy's gonna bum around for a few days until he decomposes or someone else notices the not so subtle gaping wound in his head. So I had a choice. The wound was fresh, very fresh. With a little work I could trace this freak's scent back to where it intersected with the feeder's and then track that bastard down and squelch the whole deal right away. Or I could take the time to get rid of laughing boy before he got himself noticed. I opted for the latter. That was the prudent thing to do. Take care of the problem in front of you, then move on. So I did the prudent thing.

First, I wrap the squatter's head in a dirty bandanna I find in his pocket. Then I get him up off the bench, put my arm around him and start walking him east, swaying and lurching like we're just a couple of Tuesday night drunks out for a stroll. We walk all the way out to the East River Park. I plop him onto one of the benches facing the river and go get a bunch of rocks from the kiddy park just behind us.

It's the end of the exercise hours and people are jogging, biking and rollerblading past his face. He makes little lunges from the bench, but his motor skills are too eroded for him to catch any of that fit prey.

Kinda pathetic watching this chump gibber and drool while he jerks, and grabs at the sleek spandex shapes whizzing past. I'm tempted to trip one of the yuppies so I can watch his face while laughing boy crawls up on his back and starts biting through his scalp. But that's just the reactionary in me. Fucking yuppies are ruining my whole neighborhood.

I get my rocks, take them back over to the bench and start filling up the squatter's pockets. He paws at my head and tries to take a bite. I push his hands away and shove him back against the bench, kind of like trying to get a restless child dressed for school. Soon enough I have his pockets stuffed with stones. I get him up and over to the handrailing between the river and the path. We stand there like we're enjoying the view of Queens and the Domino Sugar sign. I wait for a break in the jogging path traffic. Then I wrap my arm around his waist, lean forward and flip him up and over the railing with a little hip toss. He splashes into the water. Maybe he makes a noise before the stones drag him under, but I couldn't say for sure.

Did he feel anything? Did he panic as the water filled his lungs? Probably. It's not like I'm out here doing mercy killings. This was a sponge job. Wipe up the spill and get rid of it. So I waited to see that he didn't bob up then I trotted over the pedestrian bridge across the FDR and caught a cab. Back in Tompkins I tracked the squatter's scent to a public garden on 12th where it got mixed up with the flowers and plants and children and families and I lost it.

Anyway, that's how I got into this current mess, being prudent.

After I get back from uptown and take my bath, I stretch out on the bed to catch up on the sleep I lost this morning, but my sunburn and memories of the scolding I took off Predo keep me awake. That prick is just like any one of my foster parents, or the youth authority counselors, or the cop of your choice. He likes putting people in their place, gets a charge out of it. And me? Every time one of his kind of prick tells me to shut up or sit down or get up against the wall it just makes my stomach bunch up and boil over and I start saying things that get me into trouble.

Thinking about Predo reminds me that he knew about the carrier, knew soon enough to get a crew down here to rig the scene. And that makes me think about Philip. I slipped up and told Philip about the carrier this morning when I was still half asleep. And that gets me pretty fucking pissed at Philip. And why was Philip calling me first thing in the morning? It was like he already knew the mess was mine. Like maybe he had been following me around and maybe caught at least part of last night's action.

Philip is a turd. He's a toady weasel, likes to hang around and try to get close to the Clans or some of the Rogues. Makes him feel like he's connected, inside the velvet rope. Thirty years ago he would've been sucking up to the Studio 54 crowd. Of course he has no official status, no affiliations. He'd like to be infected, has a hard-on for the Vyrus, but the big Clans don't go in for that kind of thing, and he's too chickenshit to approach any of the small ones. Those small outfits are a little too unpredictable. Some Renfield like Philip shows up looking to be infected, they

F/2145116

say sure, and the chump ends up tapped out and floating in the river.

But the Coalition has given him an unofficial sanction. He's just servile enough for them. They hand him some shitty errands that even I wouldn't take and they slip him some cash. He's not a *total* Renfield, mind you, not a full-blown bug eater. But that's just because a bug would look a little too much like food to this pill-popping, emaciated speed freak.

Anyway, it's Philip's connection to the Coalition that's gonna keep me from wringing his head off when I get my hands on him.

And it's not like the Coalition is all I have to worry about. I haven't even heard from the Society yet. When Terry Bird and that crew find out I was involved in this, there's gonna be hell to pay. And they will find out. Anything busts below 14th and Bird knows.

After the sun goes down I cover my burns in aloe and put on a clean pair of jeans and a loose black shirt. While I'm getting ready I flick on the TV to look at the news, and there he is, the kid from last night, the one didn't get his brain eaten.

Cops are leading him up the courthouse steps downtown. He's surrounded by a press mob. The announcer is telling me his name is Ali Singh and that he's a twenty-one-year-old marketing major at NYU. Ali is being charged with a couple of last night's grisly murders. The authorities suspect the others were committed by his victims. They're looking at the whole mess as some kind of ritual-cannibal-murder-suicide pact. A murder weapon with Ali's prints was found in his room along with Satanic materials and *trophies* from one of the victims.

Ali looks drugged; slack-faced and dead-eyed. Cameras are crammed in his face and flashes explode at point-blank range. It'll only take a week or two for him to be convinced that he did it. Another couple weeks of evaluation and the case gets pleaded to insanity and Ali spends the rest of his life in a facility for the criminally insane. Could have been worse. Could have been me.

I turn off the news and walk over to Niagara at the corner of 7th and A. It's about nine and the place is dead, the hipsters won't start crowding in till eleven.

The bartender is a guy named Billy. He's floated around the East Village working the bars for the last nine, ten years. Far as he knows, I'm a kind of local tough guy does work for people who need it; some arm bending and maybe some PI type stuff. While back I bounced for a couple months at a place called the Roadhouse, Billy was working there at the time and we got to know each other a bit.

He comes cruising down the bar. Good-looking guy, thirtyish, wearing pleated gabardine pants, two-tone loafers, and a silk Hawaiian print shirt. Got his hair slicked back and tattoos of dice and eight balls and bathing beauties on his forearms. And as greasy a greaser as Billy is, he is far from the greasiest that'll be cramming into this greaseball haven come midnight.

—Yo, Joe, whaddaya know?

He stops; his face freezes.

—Jesus fuck! Whad happen ta yer fuckin' face?

—Tanning bed, those things are dangerous.

He blinks, slowly, a grin starting to tug the corner of his mouth.

—Yeah?

—Yeah, industry doesn't want you to know, but there are almost as many tanning-bed-related deaths a year as highway deaths.

—No shit?

—I barely got out, man.

He takes another look at the severe scorch on my face and nods his head.

—Bull.

—Sunlamp?

He squints his eyes. I hold up my right hand in pledge. He shakes his head.

—Hey, man, ya done wanna tell me, ya done gotta, but hey, done fuck wit' me.

I've been working on Billy's accent since I met him, and still don't know where the hell he's from. He claims to be Queens born and bred, but he sounds more like a French Canadian educated in Boston.

I shrug my shoulders in surrender.

—Kitchen accident. No shit, I fell asleep with my head in the microwave.

He laughs and wipes at the bar with the rag he keeps tucked in his belt.

—Yeah, baked ya fuckin' brains too, bub. Whad ya drinkin'? Blood.

—'Bout a bourbon? Whatever's on the rail is fine.

—Heaven Hill comin' up.

He grabs a rocks glass and fills it with whiskey while I look the place over. The Niagara is skinny around the bar then opens up into a big back room, but that area is kept roped off until the crowd builds up later and the cocktail waitress comes on. No sign of Philip. Billy plops the drink down in front of me.

—There ya go, Mr. Marlowe, one cheap bourbon onna house.

—Thanks. Seen Philip around?

—Naw, not yet. He'll be in later.

—You see him first, don't tell him I'm looking.

Billy nods his head.

—Sure thing. He owe ya money, something?

—Something.

—Well look, guy owes *me* money, two hundred fiddy and change. Get my coin outta him while yer shakin' 'im down, an I'll wipe yer tab.

—I ain't got a tab here, I pay for my drinks.

—That's right. Get my cash an I'll see ya ain't got no tab the next month or so. Everythin' onna house. Even the top shelf, you start ta feelin' fancy.

—I'll see what I can do.

Billy puts out his hand to shake, then slides back down the bar to work on a little number sporting the inevitable Betty Page cut and fishnets. I check her out. Nice package, round ass peeking over the edge of the stool, low-cut vintage dress with pale white cleavage pushed up out of a red lace bra. Billy makes out well with that kind of action. Hell, Billy makes out well with most kinds of action. Just one of those guys. Me, I haven't had a woman in over twenty-five years. Fooled around some, sure, but the whole deal I haven't had in about a quarter of a century. Long story. I look at the number's ass again then look away. I don't need to do that. I want to torture myself I can call Evie later.

I sip my cheap booze and smoke Luckys and watch the crowd build. Around ten they open the back room and I move there. All the time I'm thinking I should be out looking for the carrier. Instead I'm here in greaser heaven watching all the wannabes compare their latest Sailor Jerry knockoff tattoos while they try to hook up with chicks in vintage dresses and sling-back pumps. I'm here because the only damn lead I maybe have on the carrier is Philip. The toad knows something and I'm gonna get it out of him.

Just before eleven the cocktail waitress drifts over and

tries to hand me a fresh drink. I look at the glass she's holding and shake my head.

—I didn't order anything.

—Yeah, I know.

She puts the glass in my hands.

—It's from Billy.

She nods at the little napkin under the glass.

—I think he likes you.

I look at the napkin. It has a note written on it: *He's here.* I look up. The cocktail waitress is still standing there.

—What?

—You know, you should put something on your face for that burn.

—Great, thanks for the tip.

She snorts.

—Yeah, thank you for the tip, too. *Not.*

She starts to walk away and I put a hand on her shoulder. She shrugs it off.

—Easy, bruiser.

—Yeah easy. Wait a sec.

I dig in my pocket and come up with a few twenties and put one on her tray.

—That's for the delivery service. You know a tall skinny guy named Philip, hangs out here?

—Sure.

—He just came in, right?

—Yeah, he's in the crowd up by the door.

I drop another twenty on her tray.

—Do me a favor; take the guy a drink, one of those fancy Scotches is what he likes. Tell him it's from a chick back here, she wants him to come say hi.

She looks at the money.

—What do I tell him if he asks who she is?

—Tell him she's the one with the Betty Page haircut.

She heads over to the bar. I peek over the crowd and see Philip's pomp towering over the crowd. His hair is bleach blond, piled about ten inches high into a cliff that sticks out half a foot beyond his forehead. I see the cocktail waitress walk away from the bar with a McSomethingorother on her tray. She maneuvers through the press of bodies till she reaches Philip. His pompadour dips as he listens to what she has to say. She points in the direction of the back room and he starts to pick his way over. Someone steps out of the bathroom. I quickly pop in and stand just inside, the door half-open. A guy tries to crowd in.

—Occupied.

He looks at me standing there clearly not using the can for its intended purpose.

—C'mon, man, I got to take a leak.

—Go piss in your shoe, Jack.

He opens his mouth to say something else and I take a step toward him. I stand six three and go two hundred and change. He lines up for the ladies' room. Just then Philip sashays by looking around for whatever kind of chick would be buying him a drink. I grab a fistful of his pink Rayon shirt with a black cat motif, drag him into the john and kick the door closed. He spills his Scotch and stares at it on the floor.

—What the fuck!

Then he looks up and sees that it's me.

—Oh, Joe. Jesus, Joe, what happened to your face, man?

And I start twisting his neck, trying to decide if I should pop his head off.

The thing is, it's not as easy to pop off someone's head as

you might think. I settle for forcing his face into the toilet bowl and flushing it a couple times. He comes up gasping.

—The hair, man, the hair!

I slam him against the wall.

—That the only thing on your mind, Phil, your hair?

—Why would I have anything on my mind, Joe? You know me, I don't like to think, it just gets me in trouble.

—You got that right, buddy. Hey, I ever thank you for that call this morning?

He looks a little confused at my change in tone.

—Uh, no, no you didn't.

—Well, hell, that was sure inconsiderate of me.

I reach in my pocket, grab a few bills and tuck them into the breast pocket of his shirt.

—Well thanks, Joe, but you don't gotta do that.

Automatically, he has pulled a comb out of the back pocket of his painted-on black jeans and started to poke at his hair, trying to resculpt it.

—No, I do. I owe you one there. That was good looking out, letting me know the heat was on like that. Too bad I got a call from uptown just about a second later.

His hands are on automatic pilot, crawling over the gooey mound on top of his head.

—Yeah? Sorry I couldn't give you more of a lead there.

—Ya know the real drag about all this, Phil?

—Aw, man, don't call me Phil, ya know I hate it.

—You're right. Philip. I'm sorry. Ya know the real drag about this, Philip?

He's got one hand above his head holding the pomp in place while his other hand digs in his back pocket for his can of pomade. He's staring straight up so he can keep an eye on the overhang while the restoration continues.

—Naw, man, what's the real drag?

I grab a huge greasy handful of his hair and jerk him up onto his tiptoes.

—It's the way they made me crawl up there in the middle of the day. The way Dexter Predo knew all about the carrier when I hadn't told anyone but you. The way you called me first thing when you heard about the mess, like you already knew I was involved. That makes me wonder if maybe you were spying on me. Which makes me wonder if maybe you were spying on me for Predo and the fucking Coalition.

I let him drop to the floor, his pomp a hopeless ruin, and turn to the sink to wash the grease off my hands. Philip sits on the floor, hair finally forgotten.

—Jesus, Joe, you crazy or somethin'? Me spyin' for the Coalition? I mean, hey, even if I would do somethin' like that, you know them tight-asses wouldn't have me on the regular payroll or nothin'. You know that. I mean sure, maybe I pick up some change from them, I got a loose piece of information or they got somethin' shitty ta be done or somethin'. But spyin'? Hell, they got pros for that. And even sayin' I wanted ta spy for the Coa-fucking-lition, and even saying they would have me, I wouldn't never take a job ta spy on *you*, Joe. That's just something I wouldn't never do, you know that. Ya got ta know that.

I turn from the sink, wiping my hands on a paper towel.

—So what are you saying, Phil, you saying I'm wrong here? I'm lying?

—Aw, no, man, no. I know you know what you know and all. If you're sayin' Mr. Predo knew somethin', well, he musta known it. All I'm sayin' is, he didn't never get it from me. I'm just sayin' I didn't ever call the guy at all. I got off the phone with you I figured maybe you'd be slipping me some coin later, so I went out lookin' ta score. You know me. I didn't never even get it in my head to call Mr. Predo or none of them guys. You tell me there's a carrier? Well, hell, I just figure you must be probably takin' care of it for the Coalition anyway. No change in it for me if I give them a call, now is there? So why'd I call them? Huh, Joe, why'd I call them?

He's doing his best to come across sincere, looking me in the eyes, his pupils pinned out from whatever kind of bennies he got his hands on tonight.

—How much money you got on you, Phil?

—Well, uh.

He pulls the bills I gave him out of his breast pocket and counts them.

—Looks like I got about fifty here.

—What other money?

He pats at his pockets, gives me a hopeless look and shrugs his shoulders. I squat down and put my face close to his.

—You might be close to getting off the hook here, Phil. I suggest that now is not the time to start fucking with me.

He nods and starts digging into his pockets, turning them inside out. A handful of change, his hair goop, a pack of Dentyne, a baggie full of about twenty little black capsules, and a small wad of cash all spill out onto his lap. I grab the cash and give it a quick count. Hundred and eighty bucks. I hold the bills in front of his face.

—I'm giving this to Billy, toward what you owe him.

—Sure, sure, I mean, that's what I had it on me for was ta give ta Billy for what I owe him.

I stand up.

—Yeah, right. Do what you want with the fifty, that's for the phone call. But pay Billy off before Monday.

—Yeah, before Monday, no sweat, Joe.

I bend over, pick Philip's comb up off the floor and toss it at him.

—Fix your hair, Philip, it looks like crap.

Walking past the bar I get Billy's attention and slip him the buck eighty. He counts it and smiles.

—S'more than I thought he'd cough up.

—Yeah. He'll come through with the rest by Monday. He don't, give me a call.

—Thanks, Joe. Ya gonna stay, start runnin' up that tab? Got some sweet Betties in here t'night. I could maybe hook ya up.

—Thanks anyway, Billy, I got work to do.

He nods and waves and gets back to shaking martinis. I squeeze through the crowd, out the door and onto the hot street.

The problem with Philip is, even when he's telling the truth, it looks like lying. But he has a point. The Coalition wants to keep an eye on me they got better ways of doing it than him. They really want to keep an eye on me they'll send someone down here far more subtle and dangerous. Then again, a hundred eighty is a lot of cash for him to be packing, and he would have needed more to score the speed he was carrying. He got that money somewhere. Damn it. He's dirty on something, but I don't have time to dig it out right now. The carrier is still out there and I don't know any more than I did before. Except that maybe I do.

If Philip is telling the truth, then Predo is keeping an eye on me some other way. Which means the Coalition is keeping tabs on me personally, or the whole neighborhood, or both. Which means something is going on down here. And I don't have any idea what it is. My only move is to try and find the carrier, just like they want me to. So I go home and get my guns.

Killing a zombie isn't complicated, it's just hard. The first problem is that the damn things are not quite alive in the first place. Or not quite dead. I'm not really sure which it is. The way it is, these things, they've been infected with a flesh-eating bacteria. This bacteria is slowly consuming all their soft tissues, muscle, fat, blood, cartilage, you name it. But mostly it's eating their brains. The catch is that the bacteria can only eat living tissue. So more than anything else in the world, this bacteria wants to keep its host alive and breathing, because once the host dies, I mean really finally croaks, the bacteria goes soon after. And what this bacteria does to extend its own life span is it pumps the host body full of endorphins and adrenaline and serotonin and all kinds of naturally occurring crap that kills pain, induces euphoria, and keeps a body moving. And to replenish these chemicals the bacteria gives its zombie a taste for human flesh and, in particular, for brain matter.

So, for the sake of argument, say you have a zombie in front of you and you want to kill it. Well the best, quickest, and easiest thing to do is sever the connection between its brain and the rest of its body. This may not in actuality kill the host, but not even the zombie bacteria can move a host once its brain stem is hacked or its neck is snapped. Now, say you have two or more zombies standing there and you want all of them dead and you don't really have any practical zombie-killing experience to draw on. In that case you might try pulling out your large-caliber handgun and shooting them in the heart. You could try for the face, but unless you hit the brain stem or blow out some really enormous chunks of gray matter, they're gonna keep coming after you. So just go for the heart. Explode the heart and the machine can't run no matter how hard the bacteria works. You could also strangle or drown or burn or blow up or hang or chop up or push from a tall building your average zombie. As long as

you stop the heart or the brain or just cause massive physical trauma, you're gonna kill the thing. But we're talking
about finding a quick and easy method here. So my advice
is use a gun and a lot of bullets, just like if you were trying
to kill your wife or husband.

I keep my guns in a gun safe in the back of my closet down
in the secret Vampyre room. Not that I have any little kids
running around I need to keep away from the guns. I had
any kids I'd get rid of the guns. Nothing more dangerous to
the life of a child than a house full of firearms. Nothing
more dangerous except maybe a parent.

No, I keep my guns locked up because on bad days,
really bad days, it makes it that much harder for me to
get my hands on them and go walking through the streets
killing random strangers until the police come and shoot
me down. Not that I get that urge too often. Just when I
haven't had blood for about a week and the alien thing in
my veins starts burning me from the inside out and I start
thinking about cutting open my own wrists so I can suck
at them.

I'm not one of those guys gets all breathy over his guns.
I have two, one is a small, reliable revolver and one is a big,
nasty automatic that holds a lot of bullets. I got both of them
off of dead guys and I know just enough about the guns to
shoot them straight, keep them clean and make sure they
never get pointed at me. In the general course of life these
things never see the light of day. And I'm not just trying to
be funny. I mean things like this carrier are pretty rare even
in my life, so I don't have much use for guns and they usually
stay in the safe where they belong. The good thing about
the guns is that when you shoot someone, nobody looks twice

at the corpse. As opposed to a dead body with, say, half of its brain gone and its head chopped off.

I load the guns and pocket some extra ammo. I'm on my way back upstairs when I think about the blood in my fridge. I had a pint last night after my fight with the shamblers and another today to help with my burn. Normally I keep it to one pint every few days. That's enough to keep me healthy and take the edge off the hunger, but I'm going hunting and every little bit helps. Another pint and I'll be primed, the top of my game. I open the fridge. Eleven pints. I don't like to let my stash get much below ten pints. If I take another one I'll need to replenish the stock in the next day or two. I think about the three zombies last night and how close the girl came to cutting my eyes out. I grab one of the little bags. I suck it dry, standing there in the middle of the room, and it makes me feel the way it always makes me feel, it makes me feel alive.

There's a patrol car parked out front of the abandoned P.S. on 9th Street. A couple police barricades fence off the court-yard and the doors are sealed with yellow tape. The crime scene has been worked already, but the cops will keep it sealed until curiosity dies down and they don't have to worry about any freaks breaking into the building to party in the death room. As it is, a few people are on the sidewalk across the street, pointing at the school and taking pictures with their phones. If the Coalition hadn't fingered the kid this place would be rabid with cops and newshounds, and I wouldn't be able to get anything done at all.

I circle around to the 10th Street side of the building. The rear entrance has been long boarded up. No cops neces-sary here. A trio of club kids walks loudly west. I wait for them to turn the corner, then I take three running steps, jump six feet straight up, grab a window ledge and clamber up the security screen that protects the broken glass behind it.

It takes me less than a minute using the window screens and bricks to scuttle up the wall to the roof of the school. The two pints I drank today have me peaked. I walk on the balls of my feet to the roof access door and inspect the lock. Old, rusted, I could force it easy. Instead I slip the picks from my back pocket. I wiggle the tension wrench into the lock then tease a hook past it and rake the pins. This keyed up, I can feel and hear each tiny click as I slide the remaining pins into place. I rotate the wrench, the lock pops open and I'm inside. Pitch dark. I leave the door ajar to admit the ambient light of New York City. My pupils grow to the size of dimes. It's not exactly clear as day, but I'll be fine.

The air is dank and thick with mold. Graffiti covers the walls. I hear a scamper of rat claws ahead of me, and then the rat freezes, sensing something large and dangerous. It's right, I am dangerous, but not to it. Animal blood may as well be salt water as far as the Vyrus is concerned.

I feel a slight shifting of the air. The door I've left open is drawing the warmer air up and out of the school. I follow the draft backward and find the stairwell. I descend three flights to the ground floor, sniffing at the thin trail of air wafting up past me, picking out details from the last twenty-four hours. I can smell the decay of the zombies, the urine of Ali Singh, the nameless blood and brains of the other boy. I can smell my own slightly feral scent and the Ivory soap I use in the shower. Fresher than the rest is a heavy overlay of sweaty cop, coffee and fingerprint powder, and the excited tang of news reporters. Under it all, the heavy, damp rot of the building.

I retrace my steps to the room where the killing took place. The door has no lock, but the cops have sealed it with the inevitable yellow tape, the era's icon for tragedy. I tear it off and open the door. It reeks inside.

Normally in these things someone would have been here by now with a bucket of bleach to get things sterile, but I guess the cops want to leave the crime scene intact until they have a confession out of Singh. Result: taped body outlines, dried blood, dried urine, dried vomit from whoever found the slaughterhouse, and oh yeah, dried brains.

I pick out the zombie smell from the others and walk slowly around the room separating the scent into three distinct strands. There's the girl's musky undertone, the rank underarm stink of the one whose neck I snapped, and the hair product used by the guy I stepped on. Now that I have the zombie smell isolated into the three individuals I know of, I sniff for any other signatures hiding in the mix. It's not there. No sign of another zombie, the carrier.

But the girl's musk.

Why musky? A stale musky sex scent. That's what I smelled on her last night before I got distracted by Singh. Zombies don't have sex, do they? Shit, I don't know. I walk over to where the taped shadow of her body is outlined on the floor and take a deep breath through my nose.

I filter out the other smells and focus on hers. The youth of her flesh. She was young, maybe seventeen, eighteen. The rot under the living flesh, brought on by the bacteria that was eating her alive, eating her dead. The acid smell of the cosmetics coloring her eyes and mouth and nails midnight black. The compost odor when her bladder and bowels released after I stabbed her in the neck. Perfume, sweat, a fungus in her Doc Martens. All that, and a sweaty musk. Someone rubbed against her, touched her. Someone fucked her. Not today, but recently, since she was infected. I try to imagine the sicko that would have sex with one of these things while it pawed at him and tried to take a bite out of his brain, the bastard that would mate with the bacteria inside this dead girl.

I take one more deep breath to fix the musk smell in my mind so that I can pick it out when I find it again. That's when I notice something is missing. I take another whiff, and I catch it. An absence. Throughout the room, little patches of nothing in the matrix of odors. Slight erasures sprinkled across the air where something has absented itself from the catalogue of the room's history. I close my eyes. I inhale and try to capture one of the absences, to trace it step-by-step across the room and re-create what this thing might have done here.

And it is this deep level of concentration that allows someone to sneak up behind me and hit me on the back of the head with a somewhat immature whale.

The sound of bickering wakes me and tells me exactly where I am. I peel an eye open for confirmation, and sure enough, here I am in the squalid tenement basement headquarters of the Society. I'm on a dingy cot in an alcove. In the middle of the room three people are standing around a rickety card table under a single bare lightbulb. The two guys doing the bickering are Tom Nolan and Terry Bird.

Tom reads about twenty-five, but carries a few more actual years. He's got the blond dreads and washed-out clothes of the downtown radical, along with the requisite number of piercings and tattoos. Terry is older looking, say fifty or so. His style is more old school: ponytail, beard, John Lennon glasses, Earth Day T-shirt and Birkenstocks; that kind of thing. The third is Lydia Miles. Call her twenty, short dark hair, leather pants, white tank top, bodybuilder muscles, and an upside-down pink triangle tattooed on her shoulder. Just another ragtag band of East Village radical-socialist-anarchist-revolutionaries hanging out and plotting the overthrow of The Man. Of course this band of revolutionaries also drinks blood.

Lydia stands there watching while Tom goes at Terry and Terry pulls a passive-aggressive mellow hippie thing in response. Guess who's the topic of discussion?

—I'm telling you he's working for the fucking Coalition. Why else would he be there?

—Well, Tom, that may be. But to me, the real question here, and I think Lydia may agree with me, is what were you doing there? I was under the belief that we had agreed.

—Fuck your agreement. You agreed, I didn't agree to shit. This creep is hip-deep in the Coalition. He's their ratfink spy down here and now they have him, they intentionally have him causing trouble on our territory. He's a saboteur, he's a fucking saboteur and we should execute him right now.

Terry pushes his slipping glasses back up his nose.

—Well I, for one, certainly think that would be more than extreme. Even, for the sake of argument, even if it came to the point where we *might* execute him, I think our first step should be to question him.

—Fucking fine, let's interrogate him then. Let's wake his ass up and teach him a lesson about the revolution.

He picks up a short length of pipe from the card table.

Lydia is looking right at me. She's staring me in the eyes just as she has been since right after I opened them. She smiles and turns to the boys.

—He's awake.

They both turn to look at me sprawled on the cot. Tom

takes a quick step in my direction, the piece of pipe still in his hand.

—OK, fucker.

Terry reaches out and lays a hand on Tom's shoulder.

—Easy, Tom, just mellow out a little, guy.

Tom stops and squeezes his eyes shut. He turns to Terry as if he'd like to wrap the pipe around his head instead of mine.

—How many times do I have to tell you? How many, man? Don't tell me to mellow out. You be as mellow as you want, but don't tell me what to do.

Terry smiles.

—Sure, Tom, no prob. I'm not trying to disrespect you. I just want us all to calm down a little here and find some things out before we think about resorting to violence. There are always options, man, we just need to explore them.

I sit up.

—Yeah, Tom, let's explore some options.

He turns back to me.

—You just shut up, Pitt. You want to stay alive, you just shut up until someone tells you to speak. You got practice shutting up, taking all those orders from the Coalition.

I look at Terry.

—Hey, Terry, what are you doing letting this kid run around loose, anyway? People could get hurt.

I look at Tom again.

—He could get hurt.

Tom makes a move at me, but Terry and Lydia pull him back. I sit on the cot being bored. Some people's buttons are so easy to punch it's barely worth the effort. Terry and Lydia get Tom into a chair. Lydia stays next to him while Terry walks over and drops down on the cot, a big smile on his face.

—Tom's a hothead, Joe, we all know that, it only takes the slightest provocation to set him off. But we're adults here, so what say we put aside the immature mind games and name-calling and just have a little communication, air things out?

—How 'bout you buzz off and show me to the door so I can go about my business.

Terry shakes his head sadly.

—In a perfect world, that's what I'd like to do. After all, it was never my plan that you get dragged here, but here you are, and I have to say that as hostile as Tom is toward you, he does raise some valid points. So I think, and this is just me talking, but I think there is a real need here for some open and honest communication.

I start to get up.

—So sit here and communicate, Terr. Me, I got places to be, so I'll just be on my way.

Terry puts an oh so gentle hand on my forearm.

—Sorry, Joe, but there really are some questions I need to have answered.

He tilts his head in the direction of the stairs and Hurley steps out of the shadows. How the fuck I missed Hurley is a tribute to my lack of awareness. The guy is a giant. Really. Six eight and over three-fifty. And on top of that he just happens to be one of us. So what you got here is your basic gargantuan Irish Vampyre. Oh, and he's retarded. I shouldn't say that. What I mean is he's dumb as a sack of hammers. Whether he's actually retarded, I don't know.

I sit back down.

—Sure thing, Terry. You got questions. Shoot.

Terry smiles and nods.

—See, man, that's the way it should be, just two guys sitting and talking. People, people talking about their problems with each other, finding solutions. If everybody could do this, if we could get the world together like this, we could change everything, man. Like, for instance, my problem is this thing last night, this whole hassle over at the, well it used to be a community center, man, but pretty soon it's gonna be another yuppie co-op. But anyway, this thing over at the old center, this hassle with the kids and the zombies.

Tom jumps out of his chair.

—That's what I'm talking about, that right there. We rejected that term, man. We voted. They're not *zombies*. That belittles their status as victims, man. They're infected, not in control of themselves, and creeps like this stooge are still going around slaughtering them.

Terry bobs his head.

—Well, you have a point there, Tom, the term *zombie* does put the onus for their actions on them and implies blame. So what was the term?

—VOZ. Victim of Zombification.

Lydia finally pipes in.

—I'm still opposed to the use of the word *victim*. It suggests weakness, helplessness.

Terry holds up his hand.

—I think you may be right there, Lydia. But for now, as regards the conversation I'm having here with Joe, could we agree that VOZ is a valid term?

Tom and Lydia look at one another and nod.

—Good, good. See, Joe, people solving problems. So anyway, this hassle with the NYU students and the VOZs. Something like that happening right in our backyard is cause for concern. We can't really afford that kind of noise when we're trying so hard to integrate into the community, you know? So what can you tell me, you know anything about all this?

I sigh with regret and shake my head.

—Sorry, Terry, wish I could help you, but I really don't know anything.

Tom is back on his feet.

—Bullshit! Bullshit! He was there, man. He was poking around when I got there with Hurley to take a look. So what were you doing there, stooge? What were you doing there?

—He has a point, Joe, what were you doing there tonight?

—Same as you guys, taking a look. I live down here too, and I've done as much as anyone to keep this neighborhood a quiet place; more than my fair share. Do I do some favors for the Coalition? You know I do. Just like I do favors for the Society when you ask me. This thing last night, that kind of mess is bad for all of us. So yeah, after the cops cleared out I went over there to take a look.

—And what did you find?

—Well I don't know, Terry, I didn't really find anything. Which is not to say I wouldn't have found something if this joker hadn't popped up and had Hurley clock me. Far as I know it's like the cops said and that kid Singh did it.

—Really? Does that sound reasonable to you? I mean, knowing what we know about the world and the way it works? I mean, being an open-minded kind of guy, does that sound like a reasonable story?

I look him in the eye.

—Terry, I got no reason to lie. Far as I know the kid did it. But could this be, and this is what I think you're asking, could this be a Coalition deal? A setup? Well you know as well as I do it could be. Hell, it could be a Coalition op all the way down the line from the zombies.

—VOZs, please.

—Right, from the VOZs right down to the frame on the kid. But as far as I know . . .

—It's just like the cops say.

—Far as I know.

Terry looks down at the floor and nods his head.

—Well, Joe, that's fair enough. I respected you and asked you a straightforward question, and I can only hope that you've respected me and given me an honest answer.

—You know how I feel about you, Terry.

A slight smile visits his mouth and he looks at me from the corner of his eye.

—Yeah, I guess I do at that.

He gets up off the cot and gestures toward the door.

—Well that's it, you can take off.

I get up and brush off the seat of my pants as I head for the door.

—You mind if I get my guns back before I go?

—Hurley has them. He'll walk you out and give them to you on the street.

—Thanks.

Tom is glaring at me.

—That's it? We're letting him go after that lame bullshit?

—We're letting him go because it is not our nature to hold people against their will, Tom.

—But he knows something. Look at him, he's gloating. He knows something and he's making fun of us right now.

I glance at Tom as I walk past him.

—What's eating you, Tom? Still can't find a vegan substitute for blood?

He lunges at me and Lydia throws an arm bar on him. She locks him up tight and looks at me, tsk-tsking her head back and forth.

—Tacky, Joe.

—Yeah, well.

I'm halfway up the stairs, Hurley behind me, when Terry calls after.

—By the way, what happened to your face?

—Rolled out of bed this morning and pulled open the curtain. Don't know what it is, I just keep thinking I'm still alive or something.

—Be careful about that, Joe. Thinking like that, it gets us dead.

—So I hear.

Then I'm through the basement door, into the hallway, and out onto the street, Hurley right behind me. We're on Avenue D between 5th and 6th. Hurley starts walking north toward 6th and I follow him.

—So how 'bout my guns, Hurley?

—Terry says I gotta walk ya a ways first.

—OK.

We turn west onto 6th.

—Sorry 'bout clobber'n ya from behind an all.

—Yeah, sure.

We're about halfway down the block when he stops and turns to me.

—Sorry, Joe.

—So you said, Hurley.

—Naw, I mean sorry 'bout dis.

—Sorry about what?

—Terry says I got ta rough ya up some.

I blink.

—When the hell did he say that? I didn't hear him say that.

—He told me when ya was still out.

—What the hell for?

—He said it was fer be'n a smart mout.

—What the hell? I was out cold, I hadn't even had a chance to smart off.

—Yeah, but he said ya would. He said yer always a smart mout.

—This ain't right.

—Like I said, sorry, Joe, but I got ta do it. It's my job.

—Calling it your job don't make it right, Hurley.

—Whatever.

And he goes to work on me. He's pretty good about it, stays away from my face, and only cracks a couple ribs. When he's done I'm slumped down on the sidewalk with my back against a building. He tosses the guns on my lap and heads back to Society headquarters.

—Keep yer nose clean, Joe.

—Yeah, thanks for the advice.

I could go back, take my guns, kick down the door and blast away. With any luck I'd take out two of them. With a lot of luck I might get them all. But what would be the point? Their people would come after me. And Terry and me really do go back a ways. Hell, there was a time I almost bought all that Society line of crap. Terry's dream of uniting all the Vampyre and taking us public to live like *normal* people; maybe get the resources of the world to help find a cure for the Vyrus. Yeah, I believed all that. For awhile. Then I figured what I was around for, the kind of jobs Terry handed me, and was gonna keep handing me. So I got out.

It takes over half an hour for me to hobble home clutching my ribs. By the time I crawl into bed it's almost four in the morning and I'm not even thinking about looking for that carrier anymore.

The phone rings about an hour after I fall into a painful sleep.

—*This is Joe Pitt. Leave a message.*

—Hey, Joe, it's me. If you're in bed don't pick up.

Evie's voice. I pick up the phone.

—Hey.
—You asleep?
—Thinking about it.
—You're asleep, aren't you?
—Just barely. What's up?
—Nothing, I just got off work.
—You OK?
—Yeah, a little lonely.
—You want to come over, watch a movie?

There's a brief silence.

—No. You should sleep. You don't sleep enough.
—I'll sleep when I'm dead. Come over.
—No, I just wanted to hear your voice. I'll be OK now. You get some sleep.
—Yeah, sleep.
—You around tomorrow night?

I think about the carrier still out there and the deadline that I've already blown.

—Think I'm gonna be tied up.
—Maybe you can drop by the bar and say hi.
—I'll do that.
—OK. Sleep tight.
—You too.

She hangs up and so do I.

I met Evie about two years back. She tends bar at a place over on 9th and C. I was there looking for a deadbeat who owed a guy some money. She was behind the bar of this honky-tonk in the middle of Alphabet City. Curly red hair, freckles, twenty-two, wearing an Elvis T-shirt and a pair of Daisy Dukes.

I come in and ask her if she knows the deadbeat. She

gives me a fish eye while she digs a couple of Lone Stars out of the cooler and bangs them down in front of a lesbian couple necking at the bar. They snap out of it long enough to pay up, then go back to their alternative lifestyle.

—Who's looking for him?

I peer over my right shoulder, then over my left, and back at her.

—I guess that must be me.

—What you want him for?

—He's a deadbeat and I'm gonna collect on some debts he owes.

She looks me over.

—Uh-huh. You ever seen this guy you're looking for?

—Nope.

She smiles a little to herself.

—Well, you just sit quiet and have a drink and listen to the music. If this guy comes in, maybe I'll let you know. What're you having?

I lean over the bar to look down in the ice bin at the piles of Lone Star bottles, and nothing else.

—Guess I'll have a Lone Star.

She pulls one out, pops the cap and slaps it down.

—Man of discriminating tastes.

—Yeah.

She moves off to work the bar and I find a corner a little less crowded than the others. I do like she said, stay quiet, have a drink and listen to the music. And maybe sneak a look at her from time to time. There's a jam session going. Bunch of bluegrass sidemen pick'n and grin'n and playing up a storm. Not my usual bag, but they know what they're doing.

An hour goes by like that before I catch her looking over at me and she waves me to the bar. I squeeze through the hicks and nod. She tilts her head to the opposite side of the bar where a thick crowd of people are stuffed together.

—Over there.

—Where?

—The little guy.

—What little guy?

That's when I realize that a dude I had taken to be over six feet is actually a pudgy midget standing on the bar telling jokes to a group of seven people. She looks at me and gives me a twisted little smile.

—So how you gonna handle this one, tough guy?

I look the midget over, taking note of the large bulge in the back of his pants. I smile at her.

—What's your name?

—Evie.

—Nice name.

—Thanks.

—You got a bouncer in here?

—No, just me.

—Got a policy on fights?

—Why do you ask?

—Well I think I'm gonna have to rough that midget up and I'm trying to figure if I should do it in here or outside.

—Well, you do it in here and you're gonna get eighty-sixed.

—Uh-huh. Well I guess I better take care of it outside.

—Why's that?

—I think I'd like to come back in here sometime so I can see you again. Here's for the beer and the help. My name's Joe by the way. See you around.

I left a fifty on the bar and went outside to wait for the deadbeat. He came out a bit later with some of his normal-sized pals and there was a ruckus. He pulled a gun. I took it away and thumped him a few times. The normal-sized people got outraged and I thumped them. In the end I got the money, threw the gun down a storm drain and went home. The next night I went back to the bar and sat there and listened to the music. Evie did her job and barely looked at me, but when her shift was over I walked her home.

We sat on her stoop for awhile and talked about a book she was reading and a movie I liked. Then she got up to go in and I stood and she moved to the step above mine so she could look at me without craning her neck. She told me she was going up. She told me she'd like to see me again. She told me she had HIV and doesn't have sex with anyone under any circumstances. Then she kissed me hard on the mouth and went in. I never even had a chance to explain to her that I don't have sex either.

It's hard to explain this kind of thing to a person. That this thing called the Vyrus has taken up residence in my body. That it feeds off my blood, scours it of all impurities and weaknesses. That it wants only to survive, and to do that it needs more blood, so it gives me the instincts, strengths and senses of a predator. That if I don't feed it more blood, human blood, it will burn my body and scorch my veins and leave me a dry husk. That exposed to the UV radiation of the sun, it will rack my immune system and tumors will riot through my body in minutes. That it pumps me full of adrenaline and endorphins. That it clots in seconds and knits my flesh and that if you want to kill me you will have to blow up my heart or head or cut me in half or otherwise annihilate my body in one blow before it can heal. That I am a secret in the world and that the greatest defense I have is to remain unknown. For we are few and we are rotted by the light of the sun. That my body is as close to dead as living can get, and is kept moving only by the will and appetite of another organism. That I could walk through a ward of

AIDS patients and drink their blood and the Vyrus would eat the HIV and leave me with clean healthy blood. That I could walk through the same ward and infect the patients with my blood, and it would cleanse and heal them, but leave them with a hunger and thirst for more. That I could heal *her*.

One day, when I am a braver man, I will tell her these things, and then I will look her in the eye and tell her I love her and ask her to be only mine. But until that day, we're just friends.

In the late morning the phone rings.

—*This is Joe Pitt. Leave a message.*

—Mr. Pitt, I have a call for you from Mr. Predo. Please pick up if you are in.

Oh, shit. It's the bodybuilder from the Coalition.

—Very well, Mr. Pitt. Please be certain to return this call at the earliest possible moment.

I'm fighting to untangle myself from the sheets, grabbing at the phone. I snatch it off the cradle and drop it on the floor. I fumble with the phone and try to switch off the answering machine at the same time.

—Hello. I'm here. Hello?

The bodybuilder's voice comes over the line and I can hear his exasperation in the way he breathes.

—Good morning, Mr. Pitt, I have a call from Mr. Predo. May I connect you?

—Shouldn't you make sure it's really me, just in case?

—If I had any doubts, Mr. Pitt, you have just relieved them. I'm connecting you now.

There's a little click and then I hear you know who.

—Good morning, Pitt.

—Morning, Mr. Predo.

—All is well, Pitt?

Here it is.

—Well sure, I guess all is well.

—Then you have disposed of the problem and we can expect no further difficulties?

There are two things you do not want to do with The Coalition. The first is fail an assignment. The second is lie to them.

—Yes, Mr. Predo, all cleaned up. No problem.

—Good. In that case, I think I may have some work for you.

Shit.

—Truth is I'm pretty busy right now. Not sure I can take on anything new.

He pauses for a half moment.

—There are two ways to look at this job, Pitt. On the one hand, it is an opportunity, an opportunity you might say yes or no to as you wished. On the other hand, the cleanup we arranged after you bungled things at the school was quite expensive. In light of that, you might look at this job as a favor you owe the Coalition in return for taking care of your mess. I think the latter of these two versions may be the more accurate interpretation. What do you think?

Having just lied to the man I know that this is not the time to let pride have its say.

—I imagine you're right about that.

—That would be yes, then?

—Right.

—I thought that might be your choice.

—Yeah. So what's the job?

—A woman is going to call you today with a problem. You will offer her your assistance. Whatever it is she asks of you, you shall do it. Efficiently and, need I say it, discreetly. Yes?

—Right.

—The woman is of some prominence and breeding. Try to be polite.

—My specialty.

—Yes. Well, once again, my congratulations on taking care of the problem, and my best wishes on the swift resolution of this new endeavor.

—Thanks.

—Good-bye.

—Right.

He hangs up. I sit there on my bed and bang the back of my head against the wall over and over again. Predo thinks the carrier is dead and the fact is I don't have the slightest clue where it is. And if any new zombies start stumbling around before I find the damn thing it won't be hard to figure out where they came from. And after that it won't be long before I'm spiked to the tarmac in some New Jersey parking lot, watching the sun come up.

Joe Pitt isn't my real name. I grew up with a different name, but I changed it when I got infected. Lots of us do. It's not a rule or anything, not like you need to pick your secret-sacred Vampyre name. It's just that most of us leave our old lives behind, and the first thing to go is the name. Anyway, I grew up with a different name.

There are some great parents out there; parents who know a thing or two about loving and nurturing. I had the other kind of parent.

I was born in the Bronx in 1960. By '75 I was on my own, living with a bunch of other punk squatters in the East Village. It was alright. I panhandled and robbed, wore a Mohawk; drank, shot, snorted and sucked anything I could get. I got a rep for being twice as sick as any other punk on the scene. I'd fuck or fight anything that stood still.

In '77 I go to see the Ramones at CBGB. Great show. I get drunk, get stoned, eat speed, and in the bathroom some guy in a suit offers me twenty bucks to let him suck my dick. It was a different time. Suits would come down to slum and check out the scene, and some of them were trolls looking for rough trade. And I liked having my dick sucked; the money was icing.

He gets my tight plaid pants unzipped and goes down on his knees with a handkerchief on the floor to protect his slacks. Through the walls I can hear Joey and the band swing into "Now I Wanna Be a Good Boy" and I come in the guy's mouth. He stands up, pulls out another twenty and offers it to me if I suck him. I say no, but that I'll give him a hand job. He gives me the twenty. My hand is in his pants and he's leaning against me, his face tucked against my neck. I'm jerking him in time to the music pounding through the walls, thinking about the booze and drugs I'm gonna buy with the forty bucks. I'm so fucked up it takes me a few seconds to realize he isn't just trying to give me a hickey. By the time I try to scream he's chewed a hole in my neck.

He was sloppy. He left me folded up on the floor, didn't try to get rid of me or disguise the wound or even drain me and save some of the blood. A fucking slummer out for a cheap thrill. I lay there on the floor while people came in and out of the can, stepping over me to get to the pot. Some guy passed out on the bathroom floor was no big deal at CBGB, not even one that was bleeding. I don't know how long I was there before Terry Bird came in and saw me. He picked me up and carried me out through the crowd. I think he was just planning to dump me, but then he saw how much life I had left and took me home instead.

Terry got me healthy, explained what had happened. I didn't believe him. Big scene, lots of freaking out involved. Then he fed me blood for the first time, and I didn't care about anything else.

I was with Terry for three years. He told me about the Clans, how they run different chunks of territory in Manhattan and make sure things stay quiet, how they keep the Vampyre a secret. He told me about the Coalition.

The Coalition used to run the whole island, except for the West Village; the West Village has always been Enclave. But things changed for the Coalition in the sixties. That's when the Hood seized everything above 110th and Terry formed the Society and took the East Side turf from 14th down to Houston. That left the island's bottom cut off from the rest of the Coalition. Now all that turf down there is run by minor Clans and Rogues. As for the Outer Boroughs: Staten Island, Brooklyn, Queens and the Bronx? From what I hear, it might as well be a jungle once you cross a river. Who knows what the savages are doing out there in the bush? And who cares? But the real turf still belongs to the Coalition. They took some lumps in the sixties, got whittled down a bit, but they still control everything river to river between 14th and 110th.

They have the big turf because they have numbers. They find a role in their Clan for any Vampyre who wants to join, and keep all their members supplied with a ration of blood equal to their contribution to the Clan. And that's their real power, all that blood they get their hands on. Somehow. They'll keep you supplied so you don't go Rogue and feed on your own and cause any trouble, but only as long as you toe their line. And their line is invisibility. They cultivate influence in the uninfected world, but only to protect the Clan and its interests. Or, as Terry would say, the interests of the Secretariat.

Terry gave me the history and he explained his own philosophy, his plans to unite all the Clans and bring the Vampyre above ground. How this could never be done until the Coalition's power was broken, and that their ultimate power lay in their control of a vast and secret supply of blood. So I fought the fight, did what I could to bring all of us under one banner so we could step into the public consciousness together; undeniable and deserving the same rights as any uninfected person. I went to the meetings, helped to organize, and to find the new guys before they got themselves killed. Spent a lot of time huddled in basements talking newly infected fish off the ceiling. Spent a lot of time in those same basements hiding out from Coalition agents. Those were rough years at the end of the seventies. The Society was still coming together. The Coalition had *lost* control of the turf, but that didn't mean Terry had *taken* control of it. Wasn't until the mid eighties that he had enough of the smaller Clans pulled together into something big enough to be a major Clan. But now that turf is Society through and through. Me, I went my way when I figured what Terry had me lined up for.

Started with a couple jobs taking care of Rogues who were on the turf but didn't want to join the Society. Then there were some new fish that had trouble making the transition and needed to be put out of their own misery. Then there were members of different Society affiliates who maybe didn't always want to do things Terry's way, and they needed taking care of, too. So I took care of them. A lot of them.

One day I show up at a guy's place, a guy I know and like. I'm there to see if he wants to grab a beer, but when he sees it's me, he gets a look on his face; a look like he doesn't want to turn his back. That's when I got it that Terry was turning me into his whip, his cop. And I ain't no fucking cop.

I went Rogue, left the Society and tried to make it on my own. But you can't make it on your own as a Vampyre. You can't because the Clans don't want you out there on your own where you might cause trouble. So I kept running errands for Terry because I wanted to keep living on Society turf.

And when the Coalition came calling with their first little job, I did it. Because I know what's good for me. They knew about me going Rogue just like they know most things. And they knew I could move around below 14th. They figured to get an agent, a turncoat in the Society's house. They offered to pay for it, pay well. I counter-offered. So now they like to pretend they're pulling all my strings, and I like to pretend they're not. Who's to say who has the right idea?

I do favors for the Coalition because they have the juice to get rid of me if they decide they really want to. I do favors for the Society because this is their territory and they'll run me to the Outer Boroughs if I don't. Me, I get to stay Rogue, and that's the way I like it. It's my life, I can live it any way I want. And if I ever get tired of it, all I have to do is open the door and walk outside on a nice sunny day.

When I look in the mirror I see a face about twenty-eight. Under it I know I'm forty-five. I could stay younger. All I have to do is drink more blood. A guy like Predo, who knows how much he sucks down? But then again he has the resources of the Coalition. Sometimes the Coalition pays me off with a few pints, but mostly I scrounge my own blood, and the less I consume the less attention I draw to myself. It is our greatest vulnerability, our thirst. It identifies us and leads hunters to us. It forces us to live in highly populated areas where our foraging and aversion to the sun will draw less attention. Some run to the country and live like hermits, feeding off the occasional stray backpacker. Some move to rural communities, feeding sparingly, becoming emaciated and hiding their true nature behind a façade of eccentricity. The suburbs are hopeless, the population neither thin nor dense enough to provide cover. Vampyres in the suburbs last less than a year. Plus those places are soulless pits. Christ! Strip malls, housing tracts, business parks? Might as well pound a stake through your own heart and save some Van Helsing the work. Talk about a land of the undead.

Anyway, Joe Pitt isn't my real name. I threw away my real name. A guy like me doesn't need a real name.

In the morning I think about having a pint to help with my ribs, but I've gorged the last couple days and I don't want to overdo it. The ribs will take care of themselves. So I just hang out and watch some movies.

I mostly watch horror movies. I don't really like the things very much, but they're good research. Left to my own devices I'd probably take a look at *Treasure of the Sierra Madre* or maybe *Miller's Crossing*. Instead I watch about half of *The Abominable Doctor Phibes*, until I see it's pretty useless, then I pop in *Martin*. I've seen it a few times, but it's about as accurate as vampire flicks get. I watch some of the best scenes again. Horror movies are how most folks get their ideas about real Vampyres and the whole *supernatural* world, so I like to keep up on them. I'll see most of the new ones when they come out, even the slasher stuff, and in the meantime I pick up the older ones on DVD.

Couple years back I had some kid Van Helsing come at me with a cross and holy water. A Rogue in Jersey had wasted his sister and the kid had seen it all from the bedroom closet. Now he was on a campaign to *slay the undead*. I don't know how he got onto me, I think he was just hanging around the East Village because there are so many vampire-looking freaks down here. Somehow he locked in on me. In any case he stalked me for a few days and decided I was *an evil hell spawn*. One night outside Doc Holliday's, he comes charging across the street with this crucifix and a spray bottle full of holy water. I let him chase me down the block a little to get away from the crowds on A, then I took the cross from him and asked him to stop spraying me with water. He freaked, called me *Satan's pawn* and stuff like that. I acted dumb, drank the holy water and kissed the cross and settled him down. He was pretty embarrassed, ended up crying on my shoulder. I gave him a pat on the butt, told him to see a doctor or something and sent him on his way. Then I followed him to his flop, broke into his room after he was asleep, bled him dry in the bathtub and made it look like a suicide. Guys like that kid are dangerous and you can't let them run around causing trouble.

But I don't blame him, I blame the movies. That's obviously where he got his ideas and dialogue. Maybe if he had never seen *Horror of Dracula* he would have just mourned his sister and never went looking for trouble. But Evie likes them, the horror movies. I mean for real. So that's OK, we watch them together and every now and then I sneak in some Howard Hawks or Billy Wilder on her.

Around three the phone finally rings and I talk to the woman Predo told me about.

They say the King Cole room at the St. Regis is one of the most beautiful bars in New York. They're right. All that oak and those high-price hotel hookers and that Maxfield Parrish mural behind the bar, it almost makes it worth having to come uptown for the second time in two days. At least this time it's at night so I can leave the burnoose behind. The

hostess at the door asks me if I'd like a table and I tell her
I'm meeting someone. She smiles and indicates that I should
take a look around. I step into the room and spot her right
away. She's sitting in a corner of the room at one of the
small cocktail tables. She's the only person sitting alone. She
rises as I walk over.

—Mr. Pitt?

—Joe, you can call me Joe.

—Joseph. How lovely to meet you.

—Yeah.

She blushes just slightly.

—Oh, yes, you still don't know my name.

—Nope.

She starts to sit and releases a very genuine and slightly
embarrassed laugh.

—Sorry, I'm Marilee Ann Horde.

My jaw clenches. Marilee Ann Horde. Thank you very
fucking much Dexter fucking Predo. She watches me standing
there.

—Perhaps you'd like to sit and have a drink.

I sit.

—You must tell me, Joseph.

—Yeah?

—Whatever happened to your face?

The conversation on the phone was brief. She told me she
was uncomfortable speaking in detail over the open line and
asked if we could meet. I said sure, but it would have to be
that evening. She suggested six and I countered with nine-
thirty. She said the Cole and I said sure.

On the way up to 55th I made a plan for myself. Get the
woman's story and lay off whatever errand she needs run

until next week. Get the hell back downtown, go to the school
and pick up where I left off last night before I got waylaid.
See if I can pick up that musky sex scent the girl zombie
had and find it anywhere else in the building or the streets
nearby. That's not a dime-a-dozen scent. And all the while
keep my eyes peeled for whoever the Coalition has creeping
around. And if all else fails pick up Philip again. Nice plan,
should have got me somewhere. Then I found out I was
meeting with Marilee Ann Horde.

She's drinking ridiculously expensive designer vodka on the
rocks. I accept a glass of the same.
—You come highly recommended, Joseph.
—I get the job done. But I'm surprised Mr. Predo would
recommend me to you.
  She smiles just a bit.
—And yet.
—Uh-huh. Look, Ms. Horde.
—Marilee.
—This isn't really my kind of job.
—What kind of job is that?
—The kind that takes place in your neck of the woods.
—And what is *my neck of the woods*, Joseph?
  I look at her sitting there. Coy and quiet, a stylish thirty-
three-year-old beauty. She's wearing a tailored summer suit
in a subtle rose shade and a crisp linen blouse, her only
jewelry the engagement ring and wedding band on her left
hand. The stone in the engagement ring not the usual Upper
East Side two-carat-plus rock, but a tastefully sized blue-
white in a deco platinum setting. Her hair appears to be
naturally golden, and she has its length twirled up and pinned
neatly to the back of her head, just three perfect strands

dangling to frame her face and accent her ivory neck. Her ivory neck. I take a large swallow from my drink and lean back in my chair.

—Have you taken a look in the mirror lately, Ms. Horde?

—I said you should call me Marilee.

—Yes you did. Have you taken a look in the mirror lately, Ms. Horde?

—Yes.

—What would you say is your neck of the woods?

I look down at myself, the old suit, rumpled shirt and scuffed shoes that I dug up for the occasion.

—And what would you say was mine? And would you say, based on this, that I am the man for your kind of job?

She puts her drink down on the table.

—Actually, I would say this is exactly why you are the man for my job, Joseph. You see, my daughter has run away again, and I believe she is to be found in *your neck of the woods*.

She leans in, close to me.

—As you put it.

The cocktail waitress comes by and Marilee orders us another round.

This is taking too long. I figured blackmail. I figured drugs. I figured this woman would have some nasty little problem that needed to be swept up. I never figured missing children. I never figured Marilee Ann Horde.

The Hordes are one of New York's original families, one of the few dozen that make up Manhattan's *true society*. Their money came from the usual sources, oil, timber, and rail, but these days they're better known for their biotechnology holdings and HCN, the Horde Cable Network. Marilee Ann Dempsey's family was more than a few steps down the food chain, quite a bit more I gather. But she apparently made up for it with style enough to draw the attention of Dr. Dale Edward Horde, the only son and heir to the house of Horde, as well as founder and CEO/Chairman of Horde Bio Tech Inc. They've been married for fourteen or fifteen years and are one of those Manhattan couples who get plenty of publicity, but all skillfully crafted and honed. No Page Six blurbs for the Hordes. What it all means for me is that I can't shine this on. I have to find the damn kid, which means I have to sit here and listen to the whole story instead of being out looking for the carrier. So our second round shows up and I try not to be too fidgety while I listen to her.

She's leaning back now, holding her drink in her lap with her right hand, occasionally stirring the ice with her index finger.

—Amanda has done this before. As a small child, she's only fourteen now, but as a very small child she frequently hid in closets or in the garden until someone found her. A way of getting attention. Not that she lacked, but she enjoyed scaring us. She would do it in public places as well, museums, stores; just disappear. At first we would panic and search high and low. When we realized it was a game to her, we resolved to wait her out, wait for her to get bored or lonely and come out of hiding. But she didn't. I once spent an entire day in Bergdorf's waiting for her to come out, and she never did. She stayed hidden inside a rack of dresses until we found her just after the store had closed. But she never ran far, Joseph, just somewhere hidden so she could watch us look for her. Then last summer she ran away for real. Not all that far as it turned out, but farther than before. When we first noticed her missing we were a bit surprised, my husband and I. It had been some time since she had last played her little game. But then we realized she was truly missing. We searched the town house, we had our Hamptons house searched, as well as the Hudson River estate. After two days there was no sign. We thought she might have been kidnapped. We called the police, but no one got in touch with us about a ransom and, frankly, the police were little help. Eventually, after some days, we hired a private investigator my husband has had occasion to employ. He found her almost two weeks later. She was living in the East Village, *camping* the kids call it. They go down there in their worst clothes and live on the street and panhandle and sleep in the park and pretend to be homeless. I guess.

I nodded. It was true, there were more than a few well-off kids slumming on Avenue A in the summer. When the real squatters found them out they usually kicked the shit out of them and sent them home to mommy and daddy.

Marilee takes a sip and plays with her ice some more.

I make a little grunting noise and she looks up.

—Yes?

—No offense, but you seem pretty calm about your daughter being missing and all.

She nods.

—Well as I say, it's not exactly new to us, and it's only been a few days. But more to the point, we know she's OK.

—How's that?

—She's been withdrawing money from her account.

—That could be anyone with her card and code.

—Yes, she used her card at first, but her last two withdrawals were in person from a teller. It was her. They require photo ID.

—When and where was the last withdrawal?

—The Chase at Broadway and Eighth, two days ago.

—How much?

—Two hundred.

—How much does she have access to?

—She can withdraw up to a thousand a week, but never more than two hundred a day. If she wants more she needs her father or me to cosign.

—And she's taken two hundred every day she's been gone?

—Yes. First with her card, and the last two, as I said, from a teller. Perhaps she lost the card.

—OK. Did you bring a picture?

—Yes.

She lifts a pocketbook that matches her suit from the floor, finds the picture and passes it to me.

Her mother's eyes and neck, but the resemblance stops there. The girl in the photo is decked out in head-to-toe black with white pancake makeup on her face, hair dyed black, black lipstick, black eye shadow and black nail polish. Jesus fuck, she's a goth. Marilee sees something in my face.

—Yes, Amanda does have something of a fascination with the undead. So really, Joseph, you can see why it is I called you.

I look up from the photo, and Marilee smiles ever so sweetly.

I've been outed. Dexter Predo has outed me.

It's a given that a woman like Marilee has some sense of how things work, the exchanges that take place behind, beneath and above the scenes in Manhattan, the give and take of power. It is for that kind of favor brokering that the Coalition is known to a select few outside the Clans. But the fact that I have been outed by Predo indicates that she is operating at a much higher level of awareness, a level of knowledge at which most people are murdered to keep them silent.

There are people that know about us. But they are few and most play a specific role. There are the Van Helsings, the righteous who stumble upon us and make it their mission to hunt us down. The Renfields like Philip, who glom on to us, half servile and half envious. The Lucys, both male and female, who have romanticized the whole vampire myth and dote over us like groupies. And the Minas, the ones who know the truth and don't care, the ones who fall in love. Van Helsings are killed, we use the Renfields and the Lucys to serve us and insulate us from the world. Minas are rare and precious beyond value. There is only one way to know if you have a true Mina: tell her or him what you are and what you do to stay alive. Not many make that final cut.

Then there are the few men and women with true power and influence who know us. These are the ones to be feared. These are the ones the Coalition deals with and the Society hopes to sway. But the Society's goals will never be realized. We will never live in the open unless it is as freaks or prey. The people who might guide us out of obscure myth will never risk their positions and reputations to say to the world, *Hey, look, vampires are real!*

And Marilee is one of them, a person who knows, and knows I know she knows. And so on. And here she is in the Cole having a drink with me in public. And if I had any doubts before, I now know for certain that if I ever have the opportunity to drag Dexter Predo into the sun, I will do so gleefully.

She fishes an ice cube out of her drink, pops it in her mouth and crunches it.

—You see, Joseph, I know what you are, but I'm still not certain what it is you do. Are you a detective of some kind?

I'm still the deer in the headlights, just staring at her as she chews on ice.

—Joseph?

I blink once, slowly.

—I'm a man, does things, gets things done. I'm a handyman. Someone has a problem they maybe call me and I maybe help to take care of the problem. Sometimes that means I'm a detective, I guess, but I don't have a license or an office or anything.

She nods.

—What about a gun, do you carry a gun?

—Sometimes.

—Now?

—No.

—And what about the other things you do? I know about them in theory, but details are hard to come by. Mr. Predo and the few other Coalition members we have met are so circumspect.

I stare at her.

—What about those other things, Joseph?

—We can't talk about that here.

She inhales deeply, exhales.

—It's just that one hears the most fascinating stories. Is it true for instance about your sense of smell? Is it as acute as a dog's? Can you, for instance, tell what scent I used this morning?

—I can smell it.

—Do you know the brand?

—No. But it's lavender oil.

—You'd recognize it if you smelled it again?

—Yeah.

—Hmm.

—If you don't mind, Ms. Horde, I'm not very good at parlor tricks.

—We should talk about these things sometime, we really should.

—Ms. Horde.

—Yes?

—Your daughter?

—What about her?

—She's missing.

—Yes, she is.

—What did you mean that she is *fascinated* with the undead?

She takes another cube of ice from her drink, just sucking it this time.

—Just that. She is somewhat fascinated by the undead, and the dead for that matter. You have eyes, she's a goth. She and her friends, they are all interested in anything macabre.

—But when you say *undead*, do you mean in the abstract or in a literal sense? What I mean is . . .

—How much does she know?

—Yes.

—Nothing. I don't know what you're accustomed to, Joseph, but it's not as if I make a habit of meeting with . . . your people. This is an aberration. Dale and I and some others in our circle know, but we would hardly go about sharing that information. It would tend to brand us as something rather more than eccentric.

She smiles and licks the ice in her fingers. I can't quite get her. She's no Van Helsing, definitely not a Renfield, and lacks the proper sluttishness to be a Lucy. But she's something, she is definitely something. I slug down the last of my drink.

—Two more things.

—Of course.

—The name of the PI that found her last time?

—Chester Dobbs.

—Huh.

—You know him?

—Of him. Why didn't you call him again?

—To be honest, we did. He said he would look into it, but then called back the next evening and told us that his caseload was simply too great.

I try to feature a PI turning down a case from a cash cow as fat as the Hordes. I fail.

She's watching me.

—And the other?

—Hmm?

—The other of the two things?

—Oh, where did he find her the first time?

She finally bites down on the cube she's been sucking.

—Some abandoned building, a school I think it was, around Avenue B and Ninth Street. She was squatting in the basement with some other kids.

She looks at my face, which I'm sure looks like I just got kicked in the gut.

—Are you all right, Joseph? Is there something wrong?

I don't shake hands. I don't say goodbye. I take a pass on all the social niceties and get the hell out of there and into a downtown cab.

It's not her. I take a closer look at the picture while I ride the cab downtown, and I'm sure Amanda Horde is not the shambler chick I took care of the other night. Thanks for small blessings.

The school is as it was last night. Cop car parked out front on freak watch, police barricade across the entrance. I go in the same way as before. The wall is a little tougher this time with my ribs still healing from Hurley's beating. The roof door I left open last night is still ajar. I go in. Same graffiti, same rats, same breeze, same smells. I reach the ground floor and go to the killing room.

The scents are slightly faded, but essentially unchanged except for the additions of Hurley's and Tom's. The absences I had been so focused on when I got coldcocked have been lost as the other odors have drifted and diffused within the room. But the musk is still there, that disturbing sweaty aroma with its hint of sex and desiccation. But I'm not here for that. I'm here for the girl.

I leave the room and hunt around until I find a door leading down to the basement. It's black down there. I close my eyes tight and feel my pupils expand in response to the lack of light. I open my eyes and walk down the stairs into the complicated shadows below.

The smells are different here. Dust and damp concrete dominate with an undertone of heating oil, and rank human sweat laced throughout. A thin stream of light trickles in from the door above. Rough shapes emerge from the gloom. I skirt a pile of rotting cardboard boxes stuffed with molding textbooks, turn a corner and pass the open door of what was once the boiler room from which the oil smell creeps out. There are human smells here in thick, stale profusion. Some may be recent, but the chaos of odor keeps me from sorting them. The sweat stink I smelled on the stairs intensifies as I open a door into what used to be the boys' locker room. Most of the lockers have been removed, but in a corner I make out a dingy pile of what smells like cast-off jockstraps.

I would prefer not to announce myself to anyone lurking down here, but I'm going to have to use some light or this will take all night. From my pocket I pull a tiny Maglite. I close my eyes and switch the flashlight on, twisting the barrel until I know the light has reached its softest focus, and then opening my eyes to little slits. The illumination is sparse and gloomy at best, but to me it might as well be a flood lamp. I hold the light out away from my body so that anyone who might want to take a shot at me will blow my hand off instead of putting one in my belly.

With some visual cues to attach the smells to, it becomes easier to sort the old ones from the new. The gym smells of the boys' locker room get parsed from newer odors. I follow those fresher traces and find an abandoned shooting gallery in a storage room half-filled with broken desks.

The floor is scattered with used needles, candy bar wrappers, empty crack vials and sheets of flattened cardboard that have been used for mattresses. The scents here are fresher than those in the locker room. Chemical tang of heroin and crack, piss and crap in a corner, cheap tobacco from generic brand cigarettes, and dry blood. It's spattered on the floor in a couple spots, but that's not too unusual in a shooting gallery. The cop smells are here as well. They must have been down here when they searched the building. But something else. Hell, it's in here, too. I trace it to one of the cardboard mattresses: that rotting sex-musk from the goth shambler. Stronger here, as if some of the stains on the cardboard might be sexual in origin. As if this was the place where the living fucked the dead.

I catch a glimpse of something on the back of the door; I push it closed. It's a Cure poster. I take a closer look at the walls, and in a couple places I find tacks with the corners of torn-off posters still trapped beneath. I rummage in some crumpled paper stuffed into a bag that someone had been using as a pillow, and come up with a couple more tattered posters. The Dead. Morrissey. That tears it. Your average junkies and zombies aren't too big on interior decorating. Figure this was the same room the Horde girl and her friends were squatting in last year. After they got moved out, the junkies moved in.

I take another look at the blood. Couple days, maybe a week old. This could be where the goth shambler infected the fashion junkies she was with. Hard to say. Maybe she came down here, knew it as a hangout for squatters and campers and came here with some dull message in her brain telling her she could get food here. Maybe the junkies found her here and raped her and . . . No, it doesn't float, neither of them were carrying that smell. But something happened here. Something worse than the usual. And in a place like this the usual is pretty fucking bad.

Not that any of it gets me any closer to the carrier. Or the Horde girl.

Done with the school, I walk over to Tompkins and dig up Leprosy. He's hanging out in the corridor of benches claimed by the squatters. It runs between the kiddy park and the chess tables where most of the junkies hang out. He sees me and starts to bark at me almost before his dog does.

Dogs are amazing creatures, they can sense things, smell things that people never will. But they can't smell the Vyrus inside me, and Leprosy's dog can't smell shit. His nose is all smashed up from getting it kicked in. No, Leprosy's dog barks at me because he's a mean and vicious bastard that tries to tear the throat out of anyone who doesn't happen to be Leprosy himself.

—Fuck off, fuck face.

—Good to see you too, Lep.

The other squatters check us out. Some of them give me a little nod and some others drift away, hoping I won't notice them. As a rule I don't like squatters, but some I like a lot less than others and they know it. Leprosy jerks his dog's choke chain a few times.

—Shut the fuck up, Gristle!

He hauls on the leash until Gristle is standing on his hind legs, straining to get at me, his barks choked down to blood-thirsty growls. It's a pretty good trick on Lep's part seeing as he's all of five two and weighs in around ninety pounds, while Gristle is the product of some bizarre crossbreeding experiment that matched a rottweiler with a wolverine.

—I said fuck off, you're pissing off my dog.

—I don't know about that, Lep, I think I may be turning him on. Look, he has a hard-on.

It's true. Desperate to eat me, Gristle is still choking himself on the leash, clawing at the air with his front paws, his massive dog wood pointed straight at me.

—Down, Gristle! Put it away!

Some of the other squatters are laughing now and Leprosy is getting more pissed. He looks over at them and lets out some slack on the leash. Gristle lunges again, but this time it's at the squatters. They jump back and Lep gives a thin smile. Truth is they may be more afraid of him than of the dog. He's a scrawny little fuck, but he's probably twice as crazy and dangerous as the mutt.

—Stop fucking around, Lep. Tie the dog up and we'll take a quick walk and then the two of you can be back together.

He looks at me and glares, but he drags Gristle over to the fence, ties the leash to the iron bars and starts walking toward the kiddy park. I stroll alongside of him while the dog barks and whines in the background.

—I told you not to come around here anymore, Pitt, my dog hates you. You keep showing up and I'm gonna let him off that fucking leash one day.

—Your dog hates everyone, and if it ever gets off that leash and comes at me I'll kill it dead and you'll be out your only friend. Now tell me about this chick.

I show him the picture of Amanda Horde. He takes a quick look and passes it back.

—She's OK. I'd do her.

—Yeah, if she'd ever let your nasty ass near her.

—Shiiit. Goth chicks are ill for Leprosy. Goth chicks gotta have what Leprosy's got. Especially campers like that bitch. They gotta hit it with Leprosy. It lends au-then-ti-city to the squatting experience. As it fucking were.

—So you know her.

—Seen her around, she was camping like last fucking summer.

—You hook up?

—Naw. Camper bitches may crave what Leprosy has, but he denies them his shit. I take their money and drugs and might let one suck my dick, but Leprosy won't never fuck one of them bourgeois fucking cunts.

—So what about *this* summer, you seen her around?

He stops walking. We're by the kiddy park now. We stand next to the sign on the gate: NO ADULTS ALLOWED! PARENTS AND GUARDIANS ONLY. This is meant to keep the pederasts outside the fence so they can only watch the action within. It's too late for kids now, but any number of the creeps drifting around the park might be child molesters. If only I could smell that.

Leprosy is staring at the empty playground equipment.

—I used to come here when I was a kid.

Lep is about sixteen.

—Yeah?

—Yeah, before my folks moved us out to Long Island. I loved the park. That's why I came here when my dad kicked me out.

Lep ran away a couple years back to get away from his dad. You guess why.

—Hey, Lep.

—What?

—I look like a piece of toast to you?

—No.

—So stop trying to butter me up. You want money, tell me
you want money.

He smiles.

—I want money, fuck face.

I reach in my pocket, dig out a twenty and give it to him.

—So you seen her around or what?

He frowns at the twenty, but stuffs it in his pocket.

—Maybe.

—Don't fuck with me, that's all the cash you're getting tonight.

—I mean maybe I saw her, but I'm really not fucking sure,
OK?

—Tell me.

He leans against the rails of the fence and scratches
himself under a T-shirt that might have said something once,
but now is just the same washed-out gray-green of all squatter
clothes.

—So, like a week or two back we got a little beer bust going
at a squat on C. You know, bunch a us pooled our change
for some forties, and Fat Stinky Pete had a sack of hay and
we were just getting all fucked up. So you know Yankee Dan,
right?

—The skinny Cuban kid always has the Mets hat?

—Yeah, guy loves the Mets like life so we call him fucking
Yankee. Pisses him off. Anyway, Yankee is kind of a weasel
and nobody can really stand the fucking shit bag and now
here he shows up un-in-fucking-vited and he's towing these
fucking campers with him. I mean, they got all the right shit
on and their hair is five different colors and their lips are
pierced, but the clothes are from Urban Outfitters and their

piercings are too clean and the dye jobs are two-hundred-fucking-dollar-a-pop deals from some Upper East Side fag salon. So we know what's up even if Yankee is a fucking retard. Like the standing policy on this shit for any self-respecting punk is to stomp these pieces of shit, but we're pretty fucked up and feeling all mellow and besides we're out of beer and campers all have cash. So we give Yankee and these turds a bunch a shit, but we let 'em stay after they go out and grab some more forties and another sack.

—The girl, Lep.

—Yeah, I'm fucking getting to her.

He feels at his pockets for cigarettes that we both know aren't there. I pull out my pack of Luckys, pass him one and we both light up.

—So Lep is feeling good. And one of these camper chicks, she's digging his vibe and starts rubbin'up against it and shit. Now, like I said, these sluts from Uptown are gluttons for the real thing. They want to fuck in the dirt and get come on and shit so they can go back to fucking prep school and tell their friends about all the freaky shit they got into. Like they can all buy whatever the fuck they want, so having the latest Britney Spears CD or this year's Porsche means shit. But fucking some scabby squatter in a basement with ten people watching, that's a fucking social coup. So Lep, he's not gonna give this bitch the satisfaction, but she's pretty hot and I ain't had it for a bit so I tell her she can suck it, and down she goes.

—I can't tell you how charming this is. Now how about the girl, was it her?

He shakes his head.

—No, not that slut, but maybe her friend.

—Her friend?

—Yeah. See she finishes her job and Leprosy does his business and she's still into it, but Leprosy is not, and I repeat, not going to stick it in this cunt. So she says, what if it's her and her friend. Well, Leprosy has been around, but this piques his curiosity. So I ask her what friend and she points to one of the other camper chicks in the room. Well I check out that chick and she's OK, but Leprosy has his principles and I let this slut know it and tell her if she wants to set up a three-way or pull a train there are other guys around who don't have Leprosy's moral fiber. But at the time I think to myself that the other chick, she looked familiar. And now you show me that picture, I'm thinking to myself that that might be it, that chick might be the one in your picture.

—Might.

—Well, the hitch here is that the chick in the squat, she didn't have any makeup on. Now the chick in the picture, I saw *her* last year no doubt, and she always had all that ghoul shit all over her. But this chick in the squat? Not even nail polish. So it might have been her, but you see my fucking problem.

I nod.

—If she's around and it's the girl from last year, there are people who would know, right?

—Sure.

—Find out, Lep.

He raises his eyebrows.

—How fucking much is it worth?

—It's worth a lot. It's worth saving me a lot of hassles. Which means it's worth keeping me happy and keeping you from getting hurt. So find out for sure if it was her and then call me at Evie's bar. Now go get your dog before it kills itself or eats someone.

I turn and walk away and Leprosy shouts after me.

—Sure thing, Pitt. Hey, me, I'm at your fucking beck and

call, right, fuck face? Hey, I got an idea, why don't you go check out Realm? I hear all the hot young goths hang out there.

He laughs and I keep walking. Leprosy is a little fuck, but he'll do as I tell him. He'll do it because he owes me. He remembers the time his father came cruising in here from Long Island to get him. Comes rolling up in his stockbrokers' standard-issue Lincoln Continental and storms into the park like he owns it. Leprosy spots him and tries to run, but his dog gets off the leash and goes after the bastard. Dad doesn't even break stride, that dog runs up and he smashes the toe of his wingtip right into its nose, which is how Gristle lost his sense of smell. The dog drops, bleeding all over the concrete, and dad starts after Leprosy. Me, I'm sitting on a bench smoking, like I do, and maybe this is none of my business, but I got involved anyway. I beat the fuck out of the ass-raping son of a bitch, made his nose match the dog's. I did that for free, but it doesn't mean Leprosy doesn't owe me.

"Bela Lugosi's Dead." It's like their theme song. I'm hip-deep in Realm, watching crowds of black-garbed teenagers with pasty faces "dance" to Bauhaus. Back in my day goths were all these mopey, alienated, semi-suicidal kids. Pretty much your average teenagers, just dressed in black. Back then they were mostly hooked into the music: The Cure, The Smiths, Bauhaus, The Damned, a little Depeche Mode. Now it's gotten all tangled up in fetishism and S&M. So here's what it's like inside Realm. Over here you got your video screens showing clips from *Nosferatu* intercut with scenes from some tape of people getting their genitals pierced. Over there you got your brass chandeliers scavenged from junk shops around the Tri-State area, draped in black cheesecloth and illuminated with red lightbulbs. Along the walls you got your innumerable mirrors, brass framed and also draped in black cheesecloth. In point of fact, most everything here is draped in black cheesecloth, including half the patrons. Up on that stage you got your fetishist couple performing a rather tame S&M act. He's strapped to a big rusty steel X, wearing nothing but a black leather G-string. She's in the obligatory thigh-high boots and corset, and is sticking alligator clips connected to a car battery onto his nipples, shocking him when he fails to call her "mistress." Which is most of the time. Hot, right? Could be, except they're both middle-aged, seriously overweight and balding. Nonetheless, they're drawing a pretty big crowd, so who's to say their booking agent doesn't know what he's doing.

Over by the stage you got most of the new school goths favoring latex and studs. On the other side of the room, grooving on the music and the bootleg bottles of absinthe they scored from some guy that just got back from Brazil, are the old-school crowd. These folks lean more toward velvet and lace with a healthy dose of leather thrown in. And worn close to the heart of each, you'll no doubt find a treasured, autographed copy of *Interview with the Vampire*. This is the vampire crowd, the ones who really get into the whole undead experience. Half of them have their own coffins and the other half are saving up. These are the ones who think getting turned into a vampire will be just like *The Hunger*. Lots of hot sex with Catherine Denueve, Susan Sarandon and David Bowie followed by a centuries long, lingering, tragic, but ultimately poetic death, which is also filled with lots of hot sex with Catherine Deneuve, Susan Sarandon and David Bowie. And that's what makes these people such easy pickings for your average bottom-feeding Vampyre, because so many of them dream of being *turned*. But they don't know shit about the Vampyre, and what a pain in the ass it is to be one.

I grab a beer and eyeball the crowd. If Lep is right, Amanda Horde may have dropped the goth look. I push away from the bar and take a pass through the room. A couple chicks in full goth Kabuki-face have the right build, but a closer look tells me they're not my girl. I hang out for another half hour, keeping a close eye on the door. No dice. This is a waste of time. It's not like I can flash the girl's picture around or hang up flyers. That would pretty much go in the face of the discreet job Predo and Marilee Horde want. I'll check the basement and blow.

Realm's basement is a dark warren of small rooms, each with its own ambience, as it were. There's the Victorian Room, crammed with old sofas and cast-off end tables, all of it illuminated by oil lamps. Next to that is the Murder Room, decorated like a suburban kitchen, but with fake blood splattered across the walls and ceiling, and body outlines taped on the floor. There's the Dungeon Room and the Padded Cell and the Mad Scientist Room. I stick my head into each, take a quick look at the inhabitants and move on. Suburban goths from Long Island are sitting around the Formica-topped table in the Murder Room playing quarters. The Dungeon Room is hosting an impromptu panel discussion on spanking. And so on. I duck out of the Padded Cell, where a guy is being strapped into a straitjacket by one of his buddies, and head for the stairs. Time to get out of here.

I catch a flash of white out of the corner of my eye, turn to see what it is, see nothing, turn, and then he's right in front of me, blocking the stairs.

He squints through the grimy lenses of his glasses.

—Are you alright, Simon?

I grunt.

—I asked if you were alright, Simon?

—Yeah, I'm fine.

Christ I hate it when people use my real name.

I size him up. He's just a bit shorter than me, but more pale and skinnier than a cancer patient with AIDS and a heavy speed habit. He's wearing baggy white clothes, sporting a shaved head, and I don't know his name. I don't know him at all. But I know where he's from and who he belongs to because he knows my real name. These fuckers always know your real name. I step around him and start up the stairs. He follows.

—Are you alright, Simon?

—I said yes, for Christ's sake. Now will you stop calling me that?

—My apologies, Joe.

I get to the top and make a beeline out the front door. The skeleton stays on my heels as I walk down the sidewalk away from Realm.

—Perhaps you have a moment, Joe?

—Perhaps I have a whole shitload of moments. Perhaps I have moments squirreled away all over the place, and perhaps I plan to keep them for myself. What of it?

He laughs.

—What are you laughing at?

—I've been told about your sense of humor, Joe, how you stumble over wisdom even as you mock it. *Moments squirreled away.* Indeed, that is how so many treat time, as if it is something to be hoarded rather than a phenomenon to be experienced.

—Are you fucking serious? Is this what you have planned for me tonight? Can I just give you a donation or volunteer at a soup kitchen or something and get you off my back, or do I have to listen to this shit?

—No, Joe, you don't have to listen to anything. You don't have to do anything. But die, Joe, we all have to die. Except one of us.

—Yeah, well I already did that so maybe you can fuck off now.

—There's trouble about, Joe Pitt.

—There's always trouble around. Way I figure it, trouble just runs around this town doing what it wants.

—You are in danger and in need of allies.

—Not as far as I know.

—You do know. You know about the one you cannot smell or see.

I stop.

—Who is it?

—*It* is not a who.

Oh, Jesus. It's gonna be a ghost story.

—Bullshit.

—It watches you.

Screw this. I start to walk. He doesn't follow.

—Give them my regards then.

—Daniel wants to talk with you.

—You tell Daniel to stay out of my business.

—You are being watched, Simon. Have a care.

—I told you not to call me that.

I turn back around, but he's disappeared. Of course. That's how these Enclave guys are, dramatic entrance, dramatic exit, and a bunch of crap in between. I start walking again, and try not to feel the little tingles on the back of my neck that make me feel I'm being watched.

* * *

Evie loves me. I know she loves me because she buys all my drinks for me. I know for lots of other reasons, too, but right now this is the most important one because I want to get drunk. I took a walk around the neighborhood, looking for any indication of the carrier and coming up empty. I cruised back through the park to check on Leprosy, but the other squatters said he had split right after I did. So I heaved a sigh, said fuck it and came over here to see Evie and have a drink.

It's after midnight on a Sunday and the place is just starting to pick up. There's a late night hoedown-jam going on on the tiny stage and a few couples trying to two-step between the tables. Folks that work in the bars and restaurants in the neighborhood are getting off shift and coming in here to blow off steam. Evie likes working Sundays. She says it's the pros' night out. It's not as busy as Friday and Saturday, but she makes more money because these people know how to tip and most of them have Monday off so they're getting good and fucked up. And trust me, these people know a thing or two about getting fucked up.

Right now Evie is setting them up for the midget deadbeat I shook down the night we met. His name is Dixon and he turned out to be a pretty good guy other than being a degenerate gambler. I put another shot of Old Crow down my neck and take a sip off my Lone Star.

I can get drunk. It takes some seriously hard work because the Vyrus treats alcohol like any other poison and works quickly to neutralize it, but if I drink enough and I drink fast, I can get something resembling a buzz. And hey, no hangovers! The virtues of Vampyrism. Evie sidles back over to my side of the bar and refills my glass. She doesn't really need to do that since the bottle is right in front of me, but it's a nice gesture.

Every gesture Evie makes is a nice gesture because she's just that kind of girl. The kind I like to look at, but can't touch. I take another drink. She fills me back up. From the ground up she's wearing cowboy boots, low-cut jeans, a baby-doll T-shirt with the word TITS stretching tight as a drum across hers, and a smile that's all for me. I look her up and down and take another drink.

She fills my glass, takes a pull from the bottle and gives me the smile.

—So, can I come over tonight?

I bob my head up and down.

—Could be, could be.

She leans on the bar and puts her hand alongside my face.

—We could watch a movie maybe. Maybe play a little.

—A movie, hmm?

—Yeah.

She leans closer, puts her cheek against mine and flicks a tongue at my ear. I shiver. I almost cry. But I don't. Someone calls for a drink. Evie smiles at me and walks away down the bar. I watch her ass and take another drink.

This is what we do. This is what we do instead of sex. Not all the time, but some nights this is what we do. We flirt and tease. We slap and tickle. We go home and watch porn and make out. We jerk each other off through our clothes or sometimes we take them off and jerk off ourselves in front of each other. This is what we do because Evie will never take the chance of giving me her sickness, and it makes her feel guilty as hell that she won't fuck me, but that's just because she doesn't know that I'm afraid of giving her mine.

I don't know how to make a Vampyre. As far as I know, nobody really does. The Vyrus is certainly carried in the blood, but like HIV it might be in my come as well. I can't have sex with Evie because I might turn her into one of me, which would cure her, which would mean we could be together for . . . I take another drink.

Evie finishes up with her customer and wanders back over to me.

—So am I coming over tonight?

—I guess you are, babe, I guess you are.

—Cool. And maybe in the morning I can take you out for breakfast.

—Funny, you're a funny girl tonight.

Evie thinks I'm allergic to the sun. She thinks that because I told her I'm photosensitive and suffer from solar urticaria that would make my skin erupt in boils if I were exposed to sunlight. For that matter, that's what anyone who knows me well enough to know I don't go out during the day thinks. For that matter, I am allergic to the sun when you get right down to it.

She taps the tip of her index finger against the tip of my nose.

—I could *make* breakfast.

—And I could choke on it and die.

—Fuck you.

—You want breakfast I'll call someone and have it delivered.

—Well that's what I meant when I said I could make it.

—Silly me.

The phone rings and she grabs it off the back-bar. She talks to someone for a second then brings the phone over to me.

—It's for you.

It's Leprosy.

—What?

—Pitt?

—Yeah, what's up?

—I got something.

—What?

—Just come meet me.

—Is it the girl?

—No. I. Just meet me.

—Where?

—That garden on B.

—With the tower?

—Yeah.

—Don't fuck with me here, Lep. Is this solid?

—I'm not. Just meet me. Now.

He hangs up. I hand the phone back to Evie.

—Leprosy?

—Yeah. I got to go.

I stand up and realize I'm not packing. Not even a knife.

—You got that bat you keep behind the bar?

—Sure.

She reaches under the ice bin and comes up with a Frank Thomas edition Louisville Slugger. It's a big bat. She passes it to me.

—What's the matter?

—He didn't call me fuck face.

I walk away. She calls after me.

—I'm still coming over.

I stop and take a practice cut with the bat.

—Goddamn right you are.

And I walk out the door.

I'm pretty sure the guy who built the tower is crazy. At the very least he is amazingly skilled at being a pain in the ass. Used to be there were these little public gardens all over Alphabet City, a bunch of empty lots that people in the neighborhood split up into tiny plots for their flowers or vegetables or whatever. Nice if you're into that kind of thing. So these gardens were on land owned by the city, but Alphabet City was just a pit full of spics, niggers, junkies, queers, squatters, gangbangers and artists, so who gave a fuck. Then came the real estate boom. Pretty soon the city sells off all these lots and the gardens are paved over and another couple dozen yuppies have new condos. And once again, who really gives a fuck. But this garden on B is still there and so is the tower and the nut job who built it.

When they set up this garden they split it up into the tiny plots and everybody started growing geraniums and basil. Except this one guy was a sculptor and he didn't want to grow things on his plot, he wanted to build things. Pretty soon his little area is spilling tools and wood and mess all over the place and the gardeners are all getting pissed and want to kick him out. People are starting to threaten lawsuits and everything. Then they hit on a pretty reasonable compromise. They agreed that anyone who has a plot can do anything they want in that plot, as long as it doesn't reach anywhere *outside* of the plot. Everybody shakes on it. And then the crazy fucker builds the tower.

It's about six stories tall, made mostly out of wood, and looks kind of like the dilapidated skeleton of a very skinny pyramid. And wedged into every crack and hanging off of every plank and board, nailed to and dangling from every square foot of its surface, is a simply in-fucking-credible collection of crap. Old street signs, toilet seats, a jumbo model of an airliner, toys of every shape and size, a kitchen sink, several effigies, flags, and at least one huge stuffed giraffe. It sits there and looms over the entire garden, dominating the landscape. The one thing it most definitely does not do is reach a single inch outside the borders of its own tiny plot. You got to admire the pain in the ass that built this thing. As for me, I'm just hoping he built it well, because I'm already about ten feet up in the damn thing and if that dog jumps any higher I'm gonna have to go twenty.

It took me just a couple minutes to get over to that garden. No Leprosy. I walked around the fence for a minute, took the scent of the air and climbed on over. It's dark in there and the air is clogged with the rich, growing odors of midsummer, all that loam and sweet blossoms and bursting fruit and crap. Anyway, it wreaks havoc with my nose and as I try to sort it out I hear a little whimpering sound. I edge around a tiny stand of corn into the shadow of the creaking tower. Up against the wall of one of the tenements bordering the garden I see a dog snuffling at something and whining. I step around the corn.
—Hey, Gristle, hey there, boy.
    His head whips around at the sound of my voice.
—Easy there, Gristle.
    A growl starts up in the back of his throat.
—Let's not have any trouble here, boy. Easy. Where's Leprosy, huh? Where is he, boy?
    Why am I asking the dog where Leprosy is? Fuck do I know. Seems like the thing to do. At the sound of Leprosy's name he starts to whine again and turns back to whatever it is he's interested in, and I know things are all fucked up.
—What ya got there, boy?
    I take a step closer to get a look. Gristle's head snaps back around and the rest of his body follows. He doesn't growl or bark, just comes straight at me. I hold the bat out in front of me with both hands and his jaws clamp down on it instead of my throat. I hear his teeth crack the wood as he bites down, and his weight sends me flat on my back. He's on top

of me, his teeth planted in the bat, jerking it back and forth, trying to tear it from me while he rips at my exposed stomach with his rear claws. I push out with the bat, forcing his body up into the air. He's got the skinny part in his mouth and the fucker might just chew right through it in another second or two. Up in the air, he's lost his leverage and can't get purchase to claw me. Any time now he'll let go of the bat so he can take another crack at my neck. I twist my body to the left and throw the bat, Gristle and all, to my right. He skips and slides in the dirt for a few feet. I follow through with my roll, scramble up to my feet, run three steps, the dog just behind me, and jump up into the tower with Gristle hanging from my ankle. I manage to kick him off before he can sever my Achilles.

And here I am, sitting up in the tower with that dog down below stalking back and forth, taking the occasional jump at me and not making a fucking sound at all.

Me, I'm not what you'd call an animal person. Dogs, cats, wildebeests, it don't really matter, I don't care for any of them. But I'll give animals this over people, they just do what comes natural. Eat when they're hungry, sleep when they're tired, fuck when they're horny, protect their friends and kill their enemies. So I don't really want to hurt this dog, which is why I didn't take batting practice on his head in the first place. But getting down out of this thing without being chewed on is gonna be some kind of trick. I take out a cigarette and give it a smoke.

Gristle hasn't forgotten about me by a long shot, but instead of pacing back and forth just below me he's started covering the ground between the base of the tower and the thing against the wall. I pitch the stub of my cigarette and squat on one of the sturdier-looking pieces of lumber up here. Gristle looks up at me. The refracted light from a streetlamp turns his eyes blazing red. It's a good look for him. He turns to walk back over to the wall. I jump, land on top of him and wrap him up so that his legs are pinned beneath our bodies. He twists and writhes and wrenches his head around and snaps at the side of my face and misses and latches onto my left shoulder. He digs in. I get my hand on his throat and squeeze. He jerks his head a couple times, his teeth tearing my skin. I squeeze tighter and he starts to shudder and shake and finally pops his mouth off my shoulder and keeps it open wide and tries to breathe. I don't let him. It takes a while to knock him out, but he's still alive when I get up, and so am I. Pretty good deal for both of us.

Bruises are starting to form around the holes he put in my shoulder, but the blood has coagulated. I lift my arm over my head and stretch it out. It'll do. I pick up the bat and walk over to the wall to see what Gristle was so interested in. It's an old T-shirt, used to be kind of gray-green, but now it's mostly red. I give it a good smell, and you don't have to be much smarter than dirt to know it's Leprosy's.

In the farthest, darkest corner of the garden, where the walls of the two buildings that border it to the south and west meet, I can see an old steel basement trap. It's open. I drop Leprosy's shirt. I've been spending a little too much time in basements the last few nights, but hey, it goes with the territory. I choke up on the bat and head down the stairs.

I'm hit with that generic oily-dirt smell that permeates City basements. There's garbage down here and moldy cloth and waterlogged newsprint, and blood. Lots of blood, and it smells just like Leprosy. I follow the blood.

These East Village tenements have been torn down and

rebuilt so many times that the floor plans of the original builders have become worthless abstracts. This basement has penetrated far beyond the property lines of the building above. Many of these buildings could have had a single owner in the past and for any of a number of reasons he might have connected the basements into a single maze. Could have helped to hide a sweatshop, escape routes from a drug lab or, in a more innocent time, a speakeasy. Anything. All it means to me is that I'm getting lost down here. But the smell of Leprosy's blood is getting stronger ahead of me.

Every so often I pass a loose-fitting door that leads into someone's laundry room or the storage closet for a bodega and light from a feeble bulb leaks out. But I don't really need that light to tell me when I get to the place where someone must have cut Leprosy open because I just about slip and fall down in the puddle of his blood. He's up ahead of me. In the darkness. Alone. I tuck the bat under my arm, take out the Maglite, twist it on and shine it into the black room just ahead.

—Hey, fuck face.

He's sprawled on his ass, propped against a half-rotted wood post in the middle of the room, his arms pulled back and tied to the post. His chest is covered with dozens of slash marks and the blood oozes out and pools in his lap. My mouth begins to water. I take the bat out from under my arm and stay there in the doorway.

—Hey, Lep. You look like shit.

—Yeah, well.

His voice is choked and tight.

—I think I'm coming down with a fucking cold, so maybe that's why.

—Uh-huh. There anybody in here with you, Lep?

He moves his head around weakly, then turns it toward me and gives a shaky little smile.

—Looks like it's just me.

I take a step into the room, shine the light into the corners and crannies. It's empty. I walk over to Leprosy, drop the bat and kneel down next to him.

—Let's have a look at you.

The cuts on his chest are shallow, put there to inflict pain, not to kill. I take off my shirt and start tearing it into long strips and wrapping them around his skinny torso to bind the wounds.

—You might get lucky here, Lep.

—Yeah, lucky fucking me.

—They tell you what they wanted?

—They wanted you, fuck face. They wanted to know about you. Then they wanted me to make that fucking call, and as soon as I did they fucked off. So you get all of them?

—Who?

—It was a fucking trap, right? They made me call you and fucking jumped you, right?

—The only thing that jumped me was your dog.

—Gristle? You best not have hurt my dog, fuck face.

—Your dog is fine, the only thing that got hurt was my shoulder.

—Heh. He got you, huh?

—Fuck off, Lep.

I finish wrapping his chest.

—They get you anywhere else? They break anything?

—One of 'em stuck me in the back of my neck or something.

I take him gently by the shoulders, lean him forward until he's resting against my body and look at the back of his neck. There's a bite mark. The edges of it are a sickly greenish white. The bite of the carrier, just like I found it on the neck of the shambler chick. He's dead and rotting, and soon he'll be trying to eat me. I lean him back against the post.

—Looks OK.

—Cool. So you think they'll be waiting for us when we go out? Or maybe they wanted to get you out of the way so they could bust into your place?

I shrug.

—Whatever, we'll deal with it.

—You'll deal with it, fuck face. Not my problem.

I tear another strip from my now ruined shirt.

—Let me get another look at your neck. I want to keep your head from falling off.

—Ha fucking ha, fuck face.

I lean him against me again and use the strip of cloth to wipe the blood away from the hole in the back of his neck.

—You get a look at them, Lep?

—Naw, there was a couple of the fuckers, but it was too dark for me to see shit.

—Which one did this to your neck?

—Fuck do I know? One had me facedown on the floor, and I was screaming and shit, and one of them cut my neck with something.

—They ask you anything special?

—Couple questions. Wanted to know what you asked me. About that chick. What you wanted from me.

—What'd you tell them?

—What the fuck you think I told them? They were cutting my chest open. I told them fucking everything, which wasn't a fuck of a lot. Leprosy is no fucking hero, man, not for twenty fucking dollars.

—Yeah.

—You done patching that thing up or what?

—Just about. Hey, Lep, if your dog was sick, real sick, what would you do with it?

—What the fuck does that mean? You hurt Gristle, you shit fuck?

He struggles against me weakly and I hold him still.

—Easy, you'll start bleeding again. Naw, the dog is fine, it's like a puzzle thing, like a joke. If your dog was real sick, what would you do?

His body is leaning up against mine, his blood staining my undershirt. His head on my left shoulder, the one his dog chewed, and I'm looking into a hole chewed in his neck.

—Shit, man, if Gristle was that sick, like in pain kind of sick? I'd kill him, man, I'd just fucking kill him.

—That's what I figured.

—So what's the punch line, fuck face?

I take his head in my hands, one on the back, the other tucked under his chin. I lean him back against the crumbling post and do it while I'm looking him in the eye. It's a bad position, I'm on my knees with hardly any leverage, but I do it clean and his body slumps to the floor, head dangling at the end of his broken neck. It takes me awhile to find my way out of the basement.

Gristle is where I left him. A vicious animal that will try to kill anything that comes near it once it wakes. I could take him to the park and see if one of Lep's friends wants him, but they won't. I could take him to the pound where they'll keep him for a few days until they see the killer inside him and then put him down. I could leave him on the street to wake up and wreak havoc until he's shot by some cop. I could take him home. I could take him home and care for him until he loves me like he loved Leprosy. But he won't. He'll be a broken thing without his master. A wounded monster. I kneel in the dirt. I kill him the same way I killed Leprosy, the same sharp twist of the neck. Then I drag him down into the basement, through the warped passageways to the black room, and I drop him next to his friend. Let them be found, and let whoever finds them make of it what they will. I'm going home.

Zombies don't torture people. They don't torture and they don't interrogate and they don't set traps. Someone is fucking with me. And my people.

Evie comes by. She sees the blood and I tell her it's not mine before she can freak out. She makes me take a shower. I want a bath, but hadn't realized just how much of Leprosy's blood I have on me. She takes my clothes and stuffs them in a plastic sack while I rinse off, then she runs the tub and we sit in it naked, facing one another. I tell her Lep is dead, that some guys that have a beef with me killed him. She doesn't ask questions, just rubs soap on a washcloth and scrubs my feet.

The Cole is just the same, same oak, same mural, same high-priced clientele, but this time there's someone new.
—What I'd like to make clear to you, the one most important piece of information that you should walk away from this conversation with, is that I'd like you never to be seen with my fucking wife ever again.
  I nod. And Dale Edward Horde nods back.
  He's older than his wife, early fifties, but just as groomed. I doubt that there are designer tags on any of his clothes,

but discrete, hand-sewn labels from a bespoke shop on the Upper East Side. His haircut is flawless, a flop of graying black bangs sweeping across his forehead. He's fit and ready for the cover of *Men's Health*, but his eyes are subtly ringed and his lean muscularity speaks more of stress and intensity than of a gym.

He takes another sip of his Talisker, then leans back in his chair and taps his wedding ring against the rim of the glass.

—As public places go, this one is less public than most. It's the prices, the prices make it unlikely that you will find very many tourists popping in to gawp at the well-to-do. But they're not really the problem, tourists. The problem is the people with money, people my wife and I associate with. The problem with those people is that so few of them work, they have too much time on their hands and they like to keep up on what one another are doing. Your coming in here with my wife raised more than a few eyebrows. Honestly, I don't particularly care if they think the two of you are intimate. You wouldn't be the first roughneck from downtown with whom she's taken up. But it is something for people to talk about, and so talk they will. That talk is what concerns me. Talk circulates and becomes gossip and rumor, and gossip and rumor have wings that carry them very far indeed. No, my concern is not that I should be known as a cuckold, but rather that word of your involvement with my wife might reach the wrong ears; ears, that is, which might know about *who* and *what* you are. Ears such as those would be greatly interested in knowing that my wife and I were having dealings with you and your . . . what is the word? Brethren?

I look at my lap some more.

—Not brethren. Let's just say you and your kind. I know it smacks of racism, but there it is.

He swallows the last of his Scotch and sets down the empty glass. A waiter sweeps it away.

—Suffice it to say that you are here now because I need the gossips to see us together, speaking amiably. It will muffle any talk of my wife having an affair with you, and the gossips will quickly find some other tidbit to dwell upon. And thus our association with you will fade from common discourse. You understand my concern, yes?

I nod.

—Good. Now that we have that out of the way, you can join me in a drink.

The waiter returns with a fresh Talisker for Horde and he orders the same for me.

—Is that alright?

I nod. The drink comes and I hold it. Horde points at the glass in my hand.

—Take a drink, it will help with the façade of our knowing one another.

I lift the glass to my lips and take a sip.

—Good, yes?

I nod.

—Then business. My daughter.

I take another drink, a big one this time. It's a heavy Scotch. Wood-smoke and peat fill my nostrils, and for a moment I can't smell the odor of Leprosy's blood that clings to my hair.

—What do you want to know?

—Have you found her?

—No.

He waits for more. I don't give it to him. He tires of waiting.

—A more detailed report perhaps?

— In detail.

I gulp the rest of the whiskey in my glass.

—It looks like your daughter may be in a world of shit. It looks like she's been hanging with her squatter pals in Alphabet City. It also looks like there's some sick shit going on down there that could be very dangerous to anyone living on the street.

He grimaces and nods his head.

—As I understand it, *sick shit* is what my daughter goes down there seeking. I think it may be safe to assume that if it is about she will find it.

—No, Mr. Horde, it'll find her.

He raises his eyebrows.

—Well, in that case, and seeing as your drink is empty, you'd best go find her.

He stands. I stand.

—My demeanor can be off-putting, Mr. Pitt. People consider me cold. You might perhaps interpret this as an indication that I am less than fond of my daughter. That would be a mistake. Be assured, I love my daughter and I want her back. Unharmed. Get her, and you will be suitably rewarded. Fail, and you will be sorted out accordingly. Which brings me to my final point. I want her delivered into my arms and my arms only. You are not to hand over Amanda to her mother.

—Any special reason?

The waiter comes over with a bill, offers it to Horde, and Horde flicks a pen across it without looking. The waiter walks away.

—Yes. For the reason that my wife is a philandering lush and is becoming a singularly unhealthy influence on her daughter. Now, if you don't mind, I'd like to shake your hand. It will help to cement our deception for the audience.

I take his hand. It's just as soft as I expect it to be, but strong. He smiles broadly and claps me on the shoulder.

—Unharmed and to my arms. Understood?

He's still holding my hand, his other hand resting on my shoulder, everything about his body language and tone of voice telling the room that I am a trusted and valuable employee. I pull my hand free of his.

—Yeah, sure.

I walk out of the Cole and into the St. James lobby and don't see the stairs in front of me and trip down the first few and have to grab the banister to keep from falling. Sweat breaks out on my face. I feel drunk; very suddenly very drunk. I wipe my hand across the sweat on my face. I smell something, something on my hand, something I've smelled before. I walk past the front entrance and only realize it when I find myself standing at the elevators. I go back to the entrance and have to watch the revolving door swirl past twice before I can step into it without being crushed. One of the uniformed doormen helps me down the steps and asks me if I'd like a cab. I shake my head and his face blurs in front of me. I lurch down the sidewalk to the corner of Fifth and 55th and walk right into the moving traffic. Drivers blast their horns and curse at me as I weave my way across the street. I lean against a pole at the bus stop and look around. The world is made of blurs. I should have let the doorman get me a cab, I'll never make it home like this. I don't even know where home is right now. I need to sit down. Across 55th, people are setting up tents and sleeping bags against the wall of a building. People start crossing the street and I stagger among them and don't stop until I am clutching the wall of the building on the other side. I find an empty patch of sidewalk between a beat-up dome tent and a large cardboard box covered in sheets of plastic. I slump down between them. The world is riding a Tilt-A-Whirl. I fall onto my side and curl into a ball, my back pressed against the side of the building, against the bars covering a basement window. I ball myself tighter, my hands close to my face, and I smell something again. Something on my hands.

I know that smell.

I'm in trouble.

I try to stand up and my eyes pull themselves closed.

A monster roars. I open my gummed eyes and see a troop of lean, black-topped figures blurring up the street. Old ghosts are coming to haunt me.

The wind whips the sleep from my eyes and the thunder of a dozen Harleys pounds off the buildings lining Fifth Avenue and shatters the predawn quiet. I clutch the leather-jacketed back of the lead rider and look at the Dusters as they gun their bikes downtown. Christ, how do they keep those top hats on their heads?

Terry sent the Dusters for me.

After our bath Evie and me went to bed and didn't wake up till close to two. She ordered us some food from the Odessa Diner and we sat on my bed and ate it. After, I washed my hair again to try and get rid of the smell of Leprosy's blood, but it didn't help much. Blood is a scent that clings. Evie stuck *My Darling Clementine* in the DVD player to distract me. I sat next to her and stared at the screen, but didn't see anything. I was thinking about the night. How it couldn't come soon enough. How I couldn't wait for the sun to go down so that I could go out on the streets and kill someone. Then the call came, summoning me back to the Cole to meet the husband this time.

When I didn't come back, Evie decided to do something. My coming home covered in Lep's blood was the line for her. After that, she wasn't taking any chances.

She's met Terry a couple times. He's come into her bar looking for me and I introduced him as a player in the neighborhood's community action set. As far as she knows, he's a friend, or as much of a friend as I have. So she called Terry 'cause she didn't know anyone else who might be able to find me. Good girl.

—Bird gave us a ring. Said he wanted us to check something out for him. No biggie, just wanted us to crash Coalition turf and see if we could find you up here.

Christian is yelling over the blast of the bikes' pipes. We're below 24th now, on pretty safe ground, but the Dusters are still riding patrol style: two outriders a block up front, two as a rear guard a block behind, and the rest of the bikes clustered around me and Christian atop his chopped, jet-black '72 Shovelhead. He's hunched over the drag bars and I'm sitting behind him on the buddy seat, leaning against his back so I can hear what he's saying.

—Anyway, I threw together a squad and here we are.

There's more to it, there has to be. The Dusters are one of the small Clans from below Houston. They've managed to carve out some turf around Pike Street under the Manhattan Bridge. They don't have an official affiliation with the Society, but they're allied. The Dusters watch the Society's back door so Terry doesn't get too antsy about them being so close to his turf. But they don't generally go around running Society errands. A deal was cut. The Dusters are either paying off a big debt or getting something big for their trouble; nothing else would make them risk their president and twelve of their best riders by coming onto Coalition territory for a non-member. Whatever price was paid I'll be expected to chip in with something. We cross 14th, back on Society turf, and the bikes start peeling off in twos and threes, each rider saluting Christian with the tip of a top hat before disappearing down a side street. And then it's just Christian and me.

—Bird wants to see you.

I look at the paling sky. If I go to Terry now I'll be stuck with him all day.

—Take me to my place.

—He said to drop you at their headquarters.

—You taking orders from the Society now?

He turns left onto 10th Street. I get off the bike in front of my apartment. Christian sits on the idling machine, takes off his hat and slides his WWI–style goggles up on his forehead.

—Hear you got a problem with some shamblers.

—Where'd you hear that?

—Word gets around.

—Yeah, that's what word does.

—Need any help? That shit's no good for none of us.

—Don't know what you're talking about. Everything's cool with me.

—Yeah.

He slips the goggles down and puts his hat back on.

—Guess that's why Bird's sending us to scoop you off the sidewalk on 55th.

I stick out my hand and he takes it.

—Thanks for the ride.

He keeps hold of my hand.

—I'd say anytime, but I'd be lying. You should drop all the Coalition and Society crap, Joe. You keep playing the ends against the middle, you're gonna get fucked.

I take my hand back and keep my mouth shut.

He shakes his head.

—OK, play it that way. But you don't belong with them, man. You belong with us, down under the bridge. You belong free.

—Nobody's free.

—Just looks that way to you, Joe.

He kicks the bike into gear and blows down the street. I watch him turn the corner onto A, then go inside.

Christian's one of mine. I didn't infect him, best I know I've never infected anyone, but I found him. He and his boys had taken up on that block of Pike not knowing that the Chinatown Wall had claimed it. They rumbled with the Wall. 'Course, they had no idea the Wall were all Vampyre. The Wall savaged his gang, left most drained and walked away from the mess. That's how those animals operated back then. This was '78, '79, and I was still with the Society. I went down there with Terry to clean things up. We pitched the bodies in the East River, but Christian still had some life. Terry figured him finished and was ready to dump him. I figured I owed someone else the same shot Terry had given me.

I took him to a Society safe house and got him through it. He'd seen plenty of weird shit, he'd seen what the Wall did to his friends. That was enough for him to believe. But once he was strong enough to move he split, wanted nothing to do with Terry's peace and love agenda. He tracked down what was left of his old gang and went to work, infecting them. It took him a year to build a new gang, and then he went back to Pike Street, and the Dusters wiped out an entire generation of Wall. Only reason those Chinatown bastards are even considered a Clan anymore is because they've been around for so long. Nowadays the Dusters have their turf wired so tight that only the major Clans would think about walking Pike without an invitation.

I need to call Evie and tell her I'm OK. I need to call Terry and tell him I'll talk to him tonight, find out what I owe him for the rescue. I need to get back on the street and find the girl and the carrier. But first I need a drink. I don't know what Horde slipped me, but anything that could put me down that hard would have been lethal to someone uninfected. I still feel weak and sick as shit. So I open my fridge, more than a little concerned about how much I've been drinking, and find out I have more important things to worry about. It's gone. All my blood. Every drop. Gone.

The Enclave is set up in a warehouse on Little West 12th in the Meatpacking District. They don't lay claim to any turf outside their own front door, they don't have to. The Clans and the Rogues observe a no-man's-land that covers the entire West Side from 14th down to Houston. Nobody wants anything to do with them, least of all me. But someone was in my apartment, someone who didn't leave a trace, except for little erasures where his smell should have been. Erasures just like the ones I found in the classroom where I finished the shamblers. So it's time to go talk to Daniel.

I'm out in daylight for the second time in seventy-two hours, back in my burnoose, but I called a car service this time and specified tinted windows. I sit in the middle of the backseat, shifting from side to side as the sun strikes the windows, staying out of any direct rays. The tinting cuts down the long-wave UVs, but the shorts, the ones that really fuck us up, get through. I have the driver drop me at the corner of Little West 12th and Washington and walk down the block, keeping close to the buildings and the line of shade they cast on the sidewalk.

The Enclave warehouse looks like any of the others on this block, except for a total lack of graffiti or any other vandalism. The kids may not know exactly who those guys are in there, but they know they're bad. I climb the steps up to the loading dock and slide the huge steel door open on its tracks. They don't bother locking the door here. No one is stupid enough to fuck with them.

I step inside and slide the door closed behind me. It's dark, very dark. Nice. I take off my sunglasses.

—Simon.

I turn. I think it's the one who talked to me the other night.

—What did I tell you about that?

He smiles.

—I am sorry, it is just that you are so much more a Simon than a Joe. Which is as it should be.

—Just take me to Daniel, will you.

—Of course.

We cross the open space of the empty warehouse and shapes at the far end begin to resolve. At first it looks like rows and rows of white plaster lawn ornaments, and then they become Enclave. It looks like all of them, a hundred at the outside, the most feared of all the Clans. They sit cross-legged on the floor, motionless and silent, each of them dressed entirely in clothes as white as their pigmentless skin. My guide leads me through them. The ones in the back rows still have a bit of color to them and some flesh on their bones, but they get progressively paler and more emaciated as we move toward the front of the assembly. About halfway there my guide sits down in an empty space at the end of one of the lines. I stop, but he shakes his head and waves me forward.

At the front sits a single form, his back to me, facing the same direction as the others, but alone and separate from them. I stop. He's still for a moment, and then turns his head and looks up at me. He smiles and points at my white burnoose.

—Simon, how nice of you to dress for your visit.

Daniel looks like death. Exactly how you would expect death to look if he ever showed at your bedside with a scythe and a long list bearing your name inked in blood. Hairless, bone-white skin stretched tight over the skeleton beneath. He looks like death because he's dying. That's what they're all up to in here, slowly starving themselves to death.

We're walking up the stairs to the loft that runs along the back of the warehouse, and despite his skeletal state Daniel bounces lightly up the steps, radiating verve and barely restrained energy. At the top of the stairs he leads me down a narrow corridor that runs between a series of identical cubicles, each one containing nothing but a floor mat and a water jug. He steps into one of the cubicles on the left and I follow him in. There's an Enclave lying on the mat, shivering and sweating and nearly as wasted as Daniel. Daniel nods at him.

—He's failing.

Yeah, no shit.

Daniel points at the floor in a corner and I go sit there.

He settles himself on the floor next to the dying Enclave, placing a hand on his forehead and gently stroking the sickly skin. The Enclave stops shivering.

—Failing, Simon, as we all do.

—All except you, right, Daniel?

He smiles, shrugs.

—Time will tell. But Jorge here, he's failing very quickly.

—Why?

—He's something of a fundamentalist in his beliefs. He chose to stop feeding entirely.

—Jesus. How long ago?

—Oh, several weeks now.

—And he's still alive?

—Well, that's a subject for some debate, is it not?

I watch as Daniel strokes the brow of the dying Enclave. He's right, they do all fail, the Enclave, fail and die. That's what happens when you stop feeding. The Vyrus wants you to feed, needs you to feed. It strengthens you, sharpens your senses and motivates your body so that you will feed and consume more blood that will in turn feed it. Stop feeding and it will begin to consume your own blood, just as your body will eat itself if you deny it food. The Enclave feed only the barest amount. Are they doing it out of principle, denying themselves in order to spare the lives of others? No. They're doing it because they're a bunch of fucking spooks.

Jorge's breath is becoming more ragged, his lips peeling away from his gumless teeth, mouth stretched open, the air whistling in and out of his throat. Daniel leans forward and puts his mouth close to Jorge's ear and whispers to him. Shit, he's gonna croak right now. I start to get up to leave the room, but Daniel waves me back down. I don't want to see this, but you do what Daniel tells you when you're in his house.

Jorge's back arches off the floor and his fingers claw at the sleeping mat, digging little furrows in the thin bamboo reeds. Daniel is lying next to him now, pressing his body against Jorge's, stroking his face, whispering nonstop, chanting something. Crackling sounds are coming from Jorge's mouth, not like sounds he is making, but more as if something were breaking within him, echoing up his esophagus. His eyes fly open and thick white pus begins to ooze from their sockets. The crackling noise gets louder and his skin jumps and twitches as if bugs and snakes are trapped beneath it, struggling to burrow out. He begins opening and closing his mouth, his teeth snapping and gnashing at the air. The white pus is pouring down the sides of his face and one of his bugging eyes pops out of its socket and lolls against his cheekbone, and his head thrashes and bangs against the floor.

—Help me, Simon.

I don't move.

—Help me.

I crawl over, grab his tremoring legs and try to hold them down, but they kick loose.

—Hold him, Simon.

I grab the legs and pin them to the floor. He kicks and jerks and I force the legs back down and lie across them and he almost kicks free again. Daniel has wrapped his arms around Jorge's arms and torso. Still he beats and struggles and nearly bucks us both loose. His other eye has popped free, they both swing at the ends of their cables of nerves and blood vessels as his head shakes and twitches. He arches high in the air once, twice, and again. Each time his back cracks back down against the floor I hear bones breaking in his body. He's making vomiting noises now and it looks like he's spewing up his lungs. He arches high again, tossing both

Daniel and me off of him, and smashes back onto the floor, and that's it. He lies there, his body barely recognizable as human, still and dead. Daniel stands up and offers me his hand. I ignore it and get up on my own.

—Thank you, Simon.

I stare at the remnant of Jorge.

—Someone took my stash, Daniel, all my blood.

He gives a slight laugh.

—I'm afraid you've come to the wrong place for a free meal.

The Enclave don't believe in the Vyrus. Or they believe in it, but they don't believe that it's a natural occurrence. Or they believe that it's natural, but not physical. Or something like that. What they believe, what I understand they believe, is that the Vyrus is supernatural in origin, not of this world. They believe in a whole supernatural universe. They believe that when you are consumed wholly by the Vyrus, your physical being becomes matter in the supernatural world, but your conscious-self expires. What they aspire to, what the whole starvation thing is about, is their belief that by starving yourself gradually, you can maintain your consciousness and self, and be made over into a supernatural being that will exist in *this* world. I don't know why that appeals to them, but it does. Of course, so far they've all ended up like Jorge. For centuries they've been ending up like that. Except Daniel.

We're sitting on the bottom step of the stairs that lead up to the cubicles, watching the Enclave as they go through their exercises. They're doing some Tai Chi kind of thing. So slow and precise you can't see them moving at all.

I look at the wall where they hung Jorge. They spread-eagled

his body and spiked him to the cinderblock. Daniel is looking
at him, too.

—We'll leave him there until his flesh rots away and his
bones fall to the floor. He'll serve as a reminder and object
lesson as to the transience of the physical. We'll meditate
on his decay.

I could have been a part of this. I could have lived here
with these freaks and devoted my life to the discipline of slowly
dying. When I left the Society, Daniel sent for me. I had never
met him before, never been on Enclave turf, but I went. I had
just gone Rogue, if I wanted to survive I needed as many allies
as I could get. I thought he might be looking for an errand
boy, someone to handle security or something. What did I
know? Instead he asked me to join, offered me a place as
Enclave. It was kind of flattering, in the way it might be flattering if the craziest, baddest gang on the street offered you
their colors. I declined, told him thanks and crossed my fingers
as I went out the door, hoping they wouldn't tear me to pieces
for turning them down. But that's not how they work. The
Enclave don't take volunteers, they handpick new members,
and once you're picked you're a part of them for life, whether
you like it or not. Daniel says you're Enclave because you are
made that way, not because of anything you do.

I say that's all well and good, but I'm still not planning
on going out like Jorge did.

—The guy you sent to talk to me said someone was watching
me.

—Was that anymore than what you already knew?

—Fuck sake, Daniel, can you just give me a straight answer?

—You haven't asked any questions.

I look away from Jorge.

—You know about the carrier, about what happened at the
school?

—Yes.

—'Course you do, you know everything.

—Quite the contrary, I know virtually nothing.

—Yeah, right, in the big picture we're all fucking retards, but you know what goes down, Daniel. So the school, you know someone was poking around in there, someone who didn't leave a scent?

—Yes.

—Whoever it was is the same person who stole my stash, and I want to know who it is and why they did it. That's my question, Daniel, that's what I want to know.

He runs his spidery fingers over the top of his bald head.

—It's the wrong question, Simon.

—Then what's the right question? Will you tell me that, will you tell me that so I can ask it and get a straight answer?

—The question isn't *who*, but *what*.

—Bull.

—Someone has summoned it and bound it and sent it to do their bidding.

I stand.

—OK, time for me to go.

He reaches out and takes my hand. His skin is burning. He's starving the Vyrus, and so it has seized control of his autonomic functions, jacking his metabolism impossibly high as it compels him to feed. Dying slowly, balanced at the edge of starvation, the Vyrus gradually consuming him, he is continually in the grip of a feeding frenzy. It is the last death rattle of the Vyrus, when it empties your system of all its reserves, driving you to hunt. This is the state the Enclave cultivate, it is where Daniel has existed for no one knows how long. As strong as we may be when well fed, we are that much stronger when we are at the brink of starvation. Daniel holds my hand gently. If he twitches he'll pull my arm from its socket. I don't move.

—You aren't listening, Simon.

   I sit back down.

—How is it your mind can account for your own existence, but resist so stubbornly the idea that there are others like you, beyond you?

—Because I know I'm here and I know what I am.

—What are you?

—I'm a man. A sick man. And I want to know who grabbed my stash so I don't have to kill some jerk on the street and drink him.

—You're more than a man, Simon, much more. Your stash is gone? What of it? Stay with us. This could be a beginning, an opportunity.

   I point at Jorge.

   He smiles, nods, and lets go of my hand.

—It's a Wraith.

—Say what?

—The thing that was at the school and in your home, it's a Wraith.

   Oh, shit.

—I don't believe.

—So you say. But it doesn't care if you believe in it or not. In fact, one is the same as the other. Believe in it, and it will be just as invisible to you as if you did not. Don't believe in it, and it will kill you as easily as if you did.

   I close my eyes, rub the sweat from my forehead, and open my eyes. Crap.

—What do I do?

—Against something you say doesn't exist?

   He shrugs.

—As I said, you can stay here. That is why I sent for you in the first place, Simon, to offer you the Enclave again. You can't fight the other world, you can only strive to join it.

I think about it, about a life in here. The Enclave are circling up now, two of them walk into the middle of the circle and begin to spar. It looks like a Hong Kong kung fu movie on fast forward. I can't follow the moves of the combatants, I just see a blurred tumble of limbs, hear the whir as their arms and legs cut the air and the loud clacks of their bones striking one another. It lasts only an instant, and then one of them is down with two broken legs. The others clear him from the floor. He may decide to take a little more blood to help heal the legs, or he might not and take his chances that they never knit properly. I think about starving myself, no longer worrying about where my next meal is coming from, spending my days in meditation and martial arts, perfecting my self-discipline. No more hand to mouth. No more being on my own. No more Evie.

No. It's not for me.

I stand up.

—Thanks for the offer, but the answer's still the same.

Daniel smiles.

—That's unfortunate.

—Yeah, well, sorry.

—Nonetheless, you are Enclave, Simon, and you can't be otherwise. And I'm happy to know we have you.

—Whatever.

—That's a healthy attitude to cultivate, *whatever*.

I turn to go, then turn back to him.

—So, assuming this Wraith thing is real?

—Yes?

—Any idea who might summon something like that?

He watches as another couple of Enclave begin to spar.

—You can't simply call these things into our world and command them. It takes knowledge and power, and one must have something to offer them. There are individuals who have knowledge in this area, and certainly *we* are acquainted with the metaphysical. But in terms of relevance to you? You might look at the Clans. Ask, what is the motive for the theft? Is it to weaken or to kill you? Perhaps it is meant to punish or to motivate you? Who do you know, Simon, that deals in carrots and sticks?

I nod.

—Thanks.

I head for the door. He calls after me.

—Come again, Simon, the door is always open.

I walk past the sparring Enclave. I think about the hundred of them on the streets one day, and I do mean one day. That's what it's all about, the starving and crossing over stuff. They think that when one of them finally manifests as a meta-physical being in the physical world that not only will he become invincible here, but he will be able to imbue the entire Enclave with similar abilities. Then they will begin their crusade in earnest, take to the streets and cleanse the world of all that is not Enclave. But they won't do it until they have their Messiah. So far Daniel's as close as they've got, and he's not there. Not yet. I walk out the door and close it behind me, hoping I never have to open it again.

I don't believe in another world where boogeymen lurk about and wait for opportunities to cause trouble in our world. I don't believe in any of that shit and I certainly don't believe in Wraiths. But I do believe that someone wants me to think that's the case, someone wants me scared and more than a little desperate. So who do I know that deals in carrots and sticks? Well, that's easy enough, everyone I work for. But I don't figure the Society for a gag like this, it's not really in their interest to have me desperate and hungry on their turf.

Besides that, I don't think they have the chops or the subtlety to pull it off. No, this is a sneaky deal, and sneaky deals have one guy's name on them: Dexter Predo.

Figure Predo's not too happy with the way things are going down here. Figure he's caught on that the carrier is still out there. Figure Dale Edward Horde got on Predo's case for letting me hook up with his wife in public. Figure Predo told him he'd set it right and gave him something to plop in my drink, something to keep me down while they pulled the job on my place. Figure now Predo's got me by the shorties. He knows I'll be uptight without a stash. He knows the Society won't put up with me going on a rampage and tapping a bunch of clowns on their turf to restock my fridge. He knows I won't want to expose myself to the other Clans and Rogues by hitting on their turf. He knows pulling a job on a blood bank or a hospital takes time. And he knows I don't have that kind of time. Take all that and figure one last thing. Figure Predo's applied the stick and now all he has to do is wait for me to come to him thirsty and ragged and he can offer me the carrot, and then he'll have me in his back pocket. He can tell me just how to handle the carrier and the Horde kid and he can lock me up for a long way down the line. 'Cause restocking my stash is gonna cost and he'll make me pay with my balls. So I may as well hop on an uptown train and go get it over with. Except I don't.

I rush between patches of shade until I get to the L. I take it back across town and hurry to my pad. I still haven't called Evie to tell her I'm OK. For that matter, I still haven't cleaned up after sleeping on the sidewalk.

Out of the shower I call Evie.
—Hey, baby.

—You OK?

—Yeah, sure, babe, I'm fine.

—Was there any trouble?

Piles of it.

—Could've been, but Terry took care of it.

—Hope that was OK, me calling him. I didn't want to cause a fuss over nothing, but after that stuff with poor Lep I figured . . .

—No, it's cool. You did right.

We hang on the phone for a second, listening to each other thinking. I'm thinking this is new territory for us. She's always made a point of staying out of my business and I've always made a point of keeping her out. I don't know what to think of her talking to Terry on her own, but I don't like it much. As for her, I don't have a clue what she's thinking about.

I hear her shift the phone, her short fingernails clicking against the mouthpiece as she brushes her hair out of the way.

—I'm off tonight.

Tuesday, one of her nights off. Date night for us.

—Yeah, babe, probably not a good night for it.

She makes a little sucking sound, her tongue pulling down from the roof of her mouth. It's the sound she makes when she's starting to get bugged.

—Right. 'Cause you got the thing you're working on.

—Yeah.

—The thing that got Leprosy killed.

—Evie.

—That you won't tell me about.

—Not now, OK?

—Even though I was the one washing Lep's blood off you.

—I said not now.

—OK, then when, Joe? When do I ever get to know what you're up to?

—Just. Not now.

—Not now. Where have I heard that before?

She pushes all the air out of her lungs; it's the sound a person makes when they're trying to keep their cool, the one Evie makes when her cool's already been lost.

—There's only so much a girl will take, Joe. Even a girl you can't fuck.

She hangs up. And can you blame her?

So that's one more thing for me to deal with. I'd like it to be at the top of my list, but it's not. Instead my list reads something like this:

1) Find carrier.
2) Find Horde girl.
3) Find out who is spying on me.
4) Call Terry.
5) Deal with Predo.
6) Make up with girlfriend.

Oh, and at the top of that list you can add, GET SOME BLOOD. But the phone call is the only one that looks doable right now, so I call Terry.

—Joe, I really wanted to talk to you, man.

—We're talking, Terry.

—Yeah, but the phone. Not the same as sitting down face-to-face, you know.

—I could see you later tonight.

—No, no good, I have to go uptown tonight.

—Uptown?

—Above a hundred and tenth.

—Hood?

—Grave Digga is talking war parties again and I want to see if I can mellow him out.

—Tomorrow night, then.

—I may have to crash up there a couple nights. I got transit on a boat, but the pilot can't guarantee a return trip. And the way things are with the Coalition these days, I don't think they'll be laying any passes on me to cross their turf.

He's right about that. At the best of times the Coalition wouldn't be looking to do Terry any favors, but with all the dust being kicked up down here they'll be twice as hardcase about it. And that's assuming they don't know he's going to talk to the Hood.

The Hood is an offshoot of the Coalition. Back in the sixties, about the same time Terry was organizing the Society, Luther X organized all the blacks and Latinos in the Coalition, split them off and took control of everything above One Tenth. A truce was negotiated and the Coalition ceded the territory, but they didn't like it. All the same, things were pretty peaceful between them until last year. Last year someone stuck a couple knives through Luther's eyes and his warlord DJ Grave Digga took over the Hood. He went on a purge and claimed he found Coalition agents in the Hood who had assassinated Luther. Since then he's been sending raiding parties below the border and trying to get Terry and the Society to hook up with him to wipe out the Coalition. Not my problem.

—Then I guess we'll just have to talk now. What do you want?

—Just wanted to talk with you, have a little communication about everything that's been going down.

—I mean, what do you want for getting the Dusters to pick me up?

—Hey, Joe. That was an act of humanity. I know what it's

like up there. Your girl calls me and tells me you went to meet some *client* and you're not back? Then she tells me the meet was uptown? What am I gonna do, not care? And from what I hear, you needed the help. Christian tells me you were zonked out on the sidewalk with a bunch of homeless people, getting ready to work on your tan.

—Yeah, so what do you want?

—What I want, what I wanted, man, was to rap, make sure you're OK. You don't want to come over, that's your business. We're all free to do as we please.

—I don't like open accounts, Terry. What do you want?

He chuckles.

—I know. Joe don't take nothing from nobody, good or bad. I was just trying to do the right thing by a guy who used to be my friend. A guy, by the way, I still think of as a friend.

—Funny, last time this *friend* saw you, he ended up getting a couple ribs cracked by your mick thug.

—That wasn't personal, Joe, that was politics. I needed to throw Tom a bone to keep him from going radical on us. That was for the greater good. And I'd prefer it if you didn't use terms like *mick*.

—OK, Terry, you'll let me know when you want to collect. In the meantime I'll throw you this. Tom was right, someone else was poking around at the school, looking into what happened with those shamblers.

—Victims of Zomb—

—The fucking walking corpses, whatever you want to call them. Someone else was taking an interest.

—Any idea who?

—All I know is that it's someone very private, someone doesn't like to leave anything behind, not even a scent. Sound like anyone you know?

He's quiet for a sec. I let it dangle there.

—No, I don't think so, Joe, no one I know.

—You might want to keep your eyes peeled. Because whoever it is, they're creeping around on your turf.

I hang up. Let him chew on that. Maybe he'll poke around and find something out. Be nice to have someone doing *my* dirty work for a change.

There's still time till the sun goes down, time to kill before I can go looking for the girl and the carrier.

The girl and the carrier.

Something snaps together in my head.

Oh fuck.

I smell my hand. It's not there anymore, I washed it off in the shower. I go to the heap of dirty laundry in the corner. I throw the burnoose to the side, find the black jeans I had to wear to the Cole last night because Lep's blood had ruined my suit. I hold them to my face and sniff, cigarette smoke, the dirty pavement I slept on, my own sweat. Same thing with the shirt I wore. But he touched me, I know he did, shook my hand and gave me that fake hearty slap on the shoulder. Where's my jacket? I slide open the closet door and take my jacket off the hanger. It's the nice one, the light-weight leather sport coat Evie bought me. It's got a scuff on the sleeve from last night's nap on the sidewalk. I put my nose against the right shoulder and inhale.

There it is, that smell. The one I smelled on my hand last night after Horde and I shook. That odor from the school. That musky sex scent that was all over the cardboard mattress and the zombie girl. It was on Horde's hands. It was all over him, but I couldn't smell it because the reek of Leprosy's blood was still in my hair and nostrils.

They have names, the shamblers from the school have names.

The boys' were Joey Boyles and Zack Blake. The girl's name was Whitney Vale. That's the one I care about.

She was nineteen, born and raised in Nyack. Her mom says she split as soon as she turned eighteen and she'd only seen her a couple times in the last year when she showed up to ask for money. The dad's been a no-show since she was born. She was working part-time as a bag checker at one of the used record stores on St. Marks. The manager says she hadn't shown up for a week or two. I get all this off my computer when I check the sites for the *Times*, *News* and *Post*. I try Googling her name and get the articles I just read along with the AP coverage, and some creep claiming he has nude pics of her that he's willing to sell.

I look at the clock, it's 9:11 P.M. It'll be dark enough for me to go out now. I get up from the computer and pull on a T-shirt and the leather jacket. It's plenty hot out, but I need something to cover the revolver I stuff in the waistband of my black jeans.

My head is still aching from the mickey Horde slipped me. I open the closet door and look at the padlocked minifridge next to the gun safe. Last pint I had was Saturday. Usually I would have had a drink on Monday, but Evie was with me, and then I had to run out to see Horde and then someone stole my stash.

Maybe I missed something in the fridge.

I could open the fridge and look inside, but I know it's empty. It's just that the Vyrus is talking to me, reminding me how I'm gonna start feeling in the next twenty-four when it starts eating me.

I turn around and go up the stairs.

It's early and it's a Tuesday; St. Marks isn't in full freakshow mode, but it's summertime so you still get an eyeful. Squatters sucking on forties bought with the change they panhandled this afternoon, aged hippies who live in the same rent-controlled apartments they had in the sixties, Jersey kids clogging the side-walk booths to buy cheap sunglasses and get shitty tattoos. More than anything else it's depressing. This street used to be dangerous, now it's a mall.

Sounds is on St. Marks between Second and Third Avenues on the first floor of an old brownstone. It's one big room filled with bins of CDs, and vinyl for the classicists. Just inside the door a guy is standing in front of a bunch of cubbyholes where they keep customer's bags. He's a white kid wearing unlaced Nikes, baggy jeans, a Kobe jersey, and a Lakers cap turned sideways on his head. He's standing on a milk crate so he can keep an eye on the dozen or so customers browsing the stock. I go up to him and stand there while he checks out a chick in a camo micro-skirt who's digging through the trance bin.

—Excuse me.

His eyes flick to me and then back to the chick's legs.

—Yo?

—Manager around?

He shakes his head.

—Know when he might be around?

He shrugs.

—Anyone around I could talk to?

He shakes his head.

—Not hirin'.

—Uh-huh. You worked here long?

The chick walks up to the counter with a CD and the guy uses his position on the high ground to try and get a look down her top while the college student at the register rings her up.

—I asked if you worked here long.

The chick turns from the register and hands the guy a beat-up playing card. He turns to the cubbyholes and finds a Tibetan-style handbag with a matching card clothespinned to it. He hands her the bag, openly leering at the tops of her tits sticking out of her middy tank top.

—Whadcha buy?

She takes her bag, sticks her CD in and heads for the door.

—Music, asshole.

He watches her as she goes out.

—Yeah, fuck you, too, bee-atch.

He looks at me.

—Whaddaya want?

—Like I was saying, you work here long?

—Fuck do you care?

—I don't, I just thought you might know Whitney Vale.

He grins.

—Oh shit, man.

He turns to the kid behind the counter.

—G, fool wants ta know about Whitney.

The college kid doesn't look up from the Skinny Puppy liner notes he's reading.

—Tell him to get in line.

The box guy looks down at me, still grinning.

—Hear that, fool? Get in line.

—Yeah, I heard. You ever get to take a break in this place?

—Yeah, whatsit to ya?

—Nothing, just wanted to make sure they aren't abusing their workers.

I turn to leave.

—Yeah, fuck off, freak. Go hang with the rest of the ghouls been coming around.

I walk out.

The nice thing about St. Marks, it's easy to loiter. You can just hang out and drift up and down the same couple yards of pavement and nobody will pay you any mind. I cross the street to the deli and buy a couple packs of Luckys in case this takes awhile. Then I stand on the corner and smoke and wait.

He comes out a couple times to stand on the steps and have a cigarette himself, but it's over two hours before he takes his break. He crosses the street and heads toward my corner. I turn around and get fascinated by the beats the guy there sells out of his little stall. The box guy walks past me. He slaps hands with the doorman outside the Continental, then goes into the McDonald's next door. I walk past and watch him through the window as he gets his order to go. He comes out and turns to head back to the store and I come up behind him and take him by the arm.

—Hey, man!

—What?

I turn him around and start leading him toward 9th. I grin.

—Damn, G, it's great to see you! What you been up to?

—Wha the fuck?

He tries to pull his arm free. I squeeze it tight and put my mouth close to his ear.

—Fuck with me and I'll take you back to the store, stuff you in a cubbyhole and flush the card so no one can claim your ass.

He comes with me. I steer him around the corner and halfway down the block before I let him go. He's gone scared and babbly on me now.

—Hey, hey, man, I didn't mean anything back there, you don't gotta be a dick about it. I mean, you're not a dick.

—I could give a fuck what you said.

—So whadaya want, G? I gotta get back to the store an' shit.

I stare at him. He starts nodding.

—Right, G, right, you wanna know about Whitney.

—When was the last time you saw her?

—Got me, G. Like, maybe two, three weeks back we worked together.

—She quit?

—Naw, G, ya don't quit that job, ya jus stop goin' in.

—She have any boyfriends, anyone hanging around her?

He smiles.

—G. That chick wasn't straight enough for no boyfriends. She a mad freak. Super freakin'.

—You ever see her with a guy, fifties, a guy with money?

—Hell no. Chick never had no money, always be bummin'.

—You seen the pictures in the paper, of the guys she was with?

—Shit yeah, who ain't?

—You ever see her hanging out with them?

—Got me. Anything else, G? My McNuggets be gettin' cold.

—Yeah, that's it.

I take a twenty out of my pocket.

—Here, dinner's on me.

—Sweet.

He grabs the bill. I think of something and hold onto it.

—You know anything about a guy selling nude pics of her on the Net?

—Shiiit, I don't know 'bout that, but like I say, chick a freak. Know she most definitely picked up some change on the side doin' some freaky shit for a guy.

—What guy?

He tugs on the twenty. I let it go.

—Guy name Chubby Freeze. An' you can't find Chubby, you don' deserve to be comin' on all detective-like.

I stand there thinking as he walks away. At the corner, a good twenty yards away, he turns and points at me.

—That's right, bitch! An' done let me see your ass in the shop again or I'll buss a cap init.

He throws me the bird and turns the corner to go tell his pal outside the Continental how I tried to lean on him and how he hardcased me. I walk the other way, toward Chubby Freeze's place. Because he's right, I don't deserve to be all detective-like if I don't know where to find Chubby Freeze.

—Hey, Chubbs.

—Joe! What brings you?

Chubby Freeze isn't chubby. He may have been chubby once for a few minutes right after he was born, but now he's corpulent. A very short, very fat black man who is literally almost as wide as he is tall. He sits behind a grand but beaten mahogany desk, he and his fat sprawled on a threadbare red velvet love seat in lieu of an office chair that he would doubtlessly crush.

I point at the pretty boy perched on the arm of the love seat.

—Think he could take a walk?

Chubby smiles.

—Of course, Joe. Walking is one of the things Dallas does best. Isn't that right, Dallas?

The boy shrugs and shoots me a couple eye daggers.

—Show him, Dallas. Show the nice man how you walk.

Dallas sighs, pushes himself up and sashays past me to the door. The Chelsea gym-boy looks and booth tan don't fool me. If Chubby keeps him in his office, he's not just in here to move the desk out of the way when Chubby wants to get up; the boy is dangerous. I watch him till he's out of the room. Chubby watches, too.

—Lovely, isn't he?

—If that's how you like 'em.

—Well, Joe, I like them every which way, but the pretty ones are a particular weakness. The pretty ones and the grotesque.

He points at the cracked red leather wingback in front of his desk.

—Sit, Joe. Relax. It's ages since we had a chat.

I sit in the chair.

—What's on your mind, Joe?

—Whitney Vale.

He bows his head, closes his eyes and pats his chest with a well-manicured hand. Fat ripples beneath his three-piece suit. He lifts his head, looks at me.

—Joe, that was a sad waste.

He takes a silk handkerchief from his breast pocket.

—Such a sweet girl.

—So you knew her?

He blows his nose on the kerchief and tucks it back in his pocket.

—Before we go any further with this, Joe, it goes without saying that I am delighted that a man of your prowess is taking an interest in this child's death, and naturally I will do anything to assist whatever investigation you may be involved with, but is it safe to say that doing so will make us even on the last thing?

The last thing.

I look around Chubby's crappy little office. It's just a Sheetrock cubicle in an industrial loft on Avenue D, but he's tried to dress it up with that desk and the love seat and other touches, like a stained Persian rug and a faux Tiffany lamp. The rest of the loft is taken up by Chubby's production studio. Two tiny soundstages, a dozen editing bays where video is cut, converted to digital and compressed for the Internet, a small room of servers, and some storage space for costumes and sets. Of course the costumes are mostly slutty lingerie and leather harnesses, and the sets are mostly sheets of plywood with dungeon walls painted on them, so they don't take up much space. Chubby does a nice business in creating and distributing Internet porn. It's not classy, but it's a huge step up from where he was when I met him fifteen years ago dealing dime bags in Tompkins. It's that step up in respectability that convinced him to shed his homey gear and trade it in for the hip-hop producer look.

He's deep in the life, Chubby is, way out there on the edge of how the citizens live and he's been out there all his life. He's a hood from a hood family and he makes no bones about it. Far as he's concerned, this is just the way things are. Guys like Chubby, smart guys who last in the life, they see things and they hear things and sooner or later they start to think things. The punch line is that Chubby doesn't know everything that goes bump in the night, but he knows some of them. Me for instance, he knows I go bump. Even if he doesn't know exactly how or why. Which gets us to *the last thing*. The last thing was some trouble Chubby had some months back. He wanted someone heavy to take care of it, heavy but subtle. He called me.

He's pretty careful about the talent he hires, handles all the interviews and casting himself. But sometimes something slips through the cracks. What slipped through the cracks this time was a guy who specialized in hard-core bondage scenarios. He was an expert with ropes and racks and such. Good with a knife, too, cut so thin the marks were gone in a couple weeks. He did a couple photo sessions for Chubbs and shot a video and that was it. Few weeks later a couple of Chubby's girls went missing. Not that unusual in this business, but these were two of his regular girls, girls who were part of the family here. He gave me a call and asked if I'd take a look. I went through the employment records and checked up on the short hires over the last month. I made some house calls.

The third house I called on was on Staten Island, the bondage expert. Chubby loaned me his car and driver so I wouldn't have to rely on the ferry. We drove out and I knocked and the door was answered by the bondage guy. I didn't even need to ask any questions, I could smell the girls' fear-sweat, urine, and feces reeking all the way from the basement. He thought he was smooth. He invited me in, *anything to help*. As soon as the door closed behind us I took care of him. Then I went down to the basement, got the girls upstairs and into the car and told the driver to take them to Chubby. After he pulled away I went back in the house and rigged the creep so it looked like he had broken his own neck doing an autoerotic asphyxiation gig with one of his nooses. When Chubby asked me what he owed, I told him it was on the house.

—I told you that was on the house, Chubbs.

—Nonetheless.

—Yeah, sure, if it makes you feel better, we have a clean slate on this.

He smiles.

—Excellent. I always felt bad that you wouldn't take payment on that, Joe. I wouldn't want you thinking you owed me anything on this girl. And I know taking a freebie isn't in your nature.

—Whatever you say, Chubbs. I just need to know what you can tell me about her.

—Of course.

He inhales deeply, casts his eyes to the ceiling and exhales.

—Under normal circumstances I would not have these details in mind, but after I heard the news I thought it expedient

to review Whitney's employment records, before I disposed
of them.
—Good thinking.

He waves a fat hand in the air.
—Simple professionalism. In any case. Whitney came to me
just about a year ago. She was striking and uninhibited and
I didn't have any girls around doing the goth thing at the
time. Better yet, she looked quite a bit younger than her
nineteen years. Always a bonus.
—What did she do?
—Nothing too outré.
—Outré?
—It means—
—I know what it means, Chubbs, I'm just impressed at the
way your vocabulary is growing.
—One cannot wallow in one's past, Joe, or one will stagnate.
—Nice.

He gestures to a beat-up dictionary on his desk.
—A word a day, that's my rule. What did you think, that I
would spend the rest of my life calling people *mah nigga*?
Self-improvement is one of the few strategies a black man
can use to advance in America. And I am advancing, Joe.
—Sorry I asked.
—My apologies, I didn't mean to lecture.
—Whitney Vale.
—Yes, Whitney. Nothing too outré. As it was she was heavily
pierced and tattooed, to put her in leather would have been
redundant. In her first session we tried two styles: the Catholic
schoolgirl, and the ravishing romantic. The contrasts with
her natural esthetic were striking in both costumes, but,
unsurprisingly, she soon developed a following for the schoolgirl look. We found some counterparts for her, male and
female, and shot a few videos.

—What was her demographic?

—A young, troubled-looking girl in a plaid skirt? I assume it will come as no surprise that most of her fans had *daddy* as part of their screen names.

—Could you get me a list?

—As I said, I thought it best to delete her files and records.

He pats his slightly graying fro.

—I could perhaps put together a list of similarly inclined customers? No doubt some of them were amongst her adoring public.

I think about weeding through a list of middle-aged pervs, trying to cull something useful, being eaten from the inside by the Vyrus all the while.

—Never mind.

—Anything else, Joe?

—Know anything about the guy selling nudies of Vale over the Internet?

He shakes his head.

—I expect it is one of her fans who had downloaded her images and now wants to turn a profit off of tragedy. I of course had all of her material purged along with her records. Only prudent.

I take out the picture of the Horde girl and toss it on the desk, making sure it lands close enough to him that he won't have to stretch for it.

—Know her?

He picks it up. Looks.

—I'd say not.

—Maybe without the makeup?

He looks again, squints. Tosses the picture back.

—I'd still say not. That said?

—Yeah?

—This is a high-turnover business and I see a great many

waifs looking for a career or extra income. The ones clearly too young, such as this child, are politely rejected at the door. It is possible she crossed the threshold without my knowing.

I take the picture from his desktop and slip it back in my jacket.
—Got it.

He glances at his watch.
—If that's all, Joe?
—Yeah. Thanks.

He leans forward, extending his hand across the desk, sweating from the effort. I take his hand.
—You know, Whitney went out awfully hard for such a young thing, Joe.

I take my hand back.
—What I hear, Chubbs, it had to be that way. What I hear, she was a sick girl and she's better off the way it went.

His hand flies to his mouth.
—Oh, Joe, not that.
—That's just what I hear.

I head for the door.
—You take care of this, Joe, take care of it for good and well.

I stop, the door half open.
—I'm workin' on it.

He puts his eyes on mine.
—Mah nigga.

Dallas is sitting on an old vinyl couch in the reception area. I point toward the office.
—You can go back in.

He tosses aside the magazine he's reading and sniffs into the office. I walk past the girl at the reception desk.

—Hi, Mr. Pitt.

It's Missy. One of the girls from the bondage guy's house. She wasn't out here when I came in.

She's looking better. That ear is never gonna grow back and the smile will never be straight, but she's growing her hair out and it looks like Chubby must have popped for some good bridge-work. Not that he's an altruist or anything, he just knows what's good for business. Take Missy. The other girl disappeared soon after. Maybe she split back to wherever she came from. Maybe she's in a dark apartment right now with a bottle and a handful of pills. But Missy stuck around. The way she looks, there's a market for that, Chubby could have made some nice coin off that. But it would have drawn attention, and Chubby doesn't need attention. But she still wanted a job, so he put her on the phones. Better that than having her turn sour and maybe go talking to the cops. Just business, that's all.

I nod at her.

—Hey, Missy.

Her left hand strays to the side of her head. She tugs absently at the hair, trying to pull it down over the still livid scar where her ear had been.

—Anything I can do for you, Mr. Pitt?

She looks at my face.

I remember the Staten Island house. He'd cut them both, but it looked like he'd taken a special shine to Missy. She would have died soon. Would it be so bad now to tell her *Sure you can do something for me. You can let me hook you up to my works and let me tap you for a pint or two of that blood I saved.* Hell, she'd probably say yes.

—Tell me, Chubby says any chicken that comes through the door gets sent away?

— That's right.

—You take care of that?
—Sometimes.

I hand her the picture.
—Seen her?

She looks.
—Oh, yeah, sure.

I'm already reaching to take the picture back from her.
My hand freezes.
—What?
—Not coming in for work. Just hanging out, waiting for her friend.
—Her friend?
—Yeah, the one that . . . you know. Whitney.

I ask a couple questions and then I head for the door that will take me to the freight elevator that will take me to the street.

Behind me.
—If you ever need anything else, Mr. Pitt, I'm always here.

I go out the door without saying anything, and I try not to think about how good she smells. Just like food.

Outside I smoke a cigarette.

They knew each other. Of course they knew each other. That's exactly how fucked up this whole thing is.

Missy doesn't know much. She says the Horde girl would come in pretty much every time Whitney had a session. Says she'd wait in the reception area there, read magazines or maybe talk on her cell phone. Says she knew Chubby would be pissed if he knew a little girl was in the building, but she let her stay 'cause she figured the girl was Whitney's little sister. Later she realized they were just friends, but she says they acted like sisters. Like the girl was Whitney's little sister, a little sister who worshipped her big sister.

I smoke a cigarette and look at my watch. Midnight. Early yet.

Chester Dobbs's office is on 14th at First Ave. I get the address out of the Yellow Pages I borrow from a liquor store owner when I slip into his place to buy a pint of Old Crow. I walk over, taking sips from my whiskey in its obligatory brown paper bag. The booze is medicinal. The bite of alcohol and a slight buzz can sometimes take the edge off my hunger. Say in the same way that candy bars help a junkie when he starts to jones.

I cut through Tompkins. Going past the dog run, a girl squatter starts walking alongside me.

—Hey?

I don't look at her.

—I ain't got no change.

—Didn't ask for no fuckin' change.

—Can't have any of my booze.

—Didn't fuckin' ask.

Still walking next to me.

—So?

—You seen Leprosy?

I look at her. She's dirty, ragged, plump with baby fat, wearing combat boots, cutoff fatigues, a Rollins for President T-shirt, a heavy chain runs from one ear to a ring in her upper lip. Sixteen, tops.

—No.

—Hector said he saw you an him talkin' the other day.

—Don't know Hector.

—He says—

—Don't know him.

—Only, me an' Lep been hookin' up most nights an I ain't fuckin' seen him since Sunday. Mean, I don't give a shit 'cept he has some of my stuff an' if he gonna fuck some other chick I want it back.

But she does care. I can smell it in the salty tears at the edges of her eyes.

—Haven't seen him.

—Well if you—

—I won't.

—OK, fuckin' whatever.

She's still walking next to me.

—What?

—So can I have a drink?

I give her the mostly full bottle. She can use it more than I can.

I could have called Dobbs, PIs keep odd hours, but I plan on tossing his office whether he's in or not, so why bother. The street door is a cheap piece of crap without a dead bolt. I lean my shoulder into it and the lock pops. There's no lobby or elevator, just a dirty hallway with a hand-printed directory at the bottom of the stairs. His office is on the third floor along with American Flag Travel Inc., and DBT Theatrical Agency. Looks like the Hordes spared no expense when they hired a dick to look for their daughter.

I walk up the stairs and try to listen to the building. It sounds dead empty, but that's not right. I should be able to hear things, the whir of hibernating computers, a fan left on, the scratch of a pencil on paper from someone working late in their office, rats in the walls. But all I hear is someone coughing in an office on the second floor and the creaks of the building. It's not that the sounds aren't there, it's that I haven't been taking care of the Vyrus, and now it's starting to not take care of me. My senses are starting to fade. Another day and I'll be just like normal people, a day after that, I'll be worse. Some time after that the Vyrus will give me the last boost that will send my entire system into overdrive. Then I'll be going Jorge's route. I need some blood.

There's no light coming from under Dobbs's door. I knock to be polite. Nothing. I put my ear against the door. Just the sound of an old air conditioner, as loud and wheezy as an iron lung. I sniff the air. Dust, floral air freshener, stale farts. The door is solid and has a dead bolt. At full strength I could bust it in, but not tonight. I take out my picks. I don't have any special talent for this, I usually rely on my hearing and sense of touch to get me through. Not so much tonight. I shove the tension wrench in the keyhole and then the pick, and rake the pins. It's not locked. I try the knob, the door swings open. I put the picks away and take out my piece.

No one is in the tiny office except for Dobbs. He's on the floor behind his desk. He's ice cold, a dead man with dead blood. No use to me. Then I see the other door. I stand next to it, take a sniff, but I don't need any special sense of smell. Dobbs didn't want to share the hall bathroom with his floor mates and had his own put in. Sharp bleach with an earthy tang underneath. And? And something else. I sniff. Someone is in there. Someone I know.

I kick the door and the top hinge rips from the frame. It bangs open and hangs skewed from the lower hinge. He's sitting on the can, his hands in the air.

—I didn't do it.

—We got to stop meeting in bathrooms, Philip. People will talk.

I make him sit in Dobbs's chair while I go over the body. He was strangled. It's not exotic, but neither is it as easy as it sounds. Nothing's been kicked around in here, so it wasn't a fight that got out of hand. Someone did him. Someone got behind him in his own office. Figure it was someone he knew or someone he took at face value. He let them in the office, turned to go to his desk and got a forearm around his neck. Looks like a forearm job, lots of bruises. Someone strong and quick.

I try to get the scent, and have a bad moment when I can't find anything, but it's there, the smell of whoever did Dobbs. It's not much, someone well scrubbed, but not scented. It's not Daniel's Wraith or whoever it is that's trying to freak me out. Heck, no reason this has to have anything to do with me. Could have been Joe Blow who was screwing someone's wife and didn't want Dobbs to show the husband the keyhole pictures he'd been taking. Could have been Dobbs was working a shakedown on someone that didn't like being shook. But figure that's not likely. I toss the body. Keys, half a roll of Rolaids, lip balm, wallet with ID, couple credit cards, a few ATM receipts. No bank card.

—Where's his bank card, Phil?

—Uh, jeez, Joe, got me. I mean, I just came by to talk to the guy about a piece of work and—

—Didn't ask for your story yet, we'll get to that line of bull. I asked where's his card?

—Like I was sayin', Joe, I just came in 'cause the door was open and there he was and I turned to get the hell out, 'cause, hey, a guy like me in a room with a dead body? You got to know that ain't gonna go over well with no one. But before I could split I hear someone on the stairs, and I guess now that was you, but not knowing that, I just thought I better go hole up in the commode, and then you bust the door in and I ain't even barely looked at the guy let alone touched, I mean, rollin' a corpse is pretty low and not somethin' I'm apt to do seein' as dead people give me the heebie-jeebies.

I shift Dobbs's head to get a better look at the bruises on his neck, and a toupee slips from his head. Dobbs, you just get sadder and sadder.

—Phil. You make me come over there, turn you upside down and shake you by the ankles, and I'm gonna get sore.

He stands up and starts to dump junk onto the desk.

—Turn 'em all inside out.

On the desk is a pile much like the one he made on the floor of the Niagara's bathroom a few nights ago: baggie of pills, some scraps of paper covered in phone numbers, a creased discount admission card for New York Dolls, his tin of Nu Nile, some change and about ten bucks.

—See, Joe? Nothin'.

—Come here.

—Uh . . .

—Just come a step closer, Phil, I'm not gonna hit you.

He takes a step closer and I slap him across the face, grab the back of his neck, bend him over the desk and pat him down. Nothing. I let go of his neck. He stands up and takes a step back, rubbing the spot where I slapped him.

—Jeez, Joe.

—I'm gonna make you strip you don't come clean.

He holds his arms out to the sides. *Christ on his cross.*

—Joe, nothin', I swear.

—Strip.

He shakes his head.

—Uh-uh. I know what you think, Joe, you think I'm a coward, and sure, sure I am. But even a coward, even a coward has limits. Even a coward has pride, Joe.

He juts his chin at me. I take a step toward him. He starts to unbutton his shirt.

—I'm doin' it, I'm doin' it.

He strips to a dingy pair of boxers and points at them.

—Skivvies?

—God no.

I go through every article of clothing, run my fingers over seams and under flaps. I find a bindle of crank rolled and slipped into the stay slot on the underside of his shirt collar, but that's it.

—OK, put 'em back on.

He's wiggling his skinny ass back into those impossibly tight 501s when I remember his shoes.

—Let me see the wingtips.

—Huh?

—The shoes.

—Yeah, shoes.

He tries to dip his hand inside the right one before he passes it over and I grab his wrist and twist. A card drops out of his fingers and flips to the floor. It lands faceup. A Chase bank card: Amanda Marilee Horde.

Phil stares at the card.

—Wow, where the hell that come from?

—Where's the girl, Philip?

—I don't—

—Where?

—I don't—

—Phil, don't make the mistake of thinking I give a crap about you. I don't. At the best of times I don't like you. And right now I'm pissed. Pissed and really fucking hungry. Where's the girl?

—I don't—

I stuff Dobbs's toupee in his mouth.

—Mlumph. Mlph.

I reach in my back pocket, pull out my switchblade and thumb it open.

—I'm gonna do it old school, Phil. Poke one of your arteries, cover the hole with my mouth. It's like hitting from a beer bong.

My mouth starts to water as I talk about it. I don't want to suck on a scumbag like Philip, but I'm getting hungry enough to seriously consider it.

—Or I could haul you up to the roof, dangle you over the side and if I don't like the answers I get, I can just drop you. Let some bottomfeeder lick you off the sidewalk. You get the picture, Phil?

—Ylmph.

—So where's the girl?

I pull out the now slimy toupee.

—I swear, Joe, I swear!

I start to shove the toupee back in his mouth.

—No! Mlph. Nlmph. I swearmph.

He's trying to keep his lips pressed together so I can't get the toupee all the way in.

—Didn'tmph. No onemph. Said. Mph. About. Girlmph!

I yank it out.

—Who said what?

—They didn't say nothing about no girl!

—What did they say, Phil?

—Nothing. They said take a look, take a look around is all.

—Who, Phil?

—I don't—

—Predo?

He jumps like a cat with a cherry bomb up its ass.

—Yeah, Phil, that's what I thought.

He gets dressed and I toss the rest of the office and find nothing that helps. Dobbs was an old-timer, probably had his prime back when I was hanging with Terry and the Society. I've heard of the guy in the way you hear about people that are in similar lines of work. Dobbs was mostly a straight-up skip tracer and window peeper, but he did a little rough stuff; push a guy around, collect a debt, that kind of thing. There's no reason to think he knew much about what goes on, and no reason why the Hordes would have hired him in the first place. Take it a step further, when I look in his file cabinet there's no Horde file at all. And while Dobbs may have been old school, there's an extra phone line sticking out of the wall that's not attached to anything, and an empty laptop case in the closet. Figure whoever did the choke job took his laptop so they wouldn't have to worry about any files on the hard drive, along with whatever hard copies were in the cabinet. But the asshole missed the bank card. Or didn't know about it.

—Phil.

He sticks his head out of the bathroom where he is once again resurrecting his pomp.

—Yeah?

—What say I buy you a drink?

We go across 14th to the Beauty Bar.

We needed to get out of that office, never a good idea to hang around too long with a dead body.

A corpse in an office is going to lead to cops sooner or later. And cops are a problem. Cops get ahold of you and you're in their system: go where they tell you to go, when they tell you to go. Cops nab you and it's impossible to control your environment. Try telling a cop you're allergic to the sun and he'll make you stand outside at high noon with a tanning reflector held up to your face just to teach you a lesson about smarting off. More to the point, try getting some blood from another con in a holding cell and that's it, game over. So no cops. Ever.

At the Beauty, I take the double bourbon and the fancy Scotch to where Phil is sitting in one of the chairs with the old-fashioned hair dryers mounted on the back. I pass him his drink and sit on a stool in front of him.

—Thanks, Joe. Sure I can't have my stash back? I could sure use a little boost right about now.

Stash. We'd all like our stash back. I got his in my pocket. God knows when and where I'm gonna get to take care of mine.

—Later.

—Whatever you say, Joe.

He takes a sip of his whiskey and I take a gulp of mine.

—So what's the deal, Phil?

—Deal?

I reach in my pocket and pull out Phil's baggie of pills and the bindle of crank. I fish out one of the pills, a little white tablet stamped with a number. It'll be Dexi-something, pharmaceutical grade from the look of it. Definitely a step up from the cheap black beauties he was carrying the other night.

I show him the pill.

—Yeah, Phil, what's the deal, as in what did Predo tell you?

He jumps again.

—Jeez, Joe, you know better than to use that name. 'Specially down here where the man ain't so popular.

I squeeze the pill between my thumb and forefinger and it pops into dust. Philip's eyes bug.

—Joe!

I hold up another pill.

—I'm going cold turkey, Phil, courtesy of Mr. Dexter Predo. I thought you might want to join me.

I pop the pill. He bounces in the seat.

—Joe! Joe, God, ya ain't even askin' me any questions.

I pop another one.

—Joe! I! Whaddya?

Pop.

—Ohhhhh, maaaaan.

He slumps back in the seat, his head ducked under the hair dryer.

—Said, *Go take a look*. That's it, man.

I hold another pill before his sad eyes.

—When?

—Morning. Morning for *me*, Joe. Like four this afternoon. Got a call. Man said, *Go to this place, take a look, don't touch nothing*.

—Then what?

—Then what, nothing. *Take a look*. Period, Joe. Peer-e-ud.

—When you supposed to report?

—Said they'd call me.

—When?

—Soon.

I drop the pill back in the baggie.

—Well you better go to ground, Phil.

I stand up, drop the baggie in his lap.

—You can keep those.

He grabs the baggie and goes to stand up, but bonks his

head on the dryer. He plops back into the seat and rubs his forehead.

—I gotta be home when he calls, Joe. Worth my life if I ain't home when he calls.

—Find a hole, Phil. Find a hole, crawl in and pull it in after you. If you don't? I find out you been talking with Predo about this? I'll get you a hole. I'll dig it myself.

On the walk home I look over the ATM receipts from Dobbs's wallet. The four digits of the card number printed on the receipt match the last four on Amanda Horde's card. I look at the withdrawal amounts and I get it. Cagey kid.

With my face stuffed in the receipts I don't see the limo in front of my place until I'm right next to it. I look up. She's standing there next to my front door.

—Good evening, Joseph. May I speak with you for a moment?

I stay where I am on the sidewalk.

—I think that might be a bad idea.

—What would be a bad idea?

—You and me talking.

—Where did you get a silly idea like that?

—From your husband.

She smiles.

—All the more reason for you to invite me in.

She puts a hand alongside her mouth and stage-whispers.

—So as to avoid prying eyes.

I open the door. She follows me in.

Marilee Horde has been drinking. And she doesn't want to stop.

—Are you going to offer me a drink, Joseph?

—Bourbon's all I have.

She smiles.

—Of course it is.

She wanders around the apartment while I get the bottle and pour the drinks. We're on the ground floor. The trap that leads to my real digs is sealed. She's peeking in the bedroom. I leave dirty laundry strewn about and the bed unmade; everything meant to look lived in and well used. I hand her a drink.

—Thank you.

My senses are dull, but I can smell that she's not wearing the lavender oil she had on when we first met. She's scrubbed and clean, wearing a low-cut, sleeveless black blouse, short black skirt, and knee-high black leather boots. The uptowner's uniform for a trip to the East Village. Her bare arms are lean, cut muscle. She's not just toned by yoga classes, but hard, conditioned by hours of weight lifting. A sharp vein rides the edge of her right bicep. I can almost see the blood pumping through it. She walks to the second-hand couch and drops onto it, some of the whiskey sloshing onto her leg.

She wipes her finger through the dribble of bourbon on the bare patch of skin between the hem of her skirt and the top of her boots. She licks the finger.

—Not bad, Joseph. What is it?

—Old Grand-Dad.

—Excellent. And I should know.

—Whatever you say.

I sit in the chair across from the couch. She leans to the side and lifts the edge of a curtain to look out at the street. Her limo is gone. I asked her to send it away. Limos aren't all that rare around here, but I don't need one sitting out front collecting eyeballs. She gestures at the window.

—Aren't these a bit of a hazard?

—How so?

—You know.

She makes a little burning noise at the back of her throat and dances her fingers like flames.

I shrug.

She exhales loudly through her nostrils.

—Joseph, you are being positively . . . reticent. I'm trying to make conversation and you're being reticent.

—Sorry.

She laughs.

—Oh, you are droll.

—That's what my friends tell me.

She leans forward, elbows on knees. Her skirt creeps up a couple inches and I see the lace edge of a black silk half-slip.

—You have friends?

I shrug. She scoots farther forward. The skirt edges up another inch.

—A girlfriend?

I shrug. She shakes her head, reclines back into the seat.

—Positively reticent. So much for my morbid curiosity. I imagine you would prefer to talk professionally.

—I assume that's why you're here.

She rolls her eyes.

—Yes, I suppose it is. Well?

—Well?

—Have you found anything?

—This.

I take the ATM card out of my pocket and offer it to her. She leans forward and reaches, deep cleavage is exposed by several undone buttons on her blouse. She looks at the card. Her face shows nothing.

—So you found her?
—Just the card.
—Where was it?
—Chester Dobbs had it.
—And how did he get it.
  I take a drink.
—I'm guessing she gave it to him.
  She furrows her brow. I point at the card.
—You said you called him when she first went missing. He said he'd look for her, then called the next day and bailed. Figure he found her on that one day, but she didn't want to be found. She offered him a bribe. The card and her code. Two hundred a day for as long as she wasn't found. Damn sight better than the oneday fee he was gonna get if he turned her right over. Least that's what he thought.
  I take out the sheaf of ATM receipts, about a week's worth. All of them telling him the maximum had already been drawn for that day.
  She looks at them, starts to giggle and covers her mouth.
—Oh no. Amanda.
—Yeah. She must have been going into the bank right when it opened and getting the max from a teller.
  She's looking at the last one.
—But why didn't he just go to an ATM right after midnight?
—The real question is why he didn't stay on the job and collect from both you *and* your daughter. Looks like Dobbs had a couple holes in his game.
  She drops the slips and the card on the couch, holds her glass between her thighs and claps.
—Well done, Joseph.
  She takes the glass in her hand again, drains it.
—How much does he want to tell us where she is?
—Couldn't say. He's dead.

Not a flicker.
—Oh, my.
She holds out her empty glass.
—Would you mind?
I take the glass to the kitchen counter, toss in a couple ice cubes and fill it. When I pass it back our fingers graze.
—Thank you.
She drinks.
—How did he?
—Strangled.
She lifts her glass and presses it against her neck.
—Why?
I point at the card.
—For that.
—Did you . . . ?
—No.
—Is there reason to be concerned for Amanda's well-being?
I finish my drink.
—Yeah, there's plenty of that.

I'm fixing our fifth round. I tell myself the drunker she gets the more she'll talk. And that's true. But it's also true that the drunker I get the more I peek up her skirt.
I walk over to the couch, hand Marilee her drink. She has to try twice before she can get her fingers around it. Reclined on the couch, she props her head up with her hand and takes a sip.
—They're getting better. Why is that?
—I'm pouring more in the glass.
She laughs and a little bourbon sprays from her lips.
—A joke! Excellent, you're loosening up, getting into the spirit of things.

—Yeah, life of the party, that's me.

She gives a seal bark of a laugh.

—Another one!

She squirms around on the cushions so she can look at me. The skirt has climbed all the way to her hips and her blouse has twisted around so that I can see most of her right breast through the translucent material of her bra.

—Are you getting tipsy, Joseph?

The truth is I am. Normally, this many drinks? It might as well be lemonade. But my resistance to poisons is eroding right along with the rest of my body.

I shrug.

—Back to that, are we?

She shrugs several times, making little grunting noises. Her breast peeks further from her blouse. The edge of a nipple appears.

—Like my daughter. *Where are you going, Amanda?*

She does the shrugging grunting thing again.

—*When will you be back, Amanda?*

Shrug. Grunt.

—*Who's your new friend, Amanda?*

More of the same.

—You know many of her friends?

—Hmmn? Why? Oh right, work. Trying to find my daughter. I know some. She brings them around to raid the kitchen from time to time.

—Ever meet a girl named Whitney Vale?

She barks again.

—Oh, God. Her! Whitney.

She takes a drink, spills some down her cheek and wipes it away.

—Amanda's little idol. God save us.

—Watch the news lately, Ms. Horde?

She looks at a movie poster thumbtacked to the wall above my head, *They Drive by Night*.

—Yes.

—So you heard about what happened to Whitney?

—Of course.

—You know it happened in the same school where your daughter was squatting last summer?

Her eyes move from the poster to my face.

—Yes, I believe I made that connection.

—And it never occurred to you to mention to me that your daughter knew her?

—Joseph.

She drains her drink.

—Trust me when I tell you that what happened to Whitney Vale was only a matter of time. As for the rest. You were recommended to me as a detective of sorts. I suppose I assumed that if any of this were important, you'd detect it.

I look at the ice melting in my glass.

—Uh-huh. Your husband know Whitney Vale?

—My husband? Oh, God, yes. Dr. Dale Edward Horde makes a special point of meeting all his daughter's friends whenever possible.

—Why's that?

She looks at me, levers her upper body up from the couch. I can see the entire breast now. It's perfect.

—Joseph. I was sixteen when I first met Dale, and he was thirty-four. Why do you think he wants to meet the friends of his teenage daughter? God, didn't you know that's why Amanda ran away?

She drops flat again.

—And if you're going to fuck me you better do it now before I pass out.

She's staring at me, perfect tit hanging out, skirt so high

I can see the lower lip of a black thong that probably cost a hundred dollars. My dick is hard. I shift in my seat. I rub a hand over my unshaven face. The patch of sunburned skin is still tender. I swallow the last of my drink and stand up. I walk to the bottle on the counter.

—I'll pass.

Behind me, she sighs.

—Well, you're not the first.

I pour a quick shot, down it and pour another before I return to my chair.

—It was, I shudder to say it, '88 or '89? I was a club kid and he was slumming at Limelight. He was at a VIP table, behind the velvet rope and all that. I caught him looking at me a couple times. I thought he was attractive and, more to the point, I could tell that he had money. So I followed him into the bathroom and blew him. He came back the next night. And I followed him into the bathroom again. That was the beginning of our courtship. We kept it remarkably well concealed for the next two years. And when I was eighteen, we *met*, had a whirlwind romance, and married before the end of the year. By then I'd seen enough to know why he had fallen for me so hard, but I thought we'd bridged the gap and his attraction was now for me as a person. How profoundly naive. I got pregnant when I was nineteen. And that was probably the last time he ever fucked me. Too old, he said.

She's sitting up now, her clothes more or less straight. She finished off my bottle and now she's drinking vodka from a silver flask she had in her purse.

—I'm not certain what he did to bridge the gap until Amanda was . . . *of age*. His willpower in that area has never been great. Although he has always been very discreet. I will give him that. In any case, I don't believe he's been too successful with Amanda.

—Why?

She upends the flask, empties it, and drops it on the couch.

—You're certain you don't have anything else to drink, Joseph?

I nod. She shrugs.

—For the best, I'm certain. As to your question, he's not had great success with Amanda because I took her aside when she was ten and told her that her father would soon be trying to fuck her. Not the facts-of-life talk I had dreamed of having with my daughter, but I thought it best that she should be warned.

She gets up and walks an overly precise straight line to the window and peeks through a crack in the curtain. The back of her blouse is stretched tight over tense muscles as articulated as those in her arms.

—Don't suppose it ever occurred to you to just take her and leave?

—I'm sure it will not surprise you to discover that I have not been what anyone would call a *faithful wife*. Not that Dale cares. But I have not been nearly as discreet as he has been. And he has the evidence to prove it. That's how he knew Dobbs in the first place. The good detective has been documenting my infidelities for my husband for several years. The man has probably seen me naked more often than any of my lovers.

—So?

She turns from the window.

—If I try to take Amanda from Dale he will divorce me. He will destroy me. I will be kept from my daughter. And that will leave her alone. With him. I will not have that.

She inhales sharply and clenches her jaw.

—I think I'll be needing your bathroom now.

I stand behind her and hold her hair as she kneels on the scummy tiles and throws up into the streaked toilet bowl. She turns her head and looks up at me.
—You don't have to do that, you know. I have plenty of experience.

So I drop her hair and leave her to clean up her own mess. Everything should be so easy.

—May I get some water?
She's standing in the bathroom doorway, face damp and eyes rimmed red.
—I'll get it.
She waves me down and walks to the sink.
—My drunken seduction scene and its fallout are over, Joseph. I'm quite capable of filling a glass.

She fills the glass, shows it to me as proof. Then she sits back on the couch and opens her handbag. I watch as she takes out her compact and looks at herself in the mirror.
—Horrors.

She begins reapplying her makeup. I look at my watch, it's after two and I still have things I need to take care of.
—What about Whitney Vale?
Her eyes flick from the mirror to me and back.
—She's one of the kids Amanda had been living with in that school last summer. One of the, *squatters*, is it? Amanda was attached to her, wanted her to come stay with us. Well, that was out of the question. We told her she wasn't even to see any of those people. Naturally she did what any teenager would do and threatened to run away again if she couldn't see Whitney.

She throws up her free hand in surrender.

—Needless to say, I know where that kind of rebellion ends. It ends giving blow jobs to older men in nightclub bathrooms. I told her that Whitney could visit, but that she was not to spend time with her outside of the town house. I knew she would, but I hoped to keep a pretence of parental supervision. Doubly so when I met Ms. Vale.

—Why?

She traces a perfect line of scarlet around the edges of her lips.

—She's a tramp, Joseph, a tramp and a thief who was using my daughter's friendship to get money and anything else she could snatch on her visits to our home. I recognized her type the first time she came through the door. It was, after all, like looking into a mirror.

Her hand freezes and she stares into her compact.

—A seventeen-year-old mirror, but a mirror nonetheless.

—Your husband?

She pats powder onto her still flushed cheeks.

—Oh, yes, he saw that *quality* in her as well. And believe me, she made certain that he knew she was of legal age, despite her appearance very much to the contrary.

—She came on to him?

—Mmm. *Came on to him.* No, it was more that she performed for him. Flounced, let her skirt fly up a little too high, touched him a bit too intimately. Acted, in general, as though she were the fifteen-year-old that she appeared to be.

—How did he handle it?

She takes a last look in the mirror, flicks a strand of hair from her forehead, and snaps the compact shut.

—My husband is not a figurehead, Joseph. He is a gifted executive and businessman. He is also a medical doctor and epidemiologist. He did not simply found Horde Bio Tech, he

is its chief researcher. He is devoted to his work and rarely at home. Then Whitney started paying us visits. For the last year it has become more and more common for him to work at home or to stop in for an unexpected lunch. I was not shocked by his interest in her, only that he allowed it to be seen by others. Then again, it really isn't all that surprising.
—Why?
—Surely you noticed.
—What?
—The resemblance? To my daughter. I think they even made a game of it when they met strangers, saying they were related.

I remember Missy telling me she thought the Vale and Horde girls were sisters.
—What did your daughter think about Whitney's little act with your husband?

She takes her cell phone from her bag.
—Amanda is a very sophisticated fourteen-year-old, but she is a fourteen-year-old. I'm not certain the threat of Dale's advances is entirely real to her. Or undesired, for that matter. It would not be unusual for her to be sexually curious about her father. In the abstract.

She opens her phone and starts to dial.
—I'm going to call my car.

She makes the call and tells her driver she's ready to be picked up.
—Amanda loved Whitney. I think she thought Whitney's *flirting* was a joke, a way of making fun of her father, which pleased Amanda no end. Whitney never behaved like that around anyone else. That was the inspiration for Amanda's schoolgirl crush, Whitney was so mature and street-smart. She thought Whitney was having a laugh at Dale's expense, and I suppose she was, but she was also hoping it might pay off.

—Did it?

She gets up and begins straightening her clothes, brushing away lint from my couch, smoothing wrinkles.

—I don't know for certain. But something happened.

—What?

—Perhaps two weeks ago Whitney stopped coming over, and Dale stopped spending so much time at home. And things were somewhat normal.

I don't bother asking if she thinks her husband had anything to do with Vale's death. I don't have to. After all, the killer's hand is holding the cigarette I'm smoking.

Her cell rings once.

—That's my car, Joseph.

I get up.

—Whitney stopped coming over around two weeks ago. So what happened between then and when your daughter took off?

She walks to the door and waits for me there. I come down the hall, open the locks, and we walk to the street door.

—I came home one day and she and Dale were fighting. They stopped when I came in. Amanda ran to her room and Dale retreated to his office.

—What'd you do?

—I went to Amanda's room and asked her if her father had touched her.

—What'd she say?

—She said, *Moooom*. The next morning she was gone.

—And when you heard about Whitney you didn't call the cops? You didn't worry more about your daughter?

—No, Joseph. Something of that nature occurs and we know who to call. We called Mr. Predo. And he called you. The best man for the job is what he said, I believe.

She points at the door.

—Please.

I open the door and we stand there.

—You still want me to find her?

—Why wouldn't I?

—From what you said she might be better off wherever she is.

She glances at her limo, back at me, and puts a hand lightly on my shoulder.

—Find her, Joseph.

She leans close, her breasts press against my chest.

—Find her and bring her home. If she's out there, he might find her first.

She kisses the edge of my mouth.

—And his interests are becoming . . . baroque.

My voice husks in my throat.

—What the hell does that?

She opens her mouth, bites off what was about to come out, and shakes her head.

—Find her.

She wipes her thumb over the smudge of lipstick at the corner of my mouth, walks to the limo, and it takes her away.

Baroque.

I turn to go back inside and see Evie standing on the sidewalk just up the street. She stares at me for a second, turns and starts to walk away. But she stops. She turns back around. And she flips me off. Then she's gone.

I can't go after her now. I can't be in a scene where there'll be yelling and screaming and tears. Not when I'm this hungry. Instead I stand there and wish the guy in the bathroom at CBGB had finished the fucking job.

*   *   *

It's after four. I need to get my works together. I go down to the basement room and open the safe. I take out the thin leather wallet and unzip it. There's a new pair of rubber gloves inside, a tiny bottle of alcohol and some swabs. I fill the other slots and pockets of the kit with clean needles, some fresh surgical tubing and a couple unused IV bags. I close and lock the safe and slip the wallet inside my jacket. I have a few hours before sunrise to get some blood. I need to get it now so I can be at full strength tomorrow night when I go after Dale Horde.

There are rules. They aren't written down, but you follow them anyway.

1)   Don't hunt where you live.
2)   Don't get greedy.
3)   No gruesome kills.
4)   Don't tap anyone who will notice it.
5)   No double taps.
6)   Don't hunt Clan turf without a permit.
7)   No witnesses.

All these rules can be summed up in a single phrase: Don't shit where you eat. But that's easier said than done.

The main thing is, it takes time. Gonna go for a kill? You need time. Time to find the mark. That means someone who won't be missed soon, or so much that it raises a stink. Time to take care of the mark. That means privacy to tap the mark out, drain 'em dry. The human body holds around five to five-and-a-half quarts; that's ten or eleven pints. Only rookies or thrill seekers, like the fuck who infected me, go for a kill and leave anything in the mark. And when you're done, you got a corpse that's been sucked dry to the bone. Something like that draws a little attention. So you need a place to get rid of it, somewhere it will never be found.

Say you're like me, say you don't like the kill, say you think it's bad for business. Why is it bad for business? The Coalition is far and away the largest Clan, and Terry tells me there are just over two thousand members. All together, he figures there's four thousand of us on the island. Most slobs, the rank and file in the Coalition, bottom-feeding Rogues, small outfits like the Family down in Little Italy, most get by on a pint a week. Let's go with the low end, call it an average of four thousand pints a week. That's five hundred gallons. That's over three hundred and fifty corpses a week to keep us going. Even Brooklyn doesn't have a murder rate that high. So keeping the kills down is in everybody's best interest. Especially mine.

So you go for the tap. But that takes time, too. Got to find a mark you can knock out. That means someone you can drug or get drunk or just bash on the head. Got to make sure you can get the mark somewhere private. That usually means someplace they're comfortable, which means they're maybe comfortable with you, which means maybe they know you, which definitely means extra risks. Or it means finding the right alley at the right hour, the kind of place where you know the right kind of mark will be coming around. And what about those needle tracks? What does a non-IV-drug-user think of the new holes in his arm when he wakes up? So you have to hide the tracks, find a good vein on the ass or in the armpit. That's why junkies are a favorite. They're easy to get alone, all it takes is a dime bag. They nod as soon as they shoot up. And they're not likely to remember who the guy was that got them high or notice another track. The problem is they get tapped so much you have to worry about double tapping, and it's never a good idea to push your luck by hitting the same mark more than once.

Some guys got someone special. They got a Renfield or a Lucy that keeps them well fed and loves it. Those freaks just open their veins and let their owners fill up. They can only do it about four times a month, and that's pushing it, but it's still a good deal. Like having your own milk cow. There's other options. Guys get jobs at blood banks and hospitals, keep themselves stocked and sell a little on the side, as well. I have a hookup like that, but I'm already into him for a few grand and he won't be looking to front me anything more on credit until I pay off. Besides, he's like any other connection, never there when you need him in a hurry.

The main thing is you have to remember the numbers. Manhattan has a population of over eight and a half million. And there are four thousand of us. The odds are kind of against you.

Terry thinks the Coalition owns their own blood bank, thinks they have it outside the city, like an offshore account. He thinks they buy blood from banks around the country through blinds and cutouts, and then bring it into the city to feed their little legion. The rest of us have to walk on our toes and remember those numbers: eight and a half million vs. four thousand. We don't stand a chance.

So don't shit where you eat.

I'm shitting where I eat tonight.

I don't have a choice. I got to hit something quick. I'd like to hit a junkie. That would be the safest deal. But for that I need to have some junk to bait the mark, and I'm not holding. I could try and score and then head for a shooting gallery I know on Ludlow, but I just don't have the time. So it looks like a tap. An unplanned tap. A big turd on my dinner table.

I'm starting to get antsy. I feel little tingles and itches and I'm having trouble staying focused and the booze I drank is doing nothing to keep me mellow. It's the Vyrus coming on. Once it hits I won't be sleeping or thinking about anything else until it's fed. Soon I'll be talking to it, bargaining with it, making promises if it'll just give me a little peace. I have to deal with this now, have to get right and get some rest, have to be fresh tonight when the sun goes down.

'Cause I think I have it figured now, not all of it, but pieces. The piece where Dr. Dale Horde is fucking Whitney Vale I got figured. The piece where Amanda Horde finds out her dad is fucking her friend, freaks and splits, I got figured. And that's enough for me to go after Horde. 'Cause the other thing I got figured is that he's the one had Dobbs taken care of. Dobbs found something out, say he found out about Horde banging Vale and tried a little blackmail. That's about his speed. Horde gets rid of him and cleans out his files. And somewhere in those files is something that can tell him where his daughter is. Marilee was worried about the wrong thing; it's not about keeping Amanda away from him, it's about getting her back. Figure he's got her already, and that means she's on the clock. I don't know where the carrier gets into it, but that's one more thing the fucker's gonna tell me when I start in on him.

So here I am, walking the streets at five in the morning, watching the pale line of blue at the tops of the buildings, looking like just another sad-case junkie trying to get lucky.

I see my mark.

It's not the kind of thing I like, but it'll have to do. A girl in her early twenties wearing last night's party clothes, clearly doing the walk of shame home from some guy's apartment. Her eyes are dull and she's running her fingers along the sides of the parked cars, trying to keep her drunken balance. We're on 11th between B and C. Just up ahead, a brownstone is being gutted and made over for condos. Scaffolding canopies the sidewalk and a thin plywood fence screens the ripped-out façade of the first floor. I can catch her in that dark tunnel, kick through one of the boards, tap her in the building, and the construction guys will find her in an hour and call the cops. It's a crappy job, but hell, I'm probably doing the chick a favor getting her off the street before some nasty piece of shit grabs her and rapes her.

I come up behind her and whack her on the back of the head. I give her a good straight shot, use the pad of muscle at the base of my open hand. Her head snaps forward and her brain bangs against the front of her skull and she goes limp. She's so gone I barely had to hit her. I catch her as she goes down, lay her out on the sidewalk, get a grip on one of the four by eight plywood sheets that make up the fence, and wrench it loose. I scoop up the girl, get her inside, scrape the plywood back into place and get to work.

She has some great veins in her arm and I don't have time to get creative. I unzip my kit, roll on the gloves and put the works together. I remove the needle from the blood cup, screw it into the receiving tube and attach the hose and bag. Then I tie the tourniquet above her elbow and swab her skin with alcohol. I hold the needle in my right hand and her arm in my left, bracing the vein with my thumb, and slide the needle in. It's a good strong vein. Blood fills the tube. I release the valve and pressure from her young, healthy heart pumps blood through the hose and starts to fill the bag. I watch the rich, almost purple blood and my dick starts to get hard.

It's over in less than five minutes. I break down my works, carefully slide the IV bag inside my jacket and it's over. I'm gonna drink this straightaway when I get home so I don't even have to worry about adding anti-clotting agents. She's got a tiny mark on her arm, but her skin is dark and I don't think she'll be bruising. Little luck and she'll think it's a bug bite. Before I leave I open her handbag and shake the contents onto the ground. I take the five bucks she's got and her cell phone. I'll just dump the phone later, but it'll make it look a little more like a mugging this way. I stand up and get ready to move the plywood out of the way. I stop.

I take another look at her, limp and helpless on the ground. I should take another pint. Just to be safe I should take one more. Hell, I should just drain her. I can. I can carry her to the avenue like she's my drunk girlfriend. Get her in a cab, take her home and have all the time in the world to get it all. Fucking chick like that, walking around loaded, shit-faced out of her mind, chick like that is asking for trouble. Shit, chick like that probably has a death wish. Be doing her a fucking favor. I bend over to pick her up.

I stop.

It's the Vyrus. It's just the fucking Vyrus talking. It's not me. I know better. That's not the way to do things. It's stupid and it's weak. It's not who I am. I may not be the sharpest crayon in the box, but I'm smarter than that. And I'm not that weak. Not yet.

So I shove the plywood out of the way, step onto the sidewalk, shove it back and head for home. I get about two steps before Hurley clobbers me again.

* * *

—I fucking knew it.

Oh, hell.

—Fucking knew it. Consorting. Consorting and poaching.

I keep my eyes closed. I know who I'm gonna see when I open them and I'd just as soon put it off for another minute.

—Mr. Clean. Mr. Shit Don't Stick on Me, and there he is, consorting with the Coalition and poaching that chick.

—Don't say chick.

—Yeah, yeah. Poaching that woman. I told Terry, told him and told him, but he coddles this guy. Knows he spooks for the Coalition and he lets him stay down here anyway. Well not anymore. Wanted evidence?

I open my eyes. Closet. Dark. Dank. Dim cracks of light sneak in around the edges of an ill-fitting door.

—I got evidence.

I'm lying on my side. I go to push myself up and realize that my hands are cuffed and my ankles are shackled. I squirm into a sitting position. The brick wall behind my back sweats moisture.

—What kind of evidence?

—Well I saw him, didn't I? Me and Hurley both saw him.

—But doing what, Tom?

—We saw him take that Coalition chick . . . woman into his place, and we saw him poach that other ch . . . woman.

—How do you know she was Coalition? Are they wearing uniforms now?

—Trust me, you saw this one, you'd know she was Coalition.

—How?

—How? The way you always know. Had that attitude, that *the world belongs to me* attitude. Talk about a bitch who thinks her shit doesn't stink. This one—

—Don't call women bitches.

—Yeah, right.

I scoot closer to the door and put my eye against one of the cracks. I'm back at Society headquarters. Squares of carpet sample are spread around on the floor and handmade anarchist protest posters that look like oversized ransom notes cover the walls. I can see Tom Nolan's back. He's standing at a hot plate, stirring a big pot of something steaming and smelly.

—So you saw him with a woman who might be Coalition. And what else?

—She was Coalition. But even if she wasn't? He poached. Right on the street, just whacked that girl.

—Was she a child?

—What?

—Was she a child?

—In her twenties or something.

—So she's not a girl, right?

—Right, yeah. He whacked this woman right on the street and dragged her into a construction site. Tapped her right there for anyone to see. A total fucking abuse of Society poli-cies. On our turf. A slap in the face to our beliefs and methods. That can't be disputed, period. And besides, you're the one who's always going on about how more women are tapped than men.

Lydia comes into view and stands next to Tom.

—I'm not *going on* about anything. There is a huge imbal-ance in the number of women victimized by Vyrus-incited violence.

—That's what I'm saying.

—So you just had Hurley knock him out and carry him down the street to here?

—Hey, I had to take action. There's no telling what he's plot-ting with his bosses up there, what kind of trouble they have him stirring up. It was time to deal with it. He's a Coalition stooge and the time has come.

—Uh-huh.

She turns from Tom and faces someone I can't see.

—Hurley, did you see the woman he took into his apartment?

—Yeah.

—Was she Coalition?

—Don't know. Coulda bin.

—You think she was?

—Don't know. Tom said she wuz. Coulda bin. Nice lookin' lady.

—Uh-huh.

Tom turns from the hot plate.

—Hey, don't say lady.

—Why?

—Because it's demeaning.

Lydia looks at Tom.

—Get off him, Tom.

—What the hell, you just gave me shit for—

—Because you know better. Hurley's an old dog. Let him talk how he wants.

—Jesus! Fucking double standards. That's, you know what that is? That's counterrevolutionary. We're all equals. We're all equals or we're not. I don't like rules, but if we're gonna have them they have to apply across the board.

—Get off it, Tom.

She turns back to Hurley.

—What about the woman he tapped?

—S'a pretty good tap, all tings considered like.

—But was it by the book?

There's silence and I can hear Hurley's brain grinding away on that one. Probably trying to remember what a book is.

—Not da way Terry likes it done. Dat's why I sapped 'im.

—OK.

She turns back to Tom.

—So now what?

—Now what? Now we question the cocksucker.

—Tom!

—Sorry, sorry. You know me and my anarchists are sympathetic to the gay and lesbian community. It just slipped out.

—Slip it back in.

She walks out of view. Tom starts stirring his stinky pot again.

—Anyway, when he wakes up we put a rubber hose on him and see what starts to pour out.

—I'm awake, Tom.

He spins around.

—How long, asshole, how long you been spying?

—You mean, how long have I been awake and trying to get back to sleep so I don't have to listen to your crap?

He comes over to the closet, close enough so that all I can see through the crack is the leg of his crusty jeans.

—That's right, smart-ass, keep fucking jerking my chain. See what it gets you.

—Hey, Tom, I'd never jerk your chain. That's Terry's job.

—OK, that's it. You fucking asked and now you're going to fucking receive.

He starts unlocking the door.

—Please, man, have Hurley knock me out again so I can get some fucking rest.

The lock snaps open and I hear a chain rattling. I roll onto my back, knees tucked up against my chest.

—Hurley's not gonna do a goddamn thing, smart guy, I'm gonna take care of business myself this time.

—You planning on taking off my cuffs?

—Whatever way you want it.

The door swings open. I jackrabbit him, kicking out with both feet, and catch him in the gut. He woofs and stumbles back into the room. A spindly chair catches him across the back of the knees and splinters under his weight as he crashes on top of it. I shove myself back up on my ass and lean out the door of the closet and hold my cuffed hands out.

—Hey, Tom, I'd help you up if I didn't have these things on.

—That's it, cocksucker.

He comes at me fast. The only thing I have time for is to regret that I have such a big fucking mouth.

I try kicking him again, hoping to knock his legs out and get him down on the floor where I can wrap the cuff chain around his neck and maybe crush his windpipe. It doesn't work. He dodges the kick easily, grabs the front of my jacket, lifts me off the floor, and starts pummeling my face. Lydia grabs him and pulls him off of me almost immediately, but he's already jackhammered me ten or eleven times. I fall in a heap. Blood I can't afford to lose runs from my nose and mouth. Tom lunges at me again and Lydia easily shoves him back.

—Fuck do you think you're doing, cunt?

Her bodybuilder shoulders bunch, but her voice is calm.

—Watch the language.

—Stop telling me how to fucking talk, dyke!

—Tom, if you say girl, chick, lady, bitch, cocksucker, fag, lesbo, dyke, queer or cunt one more time, not only am I going to beat the sperm out of you, I'm going to have a couple shemale Vamps I know find you in an alley some night and open your back door. Wide.

He makes his move, and bounces off Hurley who is suddenly between them.

—Terry would'nae want yous two fightin'.

I'm on my side, spitting and snorting blood.

—Yeah, guys, dad's gonna be mad when he gets home and sees you can't get along.

Tom just about jumps out of his shoes trying to get at me, but Hurley puts a hand on his shoulder and he freezes. Hurley turns his head and looks at me.

—Maybe you best oughta shut yer trap, Joe.

I'm looking at the little puddle of blood on the floor in front of my face and thinking about sucking it up.

—Yeah, yeah, maybe you're right, Hurl. Hell, even you can have a good idea sometimes.

He grunts.

—'Member dat last time ya smarted off, Joe?

—Yeah.

—I wuz gentle on ya dat time.

I shut up. He looks from Lydia to Tom.

—Yous two oughta shake hands, show dere ain't no hard feelin's.

Tom groans.

—Fucking come on.

Lydia sticks her hand out.

—He's right, Tom. We're all on the same side here. We can't let our tempers get the better of us.

She's smiling at him. He takes her hand. She squeezes. It's not obvious, Hurley misses it. Tom yanks his hand back and takes a swipe at her.

—Fuckin' bitch!

Hurley blocks the punch and gives Tom a gentle push that sends him reeling to the far wall.

—OK, Tom, take a walk.

—The fuck?

—Terry would'nae like dis. So take a walk, get some air.

—It's light out.

—So go upstairs.
—But that fucking—
   Hurley raises a finger.
—OK, that's cool, that's cool, I'm cool. I'll go up. But I want
that fucking spy back in his cell.
   Hurley shrugs.
—Sure.
   He takes two steps, scoops me up and dumps me back in
the closet. The door closes and the chain is drawn back into
place. I hear Tom start up the basement steps and then stop.
—Lydia, you're right, we're on the same side. I'll remember
that, *baby*.
   A door opens and closes and he's gone. A chair creaks
heavily as Hurley sits down.
—See, dat's better. Everybody gettin' along.

—He says he's an anarchist, but really he's a fascist. You
know he wanted uniforms? He actually wanted to get T-
shirts or armbands or something for all the members of
the Society. Not only that, but he wanted affiliations to be
indicated on the uniforms, different symbols depending on
whether you're one of his Anarchists or in the Lesbian,
Gay and Other-Gendered Alliance or the Communist
Manifesto or whatever your Society Affiliate might be. He
said it would make for unity, so we could identify one
another on the street. What he's really after is a system of
classification. He wants to know where his enemies are so
he can take care of them when he's ready. And he says he
backs the goals of the LGOGA, but I can tell we freak him
out. I mean, before I got infected, the infected queers
weren't even organized, let alone represented on the
council. Now he has us in his face at every meeting. Little

fascist prick. And he's making a bid for Security Chief? He's already half a Stalin. Give him a badge and he'll go full-blown Hitler.

She's sitting at the table out there, eating a bowl of whatever veggie stew Tom had been mixing up.

—If he ever does take charge of security he's not gonna be too happy about having you around, Hurley. He likes using your muscle now, but if he gets the chance, he'll have his Anarchists in jackboots and carrying truncheons and he won't need your help knocking people out. That's why we need to keep an eye on each other's backs.

—I keep a eye on everybody's back, Lydia. Jus' like Terry tells me to.

—Yes, but are Terry's interests yours? Are you going to spend your whole life letting him make decisions for you?

—It's worked OK so far.

—Yes, I see that, but—

I can't listen to this with the cramps hitting me. One or the other, but please not both. I decide to do something about it.

—Hey, Lydia.

Silence.

—Lydia.

—What?

—There's nothing I'd like more than to listen to you trying to make Hurley understand the politics of personal empowerment, but I'm hurting a little in here.

—Yeah, you looked a little rough around the edges.

—Maybe I could get that blood I tapped.

—Sorry, Joe, that's Exhibit A in Tom's case against you. As much as I hate the little prick I can't mess with evidence.

—Got any you could spare?

—No.

—Uh-huh. Well seeing as I'm all cuffed up maybe you could let me out of here.

—No. I think you're going to have to stay in there until Terry gets back from the Hood.

—Any idea when that's gonna be?

—Could be tonight, could be a couple nights. Depends on when they can get him safe passage.

  Couple nights.

—So maybe you can call him?

—He doesn't want us calling him up there. He thinks the Coalition may have some people inside a couple of the service providers. They could tap landlines and cell signals. He's worried they might find out when and how he's coming back down. Sounds a little paranoid to me, like maybe he's been listening to Tom, but why take the chance.

—Yeah, that's great, Lydia, but see, there's this girl out there that I need to find.

—Woman.

—No, *girl*. The kind young enough to get raped by her daddy.

  She comes a little closer to the door.

I don't know much about Lydia, but I know enough. I know that just a couple years back she was at NYU, finishing her thesis on Radical Gender Roles. I know she was a big player in campus politics. I know she used to teach women's self-defense classes. I also know a desperate Rogue tried to jump her one night and got eye-gouged and groin-punched for his trouble. But not before he bit a hole in her cheek. What I hear, it turned out she knew some people that she didn't even know she knew. They noticed when she started getting sick. Guess these friends got her through and hooked her up with Terry. I think the biggest shock for her was discovering that

Vyrus-infected lesbians and gays were completely unorganized. She took care of that.

She's a tough enough nut, but she's young. Literally young, under twenty-five. She's still soft on the inside, still holding the values and feelings she had before she was infected. Hell, most everybody does. Then they grow up, or they die.

—So why do you care, Joe?
—Truth is, I don't. Just a job to me. But I figure you probably care.
—You're a piece of work, Joe.
—Little girl out there, no one to help her.
—A real motherfucker.
—All alone.
—So tell me where she is, I'll help her.
—Don't know where she is. That's why I need out of here. So I can find out.
—How you planning to do that?
—Gonna beat on a guy.
—So tell me the guy's name, I'll beat on him.
—Yeah, I know you'd be into that. Thing is, the guy lives above Fourteenth. And he's connected. You go up there, hand a beating to this guy, could be political repercussions.
—I see that. But there's another thing.
—Yeah?
—I got no reason to believe you. How about that, Joe? Any reason I should be listening to this?
—I got a reason to lie? Say it's crap and you let me out. Where am I gonna go? I leave the neighborhood and I'm dust. I stay in the neighborhood and you guys can pick me up whenever you want. Where do I run?
—Uptown.

—Any deals I have with those guys only work 'cause I'm down here. I try to live above Fourteenth and suddenly I'm not so useful. You hear what Dexter Predo does when someone stops being useful?
—Yeah.
—Well it ain't no lie.
   She's quiet again.
—She's fourteen, Lydia. And her name's Amanda.
   I work my fingers into my jacket pocket. They took my gun, my knife, my works and the blood I tapped, but the picture's there. I take it out and slip it under the door.
—That's what she looks like.
   The trailing corner of the picture disappears as Lydia picks it up. There's nothing but the sound of her breathing and Hurley turning the page of a newspaper, and the Vyrus whispering pain and hunger in my veins. The picture slides back under the door.
—You know what you shouldn't have done, Joe?
—What?
—You shouldn't have tapped that woman last night. That was rape, Joe, and I don't deal with rapists.
   She walks away from the door.
—I'm going upstairs, Hurley. If this asshole starts trying to soften you up with some shit about a little girl, don't listen to him.
—Shite, Lydia, Joe knows better den ta try an soff-soap me.
   He's right, I do. And that leaves me alone in the closet with no one to talk to except you know who.
   It's not a very rich or enlightening conversation. Mostly it's just the Vyrus chanting: *feed, feed, feed* over and over again, and me replying with: *make it stop, make it stop, make it stop.* Pretty boring stuff. I also do my fair share of groaning and sweating as I clutch at my cramping stomach

and occasionally bang the back of my head against the floor. Imagine the worst case of food poisoning you've ever had. It's like that except it hurts more and you don't have the relief of shitting or vomiting. But it comes in waves. So from time to time I get a little break where I can lie there and think about the next series of cramps and remember that this is just the start and that it will get much worse. And that has me worried, because it shouldn't even be this bad yet. I should have had at least another day before this kind of pain started. All I can figure is that the dose Horde gave me put more of a whammy on my system than I knew. Throw in the cuts I got from Vale, my sunburn, and the beating Hurley gave me, and I guess I've been overdoing it a bit. The Vyrus is tired and grouchy, like a small child kept up too late. For now it's just whining, soon it will start to cry. And then the shrieking and the tantrums will begin.

Pause while a mongoose crawls through my lower intestine.

I've been here before. I know I can take it. I know the cramps will get worse and then subside into a constant pain that I'll be able to cope with pretty well. After that things will start to get interesting. After that I'll be approaching the frontier of my personal experience. Not for the first time, and certainly not for the last, Jorge comes to mind. I need to distract myself.
—Hurley. Hey, Hurl!
—Yeah?
—What's, what's the longest you ever went?
—Me?
—I don't mean the other guy named Hurley that's out there with you.

—Ya gotta mouth, Joe.
—Yeah, forgive me, I'm a little tense.
—Yeah, s'tuff, ain't it?
—Uh-huh. So what's the longest?
—Almost two weeks once.
—No shit.
—Yep.
—What happened?
—Shouldn't oughta be talkin' wit' ya, Joe.
—Jesus, Hurl, what the fuck can it hurt? Oh, God!

Return of the mongoose.

—Ya OK, Joe?
—No.
—OK.
—So two weeks, huh?
—Yeah.
—What happened?
   He doesn't say anything. I press my face close to one of
the cracks at the edge of the door.
—C'mon, man, I'm just trying to take my mind off the cramps.
   His chair scrapes as he shifts.
—OK. Dis wuz way back. Sure ya wanta hear dis?
—Yeah, yeah.
—OK. Way back. I wuz workin' fer some bootleggers. Way
back. Stuff would come in onna water, onta Long Island. I
did da muscle, rode shotgun like.
—Some things don't change.
—Well ya gotta talent ya gotta stick wid it.
—Sure.

—Anyhows, no big ting, da boats is runnin' up onna shore an da guys is takin' da booze off an' we get hit.

—Another outfit?

—Naw. Law.

—Same thing.

—No lie. Specially dese coppers. Dese wuz da ones we had paid off so's we could work da beach. Decided dey'd sooner handle distribution demselves like. Did'nae even give a warnin', jus opened up. Tommy guns. Ya been shot much, Joe?

—Once or twice.

—Hurts, doan it? Kee-rist! Got me good. Riddled up me legs and me belly. Fellas got me inna car an blasted us out. Foockin' cops had a roadblock a mile up. Got us good. Blew da rig right off da road. I went out da winshield, so I missed it when dey trew a grenade inna winda. Blew dose guys ta hell. Too bad, good guys.

—What about you?

—Me? Flew twenny yards when da car crashed. Landed inna culvert next ta one a dem steel drainpipes. Used me arms ta drag meself inta it. Den, just passed out like. Time I came to, cops wuz all gone.

—Then what?

—Lied dere, Joe. Legs wuz blown ta bits. Could'nae even crawl anymore. Just lied dere and lied dere. Holes healed up quick, like dey does. But me insides wuz a mess and da bones wuz all splinered. Shite takes a little longer.

—Sure.

—So's I'm lyin' dere fer some time. A week I'm lyin' dere. Lost all dat blood, bones heelin' slow. Vyrus gettin' bad on me. Prayin like, dat da sun don't get reflected down inta dat pipe.

—Rough.

—No lie, Joe, I taught I'd bought it. Kept gettin' worse an worse. Me gut an den me head an den me skin. 'Fore it wuz over, everytin' hurt. Friggin' hair hurt.

So I got that to look forward to.

—'Bout da middle of da second week, it just stopped.

—The pain?

—Everytin'. Could'nae feel nuttin'. Taught, *Well, 'ere goes. Dis'll be it.* Did'nae feel nuttin' fer more'n a day. Strange not feelin' nuttin'. Den it got real strange.

—How so?

—Cuz suddenlike, I wuz feelin' everytin'.

Mongoose attack.

—Sorry, missed that last bit.

—Sure, I heard ya in dere. I wuz sayin' how I tink dat ting happened, how dey talk about dat place when da Vyrus is just about down an out. Cuz all a sudden, I was fine, better'n fine. Boy wuz I hungry, dough. Jus' hopped up an walked over ta da road. First car I flagged stopped fer me. Way I looked, musta tought dered bin a accident. Guess der had been at dat. Anyhows, family in dat car never got ta ask any questions. Whew! Never fed like dat 'fore or since, Joe. It wuz sumpin'.

—Enclave talk about that place. Daniel says they all live there.

—Yeah, dat's what Terry said when I got back an told 'im da story.

—Terry was around?

—Sure, we go back.

—Terry goes that far back? I thought-

—OK, dat's enough story time. Ya shut up in dere now, Joe. Ya got better tings ta worry 'bout den dat ol' histry.

And he shuts up. Fine with me, I got something new to think about. Me, I always thought Terry went back to the sixties, right about the time the Society was formed. Far as I know, that's what everyone thinks.

The mongoose comes back and I stop thinking.

—Hey, Pitt.

Time has passed. Unpleasantly.

I come out of my latest swoon and a bright light hits my face. I squint up into it and something far more substantial than light hits my face.

—Lydia went to one of her queer meetings.

I lift my head off the floor and he knocks it back down.

—And Hurley slipped out to check the message drop, see if the runners have brought any word from Terry.

I leave my head on the floor, so he kicks it this time.

—Guess who got left with guard duty?

He's at it for awhile, kicking and punching. He knows that kind of pain will only go so far with the shape I'm in. But that doesn't seem to keep him from enjoying it.

—You're looking pretty bad, Pitt. Know what's looking worse? Your future.

He kicks me again. I groan. He nods appreciatively.

—That's right, looking pretty fucking bleak. Even bleaker than it was a couple hours ago. Know why?

One of my molars has been knocked loose and hangs by a flap of skin. I bring my cuffed hands to my face, yank the tooth free and flick it on the floor.

—Didn't know you were a fortune-teller, Tom.

He laughs.

—Man, I can't wait, I can't fucking wait for it to all come down on your head. When that tough-guy shit finally cracks I just know you're gonna turn out to be the biggest fucking crybaby I've ever seen.

—You reading my future or what?

—We found the kid.

Oh, fuck.

—Yeah. Pretty messy, Pitt, pretty fucking messy.

Fucking hell. The girl.

—What was that about? You just hoping no one would find him down there?

Him?

—'Cause someone did. Couple my boys were looking for a new safe house, checking some basements on B. They smelled something. Found him tied to that pole with his neck snapped. His fucking dog, too. What was with all the cuts, Pitt? Trying to hide the pints you tapped?

Leprosy.

—You're getting greedy and sloppy. Must be all the time you're spending uptown. Shit, everyone knows you used that kid to run your errands. And everyone sure as shit knows that little neck snap is your specialty. Terry finds out you did a kid, did him sloppy like that on our turf? He won't care anymore how long you guys known each other.

I don't bother denying it. Besides, he's right, I did kill Leprosy and I should have cleaned it up. Doesn't matter if he's an idiot about everything else.

—Problem is, Terry's got that mercy streak. Someone's got to go, he likes to just put a few in the back of the head. Doesn't believe in sending a message. So me, I got to get my licks in now.

He punches my face a few more times. Stops.

—Oops. Getting late.

He rises from his squat.

—Time to make the coffee for the next shift.

He starts to close the closet door.

—Don't worry, I'll be back on in a couple hours. Maybe I'll bring a little blood. Keep your strength up. After all, Terry may not be back for days.

He closes the door, locks the chain. My face is swollen and broken. I don't have to worry about it for long. Soon enough real pain comes to call.

And Tom's right about the crying, but the tears have nothing to do with anything he did to me.

It's hard to say what the Vyrus is doing to me. Because not only do I have no idea what it's doing, but neither does anyone else. Terry spelled it out for me a long time ago. What it boils down to is that investigating and isolating a virus, even a simple one, takes a shitload of resources. Not even the Coalition has the kind of resources necessary. If the Vyrus were ever made public there would be no end of research fellows out there trying to make their name breaking open one of the strangest freaks of nature to come gibbering out of the asylum. Also no doubt that all the infected would be herded into sterile-environment camps so as to protect the general population. I was around when AIDS first dropped. I haven't forgotten how quickly human compassion flies out the window. Not that I'm looking for compassion, just that I know better than to assume it exists.

In the absence of any real knowledge about what the thing is doing inside of us, we're forced to go by what we see and feel. I know the Vyrus wants blood because I feel its thirst. I know it makes me stronger because I feel it in my muscles. I know it heals me and slows my aging because I can look in a mirror. I know it has fashioned me into a predator because I hunt and I kill. But I don't know what it is doing to me now. Terry thinks the cramps are like a cattle prod, little jabs to get you off your ass and out there feeding. He also thinks they might be the last gasp as the Vyrus scrapes the bottom of the barrel and consumes the last uninfected blood in your body. The long aching pain that follows is maybe the Vyrus beginning to feed on itself. That's what Terry says anyway. Doesn't much matter to me, all I care about is that it won't hurt quite as much as the cramps when it comes.

But it hasn't come yet.

—Joe.
   Light.
—Joe.
   In my face.
—Joe.
   I can only tell because it brightens the darkness behind my clenched eyelids.
—Damn it, Joe.
   I don't steel myself for Tom's next thrashing. The cramps are on me hard, and having my face busted some more is the last thing on my mind. My mind barely exists now except as a place for the signals from the nerves in my gut to land and wreak havoc.
—Joe, get the fuck up.
   He grabs me under my arms and yanks me to my feet. It makes it hurt worse.

—Auuuggh!
—Shut up.

He shoves me and I land in a chair. I pull my knees up and roll back onto the floor.

—Stop being such a wimp.

He grabs my hands and pulls them away from where they are clutching my stomach.

—Auuugh!

He grabs the cuff chain and yanks my arms out straight.

—Such a wimp. You know the pain of childbirth is worse than the cramps?

I open one eye a tiny bit. Lydia.

—And that's not just feminist propaganda. I know infected women who gave birth, they told me.

She sticks a key in one of the cuff locks and it snaps open. She looks at my face.

—I see Tom came by.

—Ung-hungh.

—Give me your ankle.

I roll on my back and lift my feet off the floor. The cramps lurch.

—Augh.

—Shut. Up.

I close my eyes and nod as she unlocks the shackles then pulls me up and puts me back on the chair.

—Can you walk?

—Ungh.

—Fucking wimp.

She grabs my shoulders and pulls me to my feet again.

—Can you walk?

I don't answer, just put one foot in front of the other. And fall down. She kneels next to me.

—Joe, this is it. This is the only shot you get. Tom's crashed and Hurley's hunting and the sun will be up soon. Get up.

She reaches inside my jacket, takes out the picture and sticks it in my face.

—Get up and go get the girl, Joe.

She's pulling on me again. I get up.

—Come on.

She holds my arm and walks me across the room.

—I'll rig it here, make it look like you smashed the door and blindsided me and got the keys.

We're at the bottom of the steps that lead up to the sidewalk trap. They're steep.

—It won't hold, but Tom can't make a serious move on me. He knows I can take him.

—Hurlehungh?

—Hurley won't do anything without Terry. Come on.

I crawl up the steps and she pushes the steel door open.

—Bloohnd?

—No, I don't have any here. Hit your stash, but don't stay at your place, they'll be looking there. Go on. Go.

She shoves me up onto the street, then reaches up through the trap and grabs my pants leg. I look down. Her face and one arm are stuck up through the trap, the picture of Amanda Horde in her hand.

—Take it. I wrote a number on the back. Use it if you have to.

I groan as I bend to take the picture from her.

—Help that girl, Joe. I find out different, or find out you were lying to me, and I'll come after you with my people. We'll fire-bomb your house and then we'll dog you through the streets.

—HoKugh.

—So fucking run.

I do, lurching and stumbling down the sidewalk, the loose cuffs still dangling from my wrist, the girl's picture in my hand, and no place to hide.

I make it ten yards before the heaves grab me. I bend over the hood of a parked car and choke up bile until I'm empty and gagging on air. When it stops I look around, trying to find a dark corner to creep into. But nothing will be dark for long. Home, Lydia said. Go home and hit my stash. She doesn't know there's no stash to hit. I pitch myself off the car and reel down the street.

At the end of the block I lean against a street sign: 3rd and C. Evie lives on 3rd. Just a block and a half away on 3rd between A and B. Evie will look after me, she'll take care of me.

And she has blood. Over five quarts of it.

I shake it off and take the right onto C, away from Evie and the blood that's killing her.

Christian and the Dusters would take me in, but there's no way I can make it to Pike before the sun is up. I need a hole. I need a deep hole in the ground where I can ride out the last waves of the cramps. I look up at the sky; it's already bright enough to burn my eyes and make them tear.

I need a hole.

The blue sawhorse barricades are still in front of the school on 9th, but the cop car is gone. Five-thirty A.M. traffic is on the streets, but I can't worry about that; I'm less than an hour from getting burned down. I edge between two of the sawhorses and walk hunched over to the door. There's a new chain and padlock. I'm far too weak to break it or to force the thick double doors. I won't be scaling the side of the wall, either. Maybe if I didn't have the cramps I could shimmy up a drainpipe. If I try it as I am I'll probably get hit with a cramp halfway up and fall a couple stories onto my head. That might be just enough to solve all my problems. Instead I start checking the ground floor windows. The steel screens on almost all of them have suffered some form of abuse over the years. It doesn't take long to find one where the lower right bracket has been wrenched from the brickwork.

The corner of the screen can be pulled up, but only a few inches, not enough for me to squeeze through. I squat, get a grip on it with both hands and push up with my legs and arms. The screen is made from heavy-gauge steel that's gridded in a pattern like chicken wire, the edges sharp prongs. They dig into the palms of my hands, popping holes through the photograph I hadn't realized I was still holding. The screen starts to bend. From down the street I hear the rumble of a sanitation truck. Just a few yards away from me on the sidewalk is a huge mound of trash. A cramp hits and tries to cut my legs out from under me. My knees buckle slightly and the screen starts to spring back. The truck's air brakes blast and squeal as it slows, approaching the abandoned school. I squeeze my eyes shut, muscling the screen upward, and its spiked edge pops through the skin of my hands just like it did the photograph. The cramp bundles my organs, trying to curl me into myself. The screen wrenches upward, leaving a gap perhaps large enough for me to wriggle through. I pull my hands free of the prongs as the truck grinds to a halt behind me, smash them against the window, grab the jagged-edged sill and pull myself up. Broken glass digs at my belly, offering awful relief from the cramps. My upper body flops inside and my pants get caught on the screen. I tear them loose, using my forearms to pull myself along the floor and into the empty schoolroom. I writhe to my knees on broken glass and peek out the window at the sanitation guys climbing off the truck. I reach out and lace my fingers through the holes in the screen and pull. It's easier to drag back down than it was to push up, and I get it close enough to the window that maybe it won't be noticed from the street. That done, I stick my fingers past the broken shards of glass and pull the bloody photograph from the bloody barbs. Then I fall down.

The cramps have become a huge hand that tangles its fingers in my intestines and balls itself into a fist. I crawl, leaving bloody smears on the floor from my oozing hands, and find the basement door. I look at the stairs, then let gravity tumble me down. I want to stay at the foot of the stairs in a tangled mess of blood and glass and cracked bones. Instead I take advantage of the fist relaxing for a moment and get to my feet. Anyone coming into the school will see the bloody hand-prints on the floor and follow them to the basement. I need my hole. I stuff my hands into my armpits to keep more blood from dribbling on the floor, and memory leads me through the rank blackness. I make it to the old storage room, shoulder the door open and fall behind a pile of the broken and graffitied desks, just as the fist squeezes closed.

Fuckmefuckmefuckme. Please! Makeit! Stop!

—Hey?

Stopstopstopstopstop!

—Hey.

Pleasepleasepleaseplease!

—Get out of here.

Nonononono!

—This is my place, you got to get out.

—No. Just. Just fucking leave me aughhhlone!

—No, asshole, you have to get out. I . . . Shit, you're fucked up.

The fist starts to relax, my intestines slowly slipping from its fingers. I open my eyes.

She's squatting a few yards away, shining a flashlight on me; the girl whose picture is clutched in my lacerated hand.

She points at my face.

—The cops do that to you?

—No.

—*No?*

—No.

She points at the top of my head.

—What's that?

I reach up to feel whatever she's pointing at and the loose cuff hanging from my left wrist knocks me in the chin.

She shakes her head.

—But the cops didn't do that to you.

—No.

—*Uh-huh*. Well, what*ever*. You still have to get out of here.

—You got the lease on the place?

—Yeah, *right*. *No*, I *don't* have the lease. But it's my hideout. Find your own.

I touch my face.

—Can't really see myself walking around much right now.

—Why? You *said* the cops aren't after you.

—I need to stay here.

She stands up.

—You are being *such* an *ass*hole. Look, you can't stay here. *OK?*

—I. Hungh.

The fingers start to tighten again. I pull my knees up against my chest.

—Oh, *maaan*. You're a *junkie* aren't you? You starting to jones? Here.

She pulls something out of her pocket and holds it out to me. A twenty-dollar bill.

—Go get a bag and fix. Just do it somewhere else.

—I. Uhn. I'm not. Augh.

She takes a step back.

—Don't throw up in here. Do *not* puke in here!

I clench my teeth, shaking my head back and forth; not at her but at what's happening inside me. She steps closer, shoves the toe of one of her Nikes under my ass and starts trying to shove me toward the door.

—Out. Get *out*!

My gut ripples and I heave up a final dribble of bile that lands on her sneaker.

—*Gross!* So gross! Get *out*!

She's kicking me now. The point of her toe hitting the side of my stomach is a new agony. I reach out to block her foot and the picture falls from my hand and cartwheels to the floor. She looks down at it, at the blood-smeared image of herself. I hold a hand up.

—Aughm! Amandahungh.

She bolts for the door. I grab the cuff of her jeans. She stops, lifts her other foot and steps on my arm.

—Let *go*!

I keep my grip and she tries to rip her leg free and trips herself onto the floor.

—I'm gonna *scream!* I'm gonna!

She starts screaming and reaches down, clawing at my hand, trying to pry my fingers loose from her jeans. I grab her wrist.

SNAP!

She stops screaming and stares at the cuff I have ratcheted onto her, chaining her right wrist to my left.

—That is so *wrong*.

—Take it off.

—I don't have the key.

—*Gaaaud*. So lame.

We're sitting next to each other, our backs against the wall. The cramps haven't hit me for five minutes and I'm starting to hope I might be in the lull.

—Let me see that.

She reaches for the photograph still lying on the floor.

—Don't touch it.

Her hand stops.

—Why not? It's of *me*.

—The blood, don't get it on you.

—What*ever*.

She picks it up by the edges. It doesn't matter, really. The Vyrus can't survive outside a host. But it bothers me, seeing her fingers graze the blood, knowing what was recently living in it.

—I can't *believe* they gave you this.

She drops it on the floor.

—How'd you find me? You talk to that Dobbs creep?

—Sort of.

—Talk about *lame*. That guy doesn't have a clue.

—No, he doesn't.

—Doesn't matter. I'm *not* going back.

I rattle the cuffs.

—Yeah, you are.

She rolls her head to the side and looks at me.

—You ever try dragging a screaming teenage girl down the *street*?

I remember a night over twenty years ago: a young girl screaming, a hunger I didn't know how to control. But it doesn't matter. The past is a dead thing. I can't change it.

—You ever been knocked out and hauled around in a sack?

—No *way*. My dad would *freak* and you would *never* get paid.

—Not taking you to your dad.

She bugs her eyes at me.

—Oh, *no!*

She laughs.

—*Her?* She sent you?

She picks up the picture.

—Of *course* she gave you this one. She *knows* I hate it.

She tears it in half and drops the pieces to the floor.

—*Bitch*. So what's she *want*? There a junior *deb ball* I'm supposed to go to or something?

I pick up the pieces of the picture and put them in my jacket pocket.

—She doesn't want you to end up like Whitney Vale.

She starts to say something else, closes her mouth instead. She looks at her shoes, rubbing the toe of one against the bile stain on the other.

—Whitney got what she *deserved*.

Whitney Vale, eighteen, jamming a knife into the back of a kid's skull; her body being eaten by a germ.

—For what?

—I don't *know*. Maybe for fucking my *dad*?

—Like I said, your mom doesn't want you to end up like Whitney.

—Oh. My. *God*. She told you that? She is such a *freak*. I *know* what she says about him. But my dad has never touched me. The only reason he fucked Whitney is 'cause she was all over him. So gross. The only guy who ever touched me was one of mom's creepy *boyfriends*. So what's she want to do, kidnap me to protect me from my dad? She is *so lame*.

She stands up.

—Let's go.

—Huh?

—Take me home.

I look at my watch, it's just after sunrise. She yanks on the cuffs.

—You got me, *toughguy*, now take me in.

—We can't go yet.

—Look, I'm not going to *spaz* or anything. I mean, the sooner you take me back there, the sooner I can run away again. So let's just get it *over* with.

—We have to wait.

—For *what*?

—For the sun to go down.

—*Why*?

—Because I'm allergic to it.

She stares at me.

—You are *such* a loser.

My stomach is filled with needles. They drop down my intestines and into my bowels; they drift up my esophagus and into my lungs; they seep into my veins and are carried throughout my body, filling the tiny capillaries in my face and fingertips and toes; they are in my lips and armpits and testicles; they are everywhere. And they are such a relief. This is the lull. This is the long, scraping irritation that follows the cramps. And I can live with it. I can live with it and breathe with it and walk with it. It won't wrack me with sudden crippling attacks. It will simply and slowly get worse and worse until the needles feel like they're red-hot and turning my

blood to steam. But there's time before that happens.
—I have to go.
  And I need time.
—Hey.
  I need all I can get.
—Hey!
  I need every second that I can possibly get that leaves me in control of the Vyrus.
—I *said*, I have to *go*.
  Because I'm chained to a neat little snacklet.
—He*lloo*.
  And I'm still in the dark about a lot of things, but I know for damn sure that drinking this girl is a great way to get myself right just long enough for her parents and Predo and Lydia to each grab one of my limbs and start pulling.
—I. Have. To.
—I told you we can't go yet.
—No, re*tard*. I have to *go*.
  But it might be worth it.

—Say something.
—Why?
—*Because*. It's hard to pee when you're handcuffed to some asshole and you're both just waiting for the pee.
  The door is swung open. I'm squatting on one side of it with my arm stretched out, and she's on the other side. Our hands grip the edge of the door, mine just slightly above hers.
—So say *something*.
—For a girl who has some experience living in squats, you're awfully pee shy.
—Fuck *you*.
  I chew on my split lower lip, sucking at one of the cuts,

trying to ease the prickles inside me with the dull copper taste of my own blood. It doesn't help. All it does is whet my appetite, as if I need it whetted. I stop sucking.

Blood still fills my veins and pumps through my heart and carries oxygen to my brain, but as far as the Vyrus is concerned it might as well be dust. My blood has been occupied and harvested, whatever it is that the Vyrus consumes has been stripped away. But there's more of what I need right on the other side of this door.

—Hey!

—What?

—Don't pull on the cuffs.

I look. She's right, I've been tugging her toward me from around the door.

—Sorry.

—Yeah you're sorry. And stop being so quiet, I told you to say something.

—Like what?

—Any*thing*. Tell me who busted up your face. *Not* that I don't think there's like a line of people *waiting* to bust it up.

—Guy doesn't like it.

—Your face?

—Yeah.

—*Well.* Can you blame him? Are you going to kick his ass?

—Hadn't thought about it.

—*Maaan.*

—What?

—For a big guy.

—Yeah?

—For a big guy, you're kind of a *pussy*.

—You pee yet?

—*Damn it.* I was almost there. Why'd you have to say *that*? Now talk about something else.

—How'd you get in here?

—There's like an alley around back, off of Tenth? The gate's not locked. Whitney showed me last summer. Go through the gate and there's the basement door. Squatters busted the lock off that couple years back, I guess.

My legs hurt from squatting. I'm pretty sure I fractured something in my right ankle when I came down the stairs. I shift to keep it from aching and I lose my balance for a second. Our wrists tug-a-war before I steady myself. I grab the edge of the door and accidentally touch her fingers.

—Don't *touch* me.

A moment's silence.

—*Talk*.

Jesus fucking.

—Why'd you run away?

Now it's her turn to get all silent.

—If it's like you say and your dad isn't messing with you?

—None of your business.

—OK.

More silence.

—Are you *jerking off* back there?

—No.

—Then stop getting all quiet, it's *creepy*.

—OK. Why'd you run away?

—I *told you*, none of your business.

—Fine.

Silence.

—Fuck do you *care*?

—I don't. I just want you to piss so I can stretch my legs.

She laughs.

—Stretch your legs, I just went.

She digs through her little backpack looking for something. She's holding her flashlight in her cuffed right hand as she searches with her left. She jerks my left hand this way and that as she rummages.

—Why'd you have to cuff my right hand?

—If I'd cuffed your left you would have to walk around backward.

She stares at me.

—Yeah, *right*. Like I would have done that.

Our hands bump.

—Your hand is all cold and *sweaty*.

She gives me a fish-eye.

—Are you *sick*? 'Cause if I *catch* something from you I am going to be *so* pissed.

—Just clammy by nature.

—*Gross*.

I *am* cold and sweaty. The Vyrus is downshifting, trying to save energy, storing up for its last big push. But sick is not a big enough word for what I am.

She pulls a few things out of the pack; some extra clothes, an MP3 player, batteries, a bottle of water, and finally comes up with what she's looking for: a handful of diet bars. She holds one in her left hand and tears the wrapper open with her teeth. She catches me watching her.

—You *want* one?

I do want one. I haven't eaten for awhile and I usually eat like a pig. You have to, just to keep up with the high revs the Vyrus usually runs your metabolism at.

—Sure.

—There's peanut butter or chocolate and coconut.

—Peanut butter.

She hands me the bar and we eat by the dim light cast

by her flashlight. She finishes hers, throws the empty wrapper on the floor, and picks out another.

—So my mom was the one who called you?

I chew for a couple seconds. The peanut butter was a mistake, it's hard and sticky and hurts my sore jaw as I chew.

—Yeah.

—What'd she say?

—Said you were missing, said she wanted to find you.

She's picking at her second bar, pinching tiny pieces of the chocolate coating between her fingernails and nibbling them.

—What about my dad, you talk to him?

—Yeah.

She huffs.

—*Aaand?*

I think about my meeting with Dr. Dale Horde, the way he casually put me in my place like it's something he does ten times a day. The way he mickeyed me so Predo's spook could rob my stash.

—Said he wanted me to find you.

—Yeah, *right*.

She's peeled about half the chocolate off her second bar, leaving the coconut underneath untouched.

—Mom says he wants to fuck me. Least that'd be *something*. Looks at me all the time like he can't figure out *where* I came from. Only time he pays any attention is when one of my *girl-friends* comes over. Then he tries to be all *super-cooldad* so he can impress them. *Lame*.

—That why you split?

Knowing I'm a fool for asking, knowing I don't need to know any of this stuff, knowing this stuff just makes the job harder.

—I *don't know*. Maybe because my *mom* gets drunk all the

time. Maybe because she *told me* my dad wants to fuck me. Maybe because I think that makes her *jealous*. Maybe because my dad is creepy with my girlfriends. Maybe because I stole a pair of my mom's earrings and to *punish me* she took my *computer away* and I snuck in my dad's office to use *his computer* and I found all this *porn* on it that Whitney did and that *grossed me out*. Not that she *did it*, because I knew about that, but because *my dad* was looking at it. Maybe because I looked in his drawers and found *pictures* of him *fucking* Whitney. Maybe because I was *pissed* at Whitney and came down here to kick her ass. *I don't know*. I just *ran away*.

She folds the torn ends of the wrapper around the mutilated bar and shoves it back in her bag.

—*God*. Hate it when I do that. Just eating 'cause I'm bored. Whitney says that's how you get fat.

She pulls up the bottom of her Che Guevara T-shirt, looks at her flat stomach and pinches a quarter inch of skin.

—*Fat*.

I look the other way, not wanting to see her healthy tanned skin and the flush of blood that rises as she pinches herself.

—So *she* call you after Whitney got . . . whatever? That freak her out?

—If it did, she didn't say anything.

—She *wouldn't*. Was she *drunk* when you saw her?

—Couldn't say.

—Yeah, most people can't. I can. If she's awake, she's drunk. She make a *pass* at you?

—No.

She looks at me.

—*Uh-huh*. As *if*. So'd you fuck her?

—No.

She looks at me some more.

—You'd be the first, then.
—Not according to your mom.
  She laughs. But not like anything is funny.
—So.
—Yeah?
—You know what happened to Whitney?
—I heard.
—That for real? That *Satanist* guy did it?
—That's what they say.
—Yeah. *Right*.
  She reaches in her bag and pulls out the partially eaten diet bar and starts picking at the chocolate again. I watch her. I try not to ask. I fail.
—What?
  Fool.
—Nothing.
—You think different?
  You fool.
—No.
  She picks a piece of chocolate, eats it, picks another and drops it on the floor; then goes on like that, alternating a bite for a drop.
—Just.
—Yeah?
—I got the idea that, maybe. I don't know. That maybe she was *blackmailing* my dad.
  She scrapes off a last bit of chocolate with her front teeth, looks the bar over to see if she missed any, then tosses the coconut remnant into a corner.

It doesn't make any difference.
  Say she was. Say Whitney took those pictures of them

fucking and threatened him; threatened to show them to his wife, who was looking for some kind of leverage to get Amanda away from him; threatened to take them to the papers and smear his rep. Hell, she might have threatened to just post them for anyone who wanted to gape at Dr. Dale Edward Horde, founder, president, chairman and CEO of Horde Bio Tech, as he fucked an Internet porn star. So say she was blackmailing him. So what?

I know what the kid doesn't. I know her dad and Whitney crossed paths down here, right in this room, right on that square of cardboard not ten feet away from us. But by the time they did, she had already crossed paths with something much creepier than Amanda's pederast father. By the time he found her the carrier had already taken a bite out of the back of her neck. Did he even know?

Figure it this way. He comes down here with some muscle, the same muscle that probably killed Dobbs for him, and they found Whitney. Couple days after being infected, her brain would still be pretty much intact. Her speech centers, even some of her short-term memory might work. She might even have been fighting her new impulses, trying not to become what she already was. Figure Horde and his goons confront her somewhere. She won't answer any questions. They think she's being tough, but she's just having holes bored through her brain by the bacteria. Doesn't matter, they find the pictures and whatever else she has on Horde. But he's not done, wants to teach her a lesson, but wants to do it somewhere private. Figure he remembers the place Dobbs found his daughter last year. Maybe that makes it better for him, having her on the floor in here, makes it easier to think about Amanda, makes it closer to what he really wants. Whitney wouldn't have been easy. The smell of his living flesh so close would have made her crazy. His guys would have had to hold her down while he raped her. And when he was done? What the fuck did he care. He has the evidence now and if she talks to anyone it's just the word of a teenage runaway slut against his. No contest. So he left her there. And the next people to see her were probably the two fashion junkies who came looking for a safe place to fix.

But it doesn't matter. It doesn't change anything for me, just fills in a couple gaps. It doesn't make my job any easier. It doesn't make me any less hungry. It doesn't help me forget the little girl lying on her side next to me taking a nap. It doesn't make my cold hand feel less of the warmth of her body as she curls tighter, pulling my chained arm close to her. It doesn't make me any less aware of the cardboard sheet on the other side of the room where I smelled the rank sweat of Horde fucking a still-breathing dead girl.

It makes no difference to me at all. I still have to get her home. I still have to find the carrier. I still have to do the job.

I tell myself this.

But all the while I see pictures of Horde's neck in my hands, my thumbs digging a hole through his skin and ripping open the throbbing artery. And I feel the hot blood splash against my lips and chin as I fit my mouth over the hole. As if that will make the world a better place.

Fool.

I am such a fool.

—You *really* allergic to the sun?
—It's called solar urticaria.
—Sounds like *VD*.
—It's not.
—So what happens if you go to the beach or something?

—What happens if you stick your hand under the broiler?

—No *shit*?

—No shit.

—That's so *wrong*.

—Yep.

—Were you born with it?

—Not really.

—So when was the last time you were out in the sun?

—Long time ago. You got any change?

We're on the corner of 10th and A, standing in front of a pay phone. I wiped most of the gore from my face and hands before we came up and have my jacket buttoned to hide the blood on my shirt. The holes in my hands have scabbed, but aren't healing nearly as quickly as they would if I was straight. They ache and throb like my face and ankle. But the needles keep me too occupied to worry about things like that. All my hurts will be healed when I get some blood, but I'm running out of time.

—Here.

She's holding out her hand, change pooled in her tiny palm. I pluck out two quarters.

—What's your mom's number?

—The apartment or her cell?

—Cell.

She rattles off the number and I dial. She stands on one side of the phone, trying to make it look like she's not with me. Pretty hard to do with the cuffs, even when they're covered by an extra T-shirt from her bag.

—Hello.

—Ms. Horde, it's me.

Amanda looks at me.

—Joseph. I.

—I have her.

—Oh, I. Thank you, Joseph.

Amanda raises her eyebrows.

—She's just *so* relieved, isn't she?

I ignore her.

—Do you want to come and get her?

—Yes I. No. No, you should. Can you bring her here?

Amanda is making little kissy faces.

—Is she just so grateful to you? Can she just not *wait* to see me?

—Sure. What's the address?

She gives me an address on 81st off Park Avenue. Amanda is just looking bored now, watching everything but me, and listening to every word I say.

—We'll grab a cab and be there in twenty minutes.

—Good. Good. Joseph?

—Yeah.

—Can I?

—What?

She doesn't say anything.

—You want to talk to her?

Amanda turns her head to look at me again.

—No. No. That's. Just. You better just bring her home.

—OK.

I hang up and grab Amanda's backpack from the ground.

—Let's go.

—Didn't want to talk to her *darling daughter*?

—Guess not.

—Don't be shocked.

—I'm not.

I wave the backpack at a passing cab. It stops. I open the door and wait while Amanda thinks about it. She looks inside the cab, looks at me. I gesture at the open door. She shrugs and climbs in. I get in after her and give the cabbie the address and we roll. She's looking out the window. I'm gritting my teeth and a little gasp squeezes out between them.

She turns from the window and looks at my face, looks at my swollen and scabbed lips stretched tight over my teeth.

—What's *eating* you?

—Nothing. Just shut up for awhile.

—And I was looking forward to another *chat*. As *if*.

And she goes back to the window. And I go back to feeling the pain that's building inside me. My veins have started to burn.

The hours spent in the school basement hiding from the sun have brought me closer to the next phase of Vyral starvation. The stage where my body will simply shut down as the Vyrus makes adjustments deep within my brain. I'm at the border now, this is as far as I've gone. I know I can take the pain right here in this moment, but I don't know if I can take what will come in the next minute or the minute after that or all the very few minutes remaining to me.

So I grind my teeth and clench my right fist, my fingernails digging into the scabbed palm of my hand. And I tell myself that she is not the answer. Tell myself that having the cabbie pull over and dragging her into a dark alley is not the answer. But the Vyrus is telling me a different story. That's OK, I can ignore it. I can ignore it just as easily as I ignore our hands sitting on the seat between us, the chain joining them beneath a retro Joan Jett T-shirt she picked up somewhere on St. Marks because she thought it was cool.

—*Moooom*, I'm *hoooome*.

The elevator from the lobby opens directly onto the foyer. It's no more or less than you'd expect: large, but not too large; expensively appointed, but not too expensively appointed; tasteful, but not too tasteful; boldly decorated, but not too boldly decorated. All in all, the kind of place I would expect to find a fabulously wealthy and dysfunctional family with ties to the Coalition. But not too much like that. I wait for the inevitable housekeeper to arrive, but none does. Nor does anyone answer Amanda's call. I look at her. She looks back and shrugs. *What did you expect, a victory parade?* I smear my forehead against my shoulder, wiping some of the cold sweat away.

The sweats got bad just as the cab pulled up to the Hordes' brownstone. I had to ask Amanda to pay the cab because Tom took the last of my cash. She looked at me like I was lame, but I've gotten used to that. She got a key out of her hip pocket and let us into an entryway that was similar in every way to this foyer. Then she led me into an elevator to take us the two flights to the floor her mother occupies. This accompanied by one of many sideways glances to see what I think of her folks keeping separate quarters. I notice the glances, but I'm not giving much back, focused as I am on the simmering fluid hissing through my organs. I'm starting to wish the cramps would return.

—Mom!

No reply.

—Come *on*, she's probably passed out.

She storms ahead of me, dragging me by the cuffs as I stumble clumsily behind her. She looks back at me.

—You want to try *walking* for a change?

I don't say anything.

—I *knew* it. You *are* a junkie, aren't you?

I don't say anything.

—Well come *on*, junkie. Get paid and then you can get rid of me and go fix.

She hauls me down the central hallway that runs the

length of the brownstone. I catch peripheral glimpses of a bathroom, a kitchenette, a large bedroom. All done up in the *not too* style. At the end of the hall we come up against a closed door. Amanda slaps her knuckles against it once, then shoves it open.

—Hey, Mom, I'm *hooome*.

She gives my arm a jerk and I take a lurching step into the room and she holds her cuffed hand up in the air.

—And look what *I* found. Can I keep it?

Marilee Horde looks up from the glass in her hands. She's sitting on a couch that matches everything in her little sitting room perfectly. Her red-rimmed eyes flick dully from Amanda to me to Amanda.

—Oh. Oh, Amanda. I'm. I am sorry.

Amanda drops her arm.

—You got *that* right, Mom.

Marilee's head drops back down and she stares deep into her glass.

—Sorry.

Amanda takes a step into the room.

—Mom?

The guy who knocks me out doesn't hit me half as hard as Hurley did. Then again he doesn't have to, I'm already halfway there. I go down and out. Sorry thing is, the Vyrus doesn't seem to care whether I'm conscious or unconscious. It just keeps hurting me.

Metal is rasping on metal.

—How much longer?

—Little while. Quicker if we go through his wrist.

—Just the cuffs, please.

I can hear them talking, but I can't see anything. My eyes

must be closed, but rather than darkness, they peer into a pale gray abyss. Then something bobs up out of the abyss, something dark that suddenly resolves into a man's face.

—He's awake.

The rasping stops and another face appears looking down at me. Something waves in front of my face. A hand.

—Uh-uh. His eyes are open, but he's not awake.

Yes, he's right, my eyes are open. The gray abyss is the ceiling of Marilee Horde's sitting room. I try to shift my eyes to get a look around. They don't move. I try to blink. Nothing. I am frozen. The hand that was waving in front of my eyes slaps lightly at my cheeks.

—He's out.

A third face appears. I know this one, Dr. Dale Edward Horde.

—Not to tell you how to do your jobs, but is he, perhaps, faking it?

The hand flourishes and an instrument materializes between its fingers: a stiletto long and thin, a rainbow glittering along its well-honed edge. The blade dips close to my right eye and the point hovers there, eclipsing half of the world.

—I'd say no.

—I'd like a more conclusive test.

The blade darts down and I hear the faint sound of steel entering flesh and feel the slightest tug in my cheek. No pain, but the taste of my own dead blood runs down the back of my tongue.

—He's not home.

—Very good.

The stiletto reappears, blade now lacquered with crimson. A handkerchief flutters and wipes away the blood. Then handkerchief, blade, hand, and two of the faces exit from sight. Horde remains above me, gazing down, inspecting me. He purses his lips and pokes a finger at my cheek. It comes back into view with a smear of blood on its tip. He looks at the precious drop, rubs it between his thumb and finger, sniffs at it.

—To think.

Then he shrugs, wipes his fingers on me and he, too, disappears.

I would like to have felt the blade pierce my cheek. It might have assured me that I am still alive, that the exterior world can still affect me. But I have no such evidence. Just a body that feels shot full of novocaine, immobilized and without sensation. On the outside, anyway. The inside is another matter. The inside is a cauldron of something bubbling and viscous, something that I think may be now burrowing into my bones, seeking out some last refuge of blood.

Someone tugs at my arm and my head rolls slightly to the left. I can't make my eyes focus beyond a foot or two, but I see the two men. One of them has his knee planted on my wrist, pinning it to the floor. The other kneels across from him, crouched over a blurred range of small hills on the horizon of the carpet. The girl. His picks something up from the floor, applies it to the girl's arm. Metal rasps on metal again as he hacksaws the cuffs from her wrist.

Horde stands over them, observing.

—Don't cut her.

—Like I said, be easier if we went through his wrist.

—No.

—He's not long for the world. Far gone as he is, he won't be coming back.

—No. He has a role to play, and a severed appendage will not suit.

—OK.

—I'll kill you if they hurt her, Dale.

Horde turns toward the other end of the room, where his wife was sitting when we came in.

—Something, dear?

—I'll kill you.

—I think it's safe to say that these gentlemen won't be harming our daughter in the least.

—Kill you.

Her words badly slurred.

—Have another drink, wife.

I watch the man with the hacksaw, the same one who had the stiletto. His movements are sharp and strong and he works the saw with an unnatural swiftness. My sense of smell has been dulled to near uselessness. I can't smell the man with the saw, but his movements give him away. He has the Vyrus. He could be a Rogue that Horde has somehow dug up, but he has a look I know. The expensive black suit, the conservative haircut, the carefully knotted tie, all say Coalition. One of Predo's enforcers on loan to Horde. The other has the beefy look of a stock bodyguard. One of Horde's own company men.

There's a little ping as the hacksaw parts the steel of the cuffs. The enforcer puts the saw aside, frees Amanda's wrist and starts to lift her from the floor. Horde puts a hand on his shoulder.

—I'll do that.

The enforcer and the goon stand and step out of the way, out of my view, as Horde kneels and tucks his arms under his daughter's back and legs and lifts her from the floor. Only his lower body is in focus for me now, but I can see the obscure shade of his head as he cradles the girl and puts his face close to hers.

—Home again, home again, my dear.

A glass shatters over by the couch. The smudge of Horde turns.

—Be careful, wife, you'll hurt yourself.

—What did you do to her?

—Gave her something to make her sleep, love. She was hysterical. She needs sleep after her ordeal. Imagine the trauma of being abducted by this filth.

—She wasn't.

He rocks the girl from side to side.

—Yes, love, she was. She was plucked from the streets by this man. This man who you then hired to find her.

—I?

—Strange coincidence that. Except that it was no coincidence. Was it, love?

—Dale, what are you?

—Very clever of you. Hire the same man you paid to abduct your daughter to then find her.

—No.

He's putting on a show for her now, rehearsing a story for more official recitations at later dates. I'm happy for the distraction. Anything is better than the thing with teeth inside me.

—Yes, I assure you that is exactly how it happened. How naive of me not to have seen it when I met with him to discuss the case.

—Kill you.

Something crashes.

—Gentlemen, if you would please keep my wife from hurting herself.

There is a rush of movement and the slightest of scuffles.

—Don't harm her, please.

—Fuck you, Dale, fucking fuck you!

—If one of you could simply inject her with a half cc from

the vial I used to calm my daughter? You'll find a clean syringe in the case there. Intramuscular will suffice.

—No! Fucking no!

She shrieks. Horde passes the time cooing at his daughter. I pass the time dying in horrible agony. Then Marilee is quiet.

—Better, yes? In any case, the humorous part of the whole tale is that I simply suspected you of cuckolding me with your hired hand. It was only when the men I had following you witnessed your visit to Chester Dobbs's office that I suspected the truth. I can only assume that you originally paid him off the case to make room for your own man. But as to what happened next? Did Dobbs threaten blackmail or some such?

A slight moan from the couch.

—No, do not answer, just relax. I will assume blackmail. Why else would you feel so compelled to kill him?

I'm listening to the frame Horde is building around us, around his wife and me, trying to stay a step ahead of it, trying to figure out what picture the frame will surround. His wife and I in cahoots in the kidnapping of the girl, his wife as Dobbs's murderer. I'm trying to imagine the picture such a frame would suit. It's a good problem, complex and detailed. It distracts me. But not enough.

Pain is becoming.

—The tragedy. The real tragedy of it all is that I couldn't save you from yourself. The tragedy is that, despite what you had done, trying to take my daughter from me, I still loved you and wished to save you from your own weakness. But I was too late. Too late to save you from a brutal murder at the hands of your hired thug turned lover.

Pain is eclipsing.

—How fortunate that I should remember Amanda's little hiding place from last summer. And how clever of your partner to have used the site of a recent massacre as his hideaway. Who would ever have thought to look there? Too bad, though.

Pain is not what I thought it was.

—Too bad we were not in time to spare you from your fate. But thank God.

I have never before felt pain.

—Thank God we were in time to save Amanda. Save her before he could abuse her, more than he already had. Was that it?

Pain is a new thing.

—Was that why you quarreled? Because you saw how he had misused her? I like to think so. I like to think that at the very end, your mother's instincts took over and you tried desperately to save our little girl. How brave you were to fight him. How awful it must have been when he slid the needle into your skin and left you helpless.

Pain lives.

—Helpless to do anything for your daughter as he touched her again, right in front of your eyes. Helpless as he turned his attentions to you. What a terrible end you had. If only we had arrived a few moments earlier, we might have been able to do more than to simply avenge your demise.

Pain breathes.

—But it's all over now. All over. Perhaps you'll have peace knowing that your daughter is safe now. Safe at home in her father's loving arms.

Pain has a home inside my body.

A grunt, and tumble of clumsy footsteps as Marilee stumbles into view clawing at her husband's face. The enforcer materializes, pulls her away and throws her to the floor. Horde nods as if she is reacting as he knew she would, reacting childishly to his story.

—Turn her over.

The enforcer flips Marilee to her stomach as Horde sets his daughter gently in a chair.

—Bare her neck.

The enforcer sweeps Marilce's hair from the back of her neck and pulls the collar of her blouse down. Horde steps out of view, and then back, now holding a small black cube with rounded corners. He kneels next to his wife and holds the cube in front of her face. It splits opens like a jewelry case. He shows her the contents.

—I finished.

She moans. He takes something white and pink from the case.

—I've even tried it out already.

He sets the case aside.

—Twice.

He holds the white and pink object, pinched between his thumb and middle finger.

—First on Whitney. Which was, naturally, somewhat by design.

He shifts the white and pink object to thc palm of his hand, letting it rest there.

—And later, in a spontaneous moment, on a downtown raga-muffin.

The white and pink object springs open slightly, like a clamshell.

—And now it is time for another trial. With a considerably larger dose I think.

He lifts the white and pink object to his face, opens his mouth wide and slides it inside. He bites down hard on the dentures, setting them in place. Marilee begins to thrash her head from side to side.

—Hold her still.

The enforcer pins Marilee's head to the floor. Horde leans

over the back of his wife's neck, his mouth stretched open, muscles and tendons popping from his own neck, and he bites her.

I have found my carrier. But it is too late to do anything about it.

I am pain.

And a black shroud drops mercifully over my life.

I am dead.

And so I am free to remember my life.

I remember being small and helpless in the house of my parents. How they took advantage of that helplessness, my mother and father. Hands in dark rooms, probing me. Belts like whips, lashing me. I remember the marks on my body that would be healed years later when the Vyrus took up residence and cleaned house. The marks discovered by sympathetic schoolteachers. I remember my mother and father struggling in the arms of the police. The last memory of them. And then the others. New sets of parents, none for more than a year, none a particular improvement over biology. And I remember the street where I taught other children the lessons I had learned at home. The grasping hands, the lash. I remember seeing fear in someone else's eyes, and that it made me feel larger. I remember running the streets, warlord of my tiny tribe. And then being found and being poisoned. And fear and helplessness returned. And then Terry and the Society and something new. A reason. And years of work and learning, as I am taught how to be in the world. Then the discovery that I have become Terry's favorite tool. His sharpest instrument when it is time to apply fear. When it is time for the lash. Then not wanting any longer to be the whip. I remember being alone and doing the job. The Coalition and the Society and their dirty little errands. The job that is just survival. And then Evie. And I remember her whispering to me in the dark of my room while the day was bright outside, telling me what she felt. And having nothing to say to her in return except lies about who and what I am, but telling them all the same. To keep from being alone. And then the years since, years close to the edge. Balancing between Evie and the job. Every step closer to the edge of . . . something. I remember Whitney Vale. The almost human look in her eyes when I took the knife from her, the cough when the blade went in. And Leprosy, the bite in the back of his neck reeking of rotting. And the picture of the girl, alone somewhere, helpless. And her mother's breast pressed against me as she kissed the edge of my mouth. And Philip babbling over Dobbs's strangled corpse. And Daniel asking for my help as Jorge vomited his life into the room. And Dale Edward Horde, arrogant and cruel, experienced in the use of the hands and the lash. And Amanda's hand chained to mine, close by one another, covered by cloth. And the scouring acid in my veins. And a smell that isn't there, describing something that cannot exist. And the basement of the school, scene of a crime no one has defined, but one I can too easily imagine.

And screaming. People screaming. Someone I know screaming.

And I am not dead.

Not dead.

But not alive.

The basement of the school, illuminated by a hissing camp lantern.

Marilee is screaming. She has a reason to.

—Use the condom.

—I don't like 'em.

—I gave it to you for a reason. Use it.

—Fucking. Can't feel anything.

—Neither will you leave any traces of *your* semen.

—OK.

—We can afford a certain level of contradiction in the evidence we leave behind, but let us not bow to hubris and become, dare I say it under the circumstances, cocky.

—OK, OK.

Horde's goon opens the foil packet. He's kneeling next to Marilee, his pants and drawers pushed down his thighs, struggling to roll the rubber onto his semi-hard penis. Marilee is on her stomach, skirt torn half off, panties around her ankles. She's bound and gagged and drugged, but the bacteria is running in her now and her screams pierce the room as she struggles against the belt looped around her wrists.

I am spilled against a pile of junked desks. Thrown here to be dealt with soon enough. When Horde is done with his wife and daughter.

He's naked, standing above the sheet of cardboard where I smelled the residue of his rape of Whitney Vale, his rape of the dead. His daughter sleeps peacefully at his feet. Her shoes and socks removed and set neatly to the side. He watches the goon put on the condom, tug the panties from Marilee's ankles and position himself between her legs.

—Not yet.

The goon looks at him, dick in hand.

—What?

—Wait. Turn her head. I'd like for her to see this. And keep your hand away from her teeth.

The goon shakes his head, grabs a fistful of Marilee's

hair and twists her face toward her husband. Horde is roped with lean muscle and pelted with graying hair. He squats next to Amanda, his penis sharply erect between his knees, and he begins to undo the button and zipper of her jeans.

—Self-control is a virtue. I always told you that, wife. With every one of your infidelities I would remind you that your inability to control your appetites was a weakness for which you would eventually pay.

He opens his daughter's fly slowly, then butterflies it and pauses, gazing at the triangle of white cotton beneath.

—Giving in to one's passions on a constant basis weakens the individual, as well as the passions themselves. Self-control, will-power, not only strengthen the individual, but also sharpen the appetite.

He inserts his index fingers at the waistband of Amanda's jeans and begins to tug them down over her slight hips.

—Self-control allows one the time to fully contemplate one's desires, and to imagine detailed scenarios in which those desires might be fulfilled. It also allows one the time to arrange circumstances so that the most favored of these scenarios might come to fruition.

The jeans are off now, and he folds them carefully and places them atop Amanda's shoes and socks.

—And if you look back, I think you will see how it is that your lack of self-control, and my own ample supply of this virtue, has led you to be in your current position, and me to be in mine.

He runs a finger over the elastic waistband of his daughter's panties. He nods his head.

—Now you may begin. But make sure she is watching me.

The goon grunts and clumsily tries to shove his now utterly limp penis into Marilee while still forcing her to watch her husband. Horde tucks his fingertips into the panties and begins to slide them down.

I close my eyes.

I can close my eyes.

And I can feel my body.

And it is not filled with pain.

I open my eyes.

—Hey.

No one hears.

—Hey!

They hear this time. The goon, with a handful of Marilee's hair and something less than a handful of limp dick. Horde, with his daughter's panties pulled just past the tops of her hip bones. They both stop and turn their heads to look at me where I stand leaning crookedly against the pile of desks.

—Stop that.

Horde purses his lips.

—He was supposed to be finished?

—I've got it.

The enforcer is on me. He appears before me from whatever corner he has been lurking in, seizes my throat and shoves me through the pile of half-rotted desks. The wood tops of the desks splinter and crack and he pins me to the wall, fingers digging into my neck.

Horde holds up a hand.

—Don't kill him. He needs to be shot.

The enforcer keeps his eyes locked on my face.

—I know.

He's strong.

Predo keeps them gorged on blood. That's what Terry told me. He said that short of the Secretariat, the enforcers are rationed the largest shares of Coalition blood. They feed to surfeit, their appetites always appeased. Predo keeps himself lean, hungry and subtle, but his instruments are often blunt and hard. I have likely never fed as well as this one feeds daily. He is strong, trained and experienced in the use of that strength.

Which is the advantage he retains when my heart explodes.

But first it stops.

Death has truly and finally arrived.

Good.

I have failed. Failed as a child; failed as a man; failed as a revolutionary; failed as a lover; failed as a goodguy. My only success in life has been as a pawn. Fuck it, I never asked to be any of those things. And my life was over by rights long ago. I've just been waiting to catch up to it.

Then my heart explodes, beating a manic rhythm, and I realize my life is not over.

Hell.

The world shivers and splinters, vibrates at a frequency beyond my senses' range of reception, and then resolves into clarity.

I feel the room. Cracks in the concrete walls etched in sharp detail; fecal and delicate odors both, articulated and singular; sounds enunciated perfectly, from Marilee's scream to Amanda's peacefully drugged inhalations; the taste of my own tongue; the whorls of the fingerprints on the hand gripping my throat.

My heart trip-hammers, trying to dig its way from my chest.

And all of it; cracks in the walls, smells of shit and Horde's French milled soap, sounds of scream and breath, taste of my own flesh, unique identifying ridges; all of it pales beside my hunger.

I grab at the enforcer's wrist. The movement jars the world. The room shivers again, bright trails of light tail from every object, and I miss the enforcer's arm entirely. It's too fast, I'm too fast. I try to breathe, realize I am already breathing, air desperately chugging in and out of my lungs in an attempt to keep up with my heart's need. I wait for the shock of the enforcer's clutch on my neck. But it doesn't come. He is frozen, stunned by the speed of my attack, not yet certain what has happened. I grab at him again, slowly this time. My hand clips his forearm, knocks his hand from my throat. He drops into a crouch, the thin stiletto blade sprouts from his hand, and he waits, poised for my next move.

But I am not interested in him. He has nothing for me. I can smell what is inside him and it will not nourish me or feed my hunger. But the others, three of the others in the room have what I spoil for. They are bursting with it.

The enforcer waits for my attack, but I do not attack. I charge, sweeping my left arm at him as I go past, launching him into the discarded desks, a wrecking ball through crumbling brick. The goon is the closest. I am nearly upon him before he or Horde have registered what has happened. I will drink their blood and they will die before they know death has begun.

The air at my back thrums as something passes through it.

I spin, see the enforcer leaping at me, sidestep and catch only half his blow. Still it drives me to my knees. The stiletto arcs down, a glitter that winks at my neck. I bring up my arm to block the blade. I am too fast again, my arm whistles in front of his, but misses entirely. He is again startled by my speed, and the angle of the glitter changes and it draws a line along the edge of my jaw. I jump up and he dodges back. What I need is behind me. I cannot be bothered with him now. I turn.

The goon is on his feet, pants bunched around his calves, penis shriveled inside its latex wrapper. He is holding his jacket, trying to pull something from one of its pockets, something that has snagged and will not come free. I reach for him, and instead of grabbing his shoulder I shove it. There is a dull snap as his shoulder pops out of its socket and he is sent reeling and crashes to the floor by the door. I look at the bound and half-naked woman at my feet. But she smells wrong. She has been polluted and will poison me if I try to drink her. I crouch, ready to leap on the helpless goon who now struggles with his one useful hand to pull free whatever weapon is concealed in his jacket.

The enforcer lands on my back.

One arm snakes around my throat and the stiletto thrusts at my face. I bring my hand up, the stiletto pierces the palm and juts out the back, the point halted an inch from my eye. I fall backward, lift my feet from the floor and land on the enforcer. He makes a noise and the arm around my neck loosens. I roll to my left, tumbling free of him, wrenching my hand from the blade and coming to my feet.

There is a tingling along my jaw and in my hand. I can feel the flesh knitting, the Vyrus in overdrive, closing my wounds as they are inflicted. The enforcer is up. He is between me and the goon now. No matter. There is more food here.

I turn to face Horde and his unconscious daughter. The stiletto enters my back, is plunged into my liver twice before I can seize his arm, hunch forward, and toss the enforcer to a far corner of the room.

The pain is more persistent this time. The healing tickle

not such a balm. The Vyrus is fighting a losing battle against the damage I'm absorbing. I must feed.

The enforcer is on me again, charging from the corner. He crashes into me and we sprawl on the floor. He straddles my chest, pins my arms with his knees. The stiletto comes down, drives through my left forearm and sticks in the crumbling concrete below. He covers my eyes with his thumbs and starts to gouge them out of their sockets. I wrench my head to the side and catch his wrist between my teeth.

His blood is acid. It fills my mouth, scorching my tongue. I close my throat against it. The small bones of his wrist crunch between my teeth and he howls and rips himself free and off of me. I gag and spit his torn meat from my mouth and yank the stiletto from my arm. I roll to my knees. The wound in my arm stays open, streaming blood. The Vyrus is dealing with my more mortal hurts. Ignoring that which will not kill me outright. The enforcer is between me and the others again. He comes in low, in a wrestler's crouch, the blood clotting at his wrist.

I see the Enclave in my mind. Their disciplined sparring. The control they exert over the Vyrus gone berserk in their veins. It can be controlled, this power. I have seen it.

He feints at my right arm, the arm that now holds his blade. I dodge to the left, away from the feint and into the real attack he had planned for my wounded left arm.

He cranks the arm up and back and pain explodes in my shoulder as he tries to snap it before I can react. But I am already reacting, twisting to my left, bringing the stiletto around in an arc behind his legs, and drawing it back, the blade raking the tendons just above the tops of his knees. He drops, his legs folding like marionette limbs beneath him, my arm falling from his grasp. I plant the heel of my left hand beneath his jaw as he comes down and force him back, his legs powerless beneath his body. I climb onto his stomach, still shoving his head back, baring his throat, and stab him in the neck. Over and over. Blood sprays, and air whistles from a dozen holes. I shove the blade in one final time, fixing it at the far point below his jaw, and then heave it over to the other side. I leave the stiletto lodged in his twitching corpse and stand up.

The woman on the floor has freed her hands and is clumsily trying to get to her feet, but the bacteria is still finding its place and she is delirious with it. The goon is by the door, whimpering and trying to get at his weapon.

But there is blood here at my left hand.

I turn to kill Horde and his daughter, and he shoots me in the stomach.

The gun is small, the slender European automatic of the well-to-do. The pain flares and disappears in the same instant. The tingle of regeneration fills my belly. I move at Horde, knowing I can pluck the weapon from his hand before he can fire it again.

Two vicious insects latch onto the back of my neck and I am knocked to my knees by 50,000 volts.

I open my mouth and howl silently and piss myself. Two wires run from my neck to the black box in the goon's hand. I flail at the wires, yank them from my skin and scramble to my feet. The goon is screaming, banging his head against the wall, fumbling one-handed with the Taser, trying to insert another charge. I take a step toward him.

Horde shoots me again. The bullet rips through the meat of my left thigh. I stumble but don't fall, and turn to face him again. And I am stung by the 50,000 once more.

Steam wisps from the holes in my arm, leg and stomach, and Horde adds a new hole, this one punched through my chest. I feel my right lung collapse and I echo it, keeling and folding to one side until I am supported by my right knee and hand, left hand clamped over the gasping hole in my chest. No tingling now, and no vibrant clarity of senses. The Vyrus has run its course. I am an empty and useless vessel that is beyond repair.

Naked and still erect, Horde steps over his daughter and comes close to me, the gun declined at my head.

He glances about the room, at his lost and struggling wife, the fear-crazed goon, the nearly decapitated enforcer, and his sleeping child. Then to me.

—I will not lie to you, Pitt; that was unexpected.

He tilts his head at the enforcer.

—And rather spectacular. Honestly, I've never seen the infected in action. I had no idea of the ferocity. Or the reserves you can call upon. Was your recovery typical? Or are you unique in your constitution?

I bleed.

—Regardless, I think it's safe to assume that you are beyond help at this point.

He thinks for a moment.

—But just to be safe.

He shoots my right arm. I sit there, helplessly listing on my one good limb.

—All this carnage may be oversetting the scene a bit, but I trust that Predo will be able to tidy things up. And I'm sure that the authorities will understand the excesses I took in avenging myself on you. You would understand as well if you were to stay present long enough to witness what you did to my daughter. But it is not to be.

He shakes his head.

—A shame. Nothing would please me more than to have you in my lab. But.

He heaves a sigh.

—Predo forbids it. I can experiment all I like with the . . . well, one feels comic to call it this, but with the *zombie* bacteria. But he will not allow me a subject of research for the Vyrus. No bother, I'll get one on my own soon enough.

—Husband.

He looks at his wife. Standing in clothes askew, leaning crookedly against the wall behind her.

—I think I want to eat you.

She tries to take a step and stumbles, her body, already decomposing, is arguing with the bacteria over who controls what.

Horde smiles.

—Don't worry, love. You won't have to live with that feeling for long. And who knows, perhaps I'll cut something from Amanda for you to nibble. I assure you she'd feel only the mildest pain in the state she's in. The dear won't even remember. What do you say? Something she won't miss, of course. A little finger?

He turns his eyes back to me and shrugs.

—As you can see, I have a great deal to take care of here. My family is waiting.

He presses the barrel of the gun against the top of my forehead. I watch his finger as it tightens on the trigger.

Something changes in the room.

A darkness flickers across the corner of my vision. A darkness perilously cold chills the air. A darkness passes between Horde and myself, erasing its own scent as it travels. The darkness cuts through Horde and he drops rigid to the floor. The darkness bleeds across the room, momentarily blackens the shadows in a high corner, and is gone.

And I forget about the darkness and go after what I need.

I crawl up Horde's naked body, every part as rigid as his

penis now, his skin icy to the touch, and a rim of frost on his gun. I dig my fingers under his jaw and pull. His flesh tears far easier than it should. Flesh tears with a crunch like stepping on snow. I bend my head to lap his blood. And find it frozen. His torn neck filled with dead crimson slush.

I rage.

And remember the sleeping girl.

I drag my gunshot leg toward her.

—Joseph.

The woman has the whimpering snot-faced goon. She holds his hair in her hand, his head pulled far back. In her other hand, she holds the enforcer's stiletto.

—You did a good job, Joseph.

The hard wiry muscles of her arms and shoulders flex as she pushes the knife into the artery.

Blood splashes.

From across the room I crawl until my mouth is over the hole in his neck. It has been years since I have had blood from the vein. It is just as I remember. The blood floods my throat and warmth swells in my stomach and a harsh burning tingle attacks my hurts.

A few blissful red minutes pass. They might be seconds or hours; over far too soon, a pleasure greater than their brevity would suggest. And when the man is empty and I am full and my face is rinsed in his gore, I feel as I always do when I feed, like I want more. I go for the girl.

And I am pummeled to the floor by her mother.

—Joseph.

I am fed, but weak. The Vyrus is replenishing itself, repairing its host. It wants more. I stand. She brings her doubled fists down on me again.

—Joseph!

Behind her I can see the girl's eyelids flutter. I must have her. I stand. And am hammered down again.

—Joseph.

I try to crawl past her. She is on my back and we are a pile of struggling limbs on the floor. I try to free my arms, to pull myself across the few yards between us and the child. The mother twists her legs around mine and binds my arms in the circle of her own.

—Joseph. Please, Joseph.

Her lips are on the back of my neck, and then her teeth, gnawing gently, experimenting with biting, but not breaking the skin.

The girl's eyes open blindly, close, open again and close again.

Her teeth are on my neck.

—Joseph. Help me.

Teeth carrying poison.

I forget the girl, flex the muscles in my shoulders and back, and feel Marilee's grip fail. I writhe loose of her arms and legs and scuttle away from her. She sits in the middle of the floor, arms slack, looking at me. Then she looks at her daughter. And crawls to her.

—Ms. Horde.

She kneels next to the child.

—Ms. Horde.

She touches the skinny bare legs.

—Marilee.

She picks up the folded jeans and starts fussing them back onto the girl. She gets them as far as her knees and stops. She looks up at me.

—I'm hungry, Joseph.

Her hand rests on Amanda's naked thigh, gripping it too hard, dimpling the skin.

—I'm so hungry.

She looks at her daughter.

—Help me, Joseph.

The holes in my body are all closed, blood trapped inside, but I can feel that only one lung is inflating, and poisons released from my pierced intestines and liver are pooled in my gut. The Vyrus will deal with it, given time it will make me whole. But if the woman attacks me now, with the bacteria fresh and strong in her, she will finish me.

I stand and walk to her. She reaches a hand up to me. I take it and help her to her feet. She puts a hand alongside my face, and presses her mouth against mine. When she pulls away her lips and chin are smeared with the dead man's blood.

—I had a feeling about you, Joseph.

I bring my right hand up to the back of her head.

—From the first moment I saw you, I had a feeling you were special.

I bring up my left hand, the cuffs, one bracelet sawed through, still trailing from my wrist, and cup her chin.

—Special. Like you were someone I could trust.

Her eyes drift to her daughter and back to me.

—Can I trust you, Joseph?

I run a tongue over my lips, taste the blood.

—Yeah, sure.

—Good.

And I break her neck.

It's not easy. It's very hard. I am drained and weak and she flinches at the last moment. I heave once and her spine crackles and she starts to tremor. Then I heave again and feel the clean snap and she goes still.

I lower her to the floor, and as I do I meet Amanda's open staring eyes, see her mouth gaping in a silent nightmare scream, and then her eyes close again. This moment, I hope, to be lost with the rest of her terrors.

Lydia brings three of her hammers. Two of them are diesels, beefier than her but not nearly as cut. The other is a pre-op tranny, a huge chick with a dick, shoulders and tits the size of bowling balls.
—Is she OK?
—They shot her up with something. I don't know what.
—They, who?
   I look at Amanda, limp in my arms.
—People who aren't around anymore.
   Lydia nods.
—What now?
—She needs a safe place.
—How long?
—Don't know. Couple days maybe.
   She looks at the tranny.
—Sela?
   The tranny nods and answers in a throaty rumble.
—Sure, I can take care of the sweetie.
   Lydia looks at me.
—OK?
   I look at Sela.
—People may come.
   Sela lifts both her arms, flexes them bodybuilder style and her biceps just about pop out of her skin.
—Their problem.
   I nod.
—OK.
   Sela lowers her arms.
—Let me have the cupcake.

I hold her out. Sela plucks her from my arms and tucks her easily into the crook of one of her own. I point at the bloody fingerprints on her jeans and shoes, left there when I finished dressing her.

—See if you can get her into something clean before she wakes up.

Sela is watching Amanda's sleeping face, one Lincoln Log finger brushes loose hair from her forehead.

—No problem, we'll get cupcake all sorted out. C'mon, ladies.

One of the diesels opens the door and checks the street outside, then signals an all clear. Sela follows her out and the other diesel brings up the rear, closing the door behind her. Lydia points at the closed door.

—She'll be fine with them.

—Yeah.

She goes to the door, puts her hand on the knob.

—We should get going, sunrise soon.

—Yeah.

We step out of the empty storefront onto Avenue B. Lydia locks the door behind us and we start down the street. I point back at the storefront.

—That a Society safe house?

—One of mine.

—Hn.

She's burned a safe house. Let someone outside her circle know about it. There'll be skin to pay for that. There's always skin to pay for something. Then again, chances are she won't have to worry about anything I know much longer. She looks at me from the corner of her eye, smiles slightly.

—Tom's been going batshit.

—Yeah?

—Yeah. Told him I went to give you some chow and you sucker-punched me and grabbed the key to the shackles. He

tried to track you, but I had a couple of my people out
gumming up your scent. He's frothing. Says he'll have me
up on charges when Terry gets back.
—Still not back?
—No. Got a message from the drop, though. The Coalition's
raising some kind of stink, clogging up all passages across
their turf. Know anything about that?
—Nope.
  She stops on the corner of 9th and B.
—I go this way. What about you?
  I point the opposite direction.
—Home.
—Sure about that?
—Nowhere else left.
  She nods.
—Anything else?
—Got a smoke?
  She shakes her head.
—Give my money to the death merchants at the tobacco
companies? You should know better.
—Right.
  She stuffs her hands in her back pockets.
—The girl?
—If you don't hear from me tomorrow, wait for Terry. He'll
know what to do.
—He usually does.
—Yep.

At home I get cleaned up, and in bed with a cigarette. Every
time I take a drag the cuff still hanging off my wrist bangs
against my neck. I could pick the lock, but my wallet with the
picks is on the opposite side of the room. Too far away. I put

my cigarette in the nightstand ashtray and take hold of the dangling cuff. I begin to twist it round and round. The chain bundles and knots and the cuff still locked on my wrist digs into the skin. I crank the loose cuff once more and wrench my locked wrist in the opposite direction and the chain pops, one broken link shooting across the room. I put the sawn-through cuff on the nightstand and pick up my cigarette. I rub my wrist, massaging the red skin under the single cuff I now wear like a bracelet. I spin the bracelet around and around and think about the girl that it had been locked to.

And I lie in the dark, sucking smoke into my one good lung.

When I finally sleep I dream. I don't dream about the girl or her mother or her father. I don't dream about Whitney Vale or Evie or the wretched things that raised me. I dream about a darkness. And I see all the details I had only glimpsed in that room.

The way the darkness seeped into the room through a crack in the air. How it cut the space between Horde and myself. How it passed through Horde, passed through him as he would have passed through a mist. How it flapped and shivered as with pleasure, gliding up to the shadows in the corner of the room. The things bulging from within the darkness, trying to get out. The shapes bulging from it, pressing it outward from the inside, like people trapped inside a black sheath of rubber. The hole it cut in the shadow. The last shape, digging from within it, before it inked the shadow black and disappeared.

The shape like an oily black relief of Horde's screaming face.

—Stop screaming, Pitt.

I open my eyes. They're already here.

—Little early, guys.

Predo has set the chair from my desk next to the bed and is sitting in it. He looks at his watch.

—It is nearly midnight. You have slept all day. Now it is time to get up.

—Yeah, guess you're right.

I sit up in bed and stretch.

—I'd offer you guys some coffee or something, but I don't like you. So.

I throw off the covers and move to get up and Predo's giant holds up a hand.

—If you could just stay on the bed for now, Mr. Pitt.

—Yeah, sure.

I grab my smokes from the nightstand, light up, lean my back against the wall and sit there in my shorts and undershirt, and smoke. Predo lets it go for a minute, then gets tired of it.

—Where is the girl?

I take a drag. I think I can feel some of the smoke going into my right lung. A good sign.

—Say, Mr. Predo.

His eyes tighten, but he waits for it.

—Know what I'm noticing?

He waits.

—No? OK, I'll tell you.

I stub my cigarette in the ashtray.

—I'm noticing how you're not asking what happened to the Hordes.

I grab the pack of Luckys and knock a fresh one out.

—When last seen, one of your enforcers was with them. You'd think he'd have called in by now. But he hasn't. Know how I know he hasn't?

I flip my Zippo open.

—Because I killed him.

I thumb the wheel.

—But I have a feeling you already know that.

I light the butt.

—And that you don't give a fuck.

I close the lighter with a snap.

—Care to comment?

He temples his fingers and presses them to his lips.

—May I have a cigarette?

I pass him one. He taps it against his thumbnail then places it carefully between his lips and leans forward. I flick the Zippo to life and hold it out. He dips the tip of the cigarette in the flame, inhales, leans back and exhales with a slight cough.

—Filterless.

I close the lighter and put it back on the nightstand.

—Yeah.

He takes another drag, exhales without coughing this time.

—One of the advantages of the Vyrus. I do not personally take advantage of it often, but when I do, I prefer filterless. More flavor.

—Yeah.

—You are right.

He picks a flake of tobacco from his tongue.

—My agent did fail to report when expected.

He shakes the tobacco from his fingertip.

—Another of our agents went to the Horde residence and reconstructed some of the action that had taken place there. Based on that reconstruction, and my knowledge of Dr. Horde's predilections, I was able to make an assumption as to where he had taken his . . . party. The agent went to the school. Yes, I do know about the Hordes and their man. And my agent. And you are correct about something else, as well. I do not give a fuck.

He takes another drag, but pulls a sour face this time and shakes his head.

—What does that say as to how I feel about you?

He drops the freshly lit cigarette to the floor and steps on it.

—You see, you are mistaken about what is happening in this room, Pitt. You think you are maneuvering yourself into position for some kind of bargain. You hope to leave this room not only with your life, but with information, and perhaps some kind of profit. It is true that there is a bargain to be struck here, but what lies in the balance is not your life, but rather the manner of your death.

My cigarette burns a little closer to my fingers.

—You have killed an agent of the Coalition. And so you will die. Put simply, you can tell us where the girl is right now, and we will kill you in some quick and relatively painless manner. Or, if you prefer, you may withhold that information, and force us to extract it from you. After which, we will drive to a location in New Jersey which I understand is excellent for viewing the sunrise. Need I be any more blunt?

The heat of my cigarette's cherry reaches my fingers. I bring it up to my face and eke out a last drag before putting it out. I hold the smoke from that last drag, then jet it out my nostrils.

—I know Horde was the carrier.

I pick up the cigarette Predo crushed on my floor.

—Yeah, I know, a statement like that is pretty much a conversation killer.

I drop the crushed cigarette in the ashtray.

—Where do you go from there? So let me expound a little bit. Just so you know I know what the fuck I'm talking about.

I gather my thoughts. And hope they don't fall apart too quickly.

—Say you're a man like Horde. Say that in addition to owning a company like Horde Bio Tech, you are also its top researcher. And just for the sake of argument, say you also happen to be a very sick motherfucker who happens to have access to certain facts about how things work on the darker side. That's our side, Predo. Oh, I'm gonna get dressed now.

I scoot to the edge of the bed. The giant takes a step toward me, but Predo shakes his head and he stops. Standing is tricky, but I manage. Predo watches as I shuffle to the closet.

—Not feeling well, Pitt?

—Been better.

I stand in front of the closet for a moment and look at myself in the mirror on the door.

Predo continues to watch the space where I had been sitting on the bed.

—You were saying?

Not surprisingly I look like shit. The bruises around my eyes and nose aren't so bad, but the tooth Tom knocked out is still gone. The Vyrus will knit bone, but it won't grow new ones.

—Yeah. So say you're Horde, and everything I've said is true of you. And it is true. We know that. So that all being the case, who could blame you for taking a professional interest in something like a very bizarre and dangerous bacteria? A bacteria that, I don't know, say a bacteria that consumes its host and compels him to eat human flesh.

The wounds in my arms and left leg are corked with plugs of brick-red scab. I pull off my undershirt.

—It would just make good business sense to look into something like that.

The holes in my belly and chest are scabbed as well and surrounded by angry red skin. If I can get some more blood they'll be gone in a couple days. If I get out of this room alive.

—Just imagine if something like that were to become widespread. Situation like that, the first company on the block with a vaccine would clean up. Face it, who's not gonna pay top dollar to get a shot that's gonna keep them from eating their neighbor's brain?

I open the closet, grab a pair of old jeans, pull them on and get a black T-shirt from the shelf. I face Predo as I shrug into the shirt.

—But where to start? How do you develop that vaccine?

I go to the desk, scoop up my wallet, keys and loose change, and put it all in my pockets.

—Now I don't know much about this kind of thing, but I'm guessing the first thing you'd need is someone already infected with the bacteria. The technical term would be *zombie*. Not many people know how to come by a zombie, Mr. Predo.

I go sit back on the edge of the bed and wiggle my feet into a pair of socks.

—You know where to get one?

I reach under the bed for my shoes.

—Sure you do. If anyone knows where to get a shambler, it'd be Dexter Predo.

I lace my shoes.

—But then things get really tricky. Way I hear it, the bacteria only lives in the human body, and sooner or later it kills its host. So what's a brilliant millionaire researcher to do?

I grab my smokes and get a fresh one going.

—Some people might say, *fuck it, I'll just keep making new zombies*. Every time one is ready to kack, just have it bite a new subject and, presto: new zombie. Hell, some folks might extend the life of their subject by feeding it some brains. But really, how long is that gonna work? Gonna be a whole lot of bodies going in and out of that lab. Might raise a couple eyebrows. And this.

I jab my cigarette at him.

—This is where being a brilliant epidemiologist comes in handy. 'Cause it turns out the bacteria *can* exist outside a host. How? Fucked if I know. But it can. I've seen it. Which means you can get it under a microscope and look at it all you like without needing to make any new shamblers. Unless you have a reason for making new shamblers. Now what could possibly be a good reason for making new shamblers?

I blow some ash from the tip of my smoke.

—Any ideas?

He stares through me, studying the wall behind me. The giant just stands there like a good boy and waits for Predo to order him to tear my fingers off for being an asshole.

I point a single finger at the ceiling.

—Here's a thought.

I aim the finger at Predo.

—What if you had the idea to study the bacteria in the wild? What if, now that you had it isolated, you wanted to see how it spreads, how quickly? For a man looking to cure a *potential* zombie epidemic, that could be valuable information. Especially if you're thinking about starting the epidemic yourself.

I tap the finger against the side of my head.

—But, can't have something like a zombie epidemic getting out of hand before you're ready to deliver your vaccine and make your billions. That would suck. So what do you do? Oh, you go ahead and make a plan to put it out in the general population. But it needs to be a very special population.

I put the finger away and smoke.

—See, nobody wants that kind of experiment on their turf. That shit gets even a little out of hand and next thing you know, there's a lot of attention focused on your yard. Nope, something like that doesn't get tested on Coalition turf. And not uptown, things are too tense with the Hood. Not on Enclave turf. Nobody fucks with Enclave turf. Sure, things are pretty open below Houston or in the Outer Boroughs, but it's just about impossible to keep an eye on things out there. Tough to collect data. And the experiment could fly off the handle. But what about *Society turf*? Hell, why not? Everybody wins. Horde gets to watch the bacteria move around in a population, and the Coalition gets to cause a little trouble below Fourteenth. A little sand in the Vaseline to keep Terry and his crew busy. That'd be good, what with DJ Grave Digga trying to stir up trouble. And after all.

I blow a smoke ring.

—You got a jerk like me down here to handle things in case the shit hits the fan. And a toady like Philip to keep an eye on me.

I blow a stream of air that rips my smoke ring to shreds.

—So Horde goes to work. He infects Whitney Vale. Tell me?

He focuses his eyes on me.

—Did you know he had been fucking her and that she was blackmailing him? 'Cause I'm guessing you never would have signed off on her as patient zero if you had known.

He blinks, slowly.

—Let's call that no. He probably sold her to you as a porn hustler no one would miss. When you found out the truth you must have flipped. And when I stumbled across Vale, you must have shit a brick. Metaphorically speaking.

Predo taps an index finger on his thigh.

—Will you be concluding soon?

I nod.

CHARLIE HUSTON

—I'll pick up the pace. How 'bout this? Horde fucks Vale;
Vale blackmails Horde; Horde has one of his goons hold
down Vale while he rapes her and infects her with the bacteria;
Vale shambles around; I catch sight of one of Vale's victims
and start tracking a carrier; I catch up to Vale and her pals
at the school; shit hits the fan; Philip lets you know shit is
hitting the fan; you call me in. You have to call me in, a
scene like that one at the school, the TV news involved and
all, if you don't call me in I'm gonna start wondering why,
and you don't want me wondering shit. Back at the ranch,
Amanda Horde finds out about daddy and her buddy fucking,
and runs away; Horde calls Dobbs; Dobbs finds the girl; the
girl bribes Dobbs off the case; Ms. Horde hears about Whitney
being killed and gets a little more worried about her husband
than usual, and she asks for help; you give her me to keep
me . . .

I stop, smoke in my lung. I blow the smoke out.

—You give her me?

Predo scratches his upper lip.

—Lost your thread, Pitt?

He puts his hand back in his lap.

—Not as easy as you thought?

I look at him.

—You gave her me. But you shouldn't have wanted me
anywhere around the Hordes. I was looking for the carrier
already. Get me looking for the girl and I might put it all
together. I *did* put it all together.

The slightest smile creases the corners of his mouth.

—Apparently not.

He stands.

—Are you done showing off now? Would you like to know
what it is you are missing?

I nod.

—All you had to do was ask, Pitt. Why should I have secrets from a dead man?

He pushes the chair back to its place next to my desk.

—What you are missing, Pitt, is information you could not possibly have in the first place. That being the case, I do not think you should be at all embarrassed. You did quite well, all things considered. The information you are lacking has to do with Horde Bio Tech and the disposition of that company's stock. HBT is not a publicly owned company. Indeed, until recently it was owned entirely by the Horde family. They still control the majority of the stock. Specifically, preferred stock shares that carry weighted voting rights, the shares that control the company. Those shares comprise sixty percent of HBT's total value, and Dale Horde owned all of them. Of the remaining forty percent, the non-preferred shares, the vast majority are held by elements of the Coalition. We came into possession of these shares at a time when Horde was in need of funding, and not quite as liquid as he might have liked. Fortunately, we were able to help. Does the picture begin to leap into clarity?

I stare at him.

—I think it does. Horde owns and controls HBT, controls every aspect of its operations, including to what questions it may or may not devote its considerable research laboratories. Those laboratories are central to the Coalition's interest in Horde and HBT.

He leans down a bit, looks at my eyes.

—I think I may see a little light dawning in there, Pitt. Good. Let me be brief before that light dims. It is true that Dr. Horde wished to research the bacteria, but his true interest was in the Vyrus. That was an interest we were unwilling to allow him to pursue. There is so little we know about the Vyrus, it would never have done for Horde to perhaps make significant discoveries. Discoveries we could not be certain he would share with us. Discoveries he might use against us. Still, the resources HBT can bring to bear far outstrip any that we have previously had at our disposal. Which led to the proposal that we should investigate strategies which would allow the Coalition to take control of those resources.

I watch the smoke drift off my cigarette.

—The stock.

Predo wags a cautioning finger at me.

—Careful, Pitt, a little knowledge is a dangerous thing. But yes, the stock. If the Coalition were in control of HBT, we might steer whatever course of research we wished, secure in the knowledge that we had installed our own people in the key positions necessary to protect the nature and results of that research. How to take control? We thought to take advantage of Dr. Horde's appetites and maneuver a subject not unlike Ms. Vale into his path. That plan was discarded. If cornered by blackmail, Dr. Horde might become a fierce adversary, an adversary with knowledge of far too many of our secrets. So we came to assassination. If Dr. Horde should die, his shares would fall to his wife. And she, we felt, would be quite easily convinced to relinquish control of them. But even with our advantages, assassination is difficult, much more difficult when the subject is a man like Dr. Horde. Any investigation into his death would be exhaustive. And if an assassination should go awry, he would certainly retaliate against us. We were, in fact, mired in the planning stages when you became involved. And I had a thought. Why should the Coalition assassinate Dr. Horde when you might be made to do it for us?

I lick my fingertips.

—It is not generally in my nature to work on the basis of instinct, but I felt this was an opportunity that warranted some little risk. The question was whether or not you could be depended on to act in a predictable manner. I felt certain that you could.

I pinch out the cherry at the end of my cigarette.

—You are, as you have proven, not an utter fool, and could therefore be expected to discover a certain amount of the truth. You have a notorious temper. And though you seem to be the only one not aware of it, you are famously unmerciful with those who abuse children. Was there any doubt that when you learned some very little about Dr. Horde that you would lose that temper? Very little doubt. You are an independent contractor. If you failed, Dr. Horde could not hold us accountable for your actions. If you succeeded, we would be prepared to conceal the few threads that connect you to the Coalition. If captured, the authorities would likely interpret Horde's murder as the action of a madman. Once in the hands of the police there would be little you could tell them before you expired in custody. And if you survived and found yourself at large?

He gestures to the room.

—Well, here we are, tying up loose ends. Is there anything else you would like clarified, anything that might make your position more apparent to you so that we might move ahead with the unalterable course of events?

I drop the snuffed butt into the ashtray.

—Why'd he cut Leprosy?

He looks at the ceiling.

—Leprosy?

I rub my thumb and index finger together, brushing the gray ash from them.

—The kid.

He looks back down.

—Yes. The one you had asking about Dr. Horde's daughter.

Well, I can't say for certain, but I think he viewed your involvement as a balm to his wife. He never intended that you should lay hands on the girl. He hoped perhaps to track your progress so as to find young Amanda first. For himself. I think it likely that he got carried away questioning the boy. His taste for youth seemed to have more to do with inflicting pain than with receiving pleasure.

I think about lighting another smoke, decide not to.

—Why infect him?

—He infected the boy?

I nod. Predo shakes his head.

—To play with his toy? He was quite proud of having isolated the bacteria. I am just as curious about why he killed the detective Dobbs. Do you know?

I rub my forehead.

—He didn't.

—Who did?

—Dobbs was Horde's peeper. He had all the goods on his wife and her lovers. She had her own plan. Wanted to take off with her daughter, but knew Horde could make her out as an unfit mother. She went to Dobbs for the pictures and whatnot, and he balked. So she choked him to death and grabbed the stuff.

—You are certain?

—When we met she asked about my sense of smell. Could I tell her scent? Next time I saw her she was scrubbed and clean. Just like whoever did Dobbs. It was her. She wanted to get her daughter out.

—Yes, I can see that. And it brings us back around to where we started. Back to my question. *Where is the girl?*

—You don't need her.

—The girl.

—Let the girl be, she doesn't know anything. She was fucking unconscious when it happened. I got rid of Horde, let the girl be.

—Yes, Pitt, you got rid of Horde. And you got rid of his wife, as well. Which leaves the girl as Horde's heir, heir to the stock, Pitt.

He takes off his jacket.

—An underage girl.

He tucks his tie inside his shirt.

—For whom that stock will now be held in inviolable trust.

He unclips his cuff links.

—Controlled by the Horde family's rather too incorruptible lawyers.

He rolls up his left sleeve.

—Until she comes of age at twenty-one.

He rolls up his right sleeve.

—Unless she dies in the same horrible, disfiguring fireball of an automobile accident in which her parents will be shortly dying.

He puts his hand out to the giant.

—In which case the stock will be made available to the other shareholders. And, I believe, I have already told you who those shareholders are.

The giant places a pair of black leather gloves in his hand.

—So.

He pulls the tight gloves on and snugs them over his knuckles.

—Where? Is? The? Girl?

I look at his hands, then his face.

—I gave her to Lydia Miles.

He doesn't move.

—Lydia Miles?

—You know, the Society's resident gay rights loudmouth.

—Where did she take the girl?

—Got me. But if I don't call in a couple days she'll give her to Terry Bird.

I decide it's time for another smoke, so I get one ready.

—And did I mention that I have Horde's teeth?

Light it.

—Not his real teeth mind you, just those fancy fake dentures of his. Now those are some interesting dentures. Not too many reasons for dentures like those, full of a nasty bacteria and all. Unless you plan on making a bunch of zombies on someone else's turf and you want them to look normal. Normal for zombies, I mean. Shit like that would be just the thing to make Terry ready to hook up with Grave Digga and launch a two-front offensive on the Coalition. Something like that he could take to all the small Clans. The Dusters, the Wall, even the Outer Borough freaks, they'd all flip. Hell, Daniel might be interested in something like that. Picture that: Daniel and a dozen Enclave knocking on your door. Gives you the chills.

Predo's fists close tight. I can hear the leather squeak.

—Where are the teeth?

After I got Amanda dressed, I stripped and wiped blood from myself with Horde's clean undershirt. He was far too skinny for anything of his to fit me, but I managed to scavenge an outfit from the enforcer and the goon. Then I went through the pockets of my own discarded clothes and found the picture of Amanda, the one she had ripped in two. I fit the halves together and translated the torn and stained phone number on the back. I had the girl in my arms when I remembered the teeth.

I found the case in Horde's clothes. The hinge creaked slightly when I opened it. Inside, the teeth were fitted snugly in a foam rubber nest. They gleamed. He must have cleaned off Marilee's blood before he put them away. I eased them out, careful not to touch the biting surfaces. They looked perfect, like the healthiest teeth in the world, a bit on the sharp side perhaps. I opened them. The canines had tiny black dimples at the tips, holes smaller than those of syringes. Inside they would be hollow, a delivery system for something that isn't supposed to exist outside a human body. I closed them and returned them to the case.

I collected the girl, found the door she had told me about and carried her out of the school. It was raining, hours after midnight and the street was empty except for a couple scuttling past, trying to share a too-small umbrella. I got to the pay phone on the corner, called Lydia and gave her the girl.

Then I came home, got cleaned up, left the teeth sitting on the bathroom sink, and forgot about them until right now.

—The teeth are someplace safe. Someplace they'll stay as long as the girl stays safe. Something happens to her, I send the teeth to Bird.

He frowns.

—Who sends them if anything happens to you?

I blink. And that's enough for him to know. He smiles.

—You did not give them to anyone. They are simply hidden someplace, are they not?

Quickly, you only get one chance at this.

—I gave them to Lydia with the girl.

He shakes his head.

—No. You did not. They are hidden someplace. Someplace close at hand, I would say.

He exhales.

—And so. Here we are again. But with a variation. Where is the girl, *and* where are the teeth?

I think about making a break for it, but I'm done. So I take a drag instead and say what's on my mind.

—Predo, you're a dick.

The uppercut catches me under the jaw and dislocates it. I fly into the air, across the bed, crash into the wall and tumble onto the mattress. He's stronger than the enforcer was.

The giant scoops me up and full nelsons me in front of Predo. Predo squares up.

—Where?

I try to say something smart, but can't get my jaw to move, so I just shake my head. Predo cocks his fist. He'll knock my jaw clear off this time.

—'Lo, Joe.

We all look up to the top of the little circular stair that leads down to this room. I grind my jaw and it pops into place.

—Hurley. How you doing?

He stands at the top of the stairs looking down at us, a huge hammerlike .45 held casually in either hand, neither of them pointing at anything, yet.

—OK. Door's unlocked up 'ere.

—Yeah?

—Tought I'd come in. Ya don't mind?

—Naw.

He nods at Predo.

—Mr. Predo.

Predo lowers his fist.

—Hurley. It has been a long time. How is Terry?

—Same. But he won't like yer bein' down 'ere none, Mr. Predo.

—He'll be understanding on this occasion. Trust me.

The giant is eyeing Hurley, wearing the unmistakable expression of a big man who wants to prove he's the most dangerous guy in the room. Hurley keeps his eyes on Predo, wearing the expression of a man who *knows* who the most dangerous guy in the room is. Predo's face shows nothing.

Hurley lets the barrel of one of the forty-fives wave in my direction.

—Terry sent me over. Wants ta see ya.

—He's back?

—Yeah, wants ta see ya.

—Well, I'm busy, but I think I can get away.

I look at Predo. He lifts his chin at the giant, and the giant releases my arms.

—Let me just go to the can.

I walk into the bathroom, pick up the case and stuff it in my back pocket. The tableau in my bedroom remains in place. I stand at the foot of the stairs.

—Don't worry, Mr. Predo, I'll take care of what we were talking about. Get it to someone who can handle the responsibility like you suggested. And you look after my friend. OK?

He doesn't say anything.

—OK, Mr. Predo?

He nods, begins stripping the gloves from his hands.

—Yes, I suppose that will have to do.

—Yeah, I suppose it will.

Halfway up the stairs I get hit with a last piece. I pause and look back down.

—I took care of business, didn't I, Mr. Predo? Did that job you wanted done?

He rolls his sleeves back into place and begins to fit the cuff links to their holes.

—Yes, you did.

I'm thinking fast, trying to make it fit, trying to get something out of this.

—*I* killed Horde?

—Yes.

He is straightening the knot in his tie and pauses to look at me.

—Rather esoterically, I am told. How did you go about freezing his blood?

I'm watching him close.

—Figure you know more about that than me.

He looks down at his tie.

—I assure you, I do not.

I play it as it lies.

—However I did it, I figure I'm owed.

He smoothes the tie down his shirtfront.

—You were thinking?

—I'd like my stash replaced.

He picks up his jacket.

—Replaced?

I dangle it one more time.

—Yeah, from when your guy without a smell snatched it.

A spark of interest flares across his face, and dies in the same instant as he snuffs it.

—I don't employ such things, Pitt.

I leave it there. He slides his arms into the jacket.

—You are correct however, you did provide a service. I will arrange delivery of compensation.

He tugs on the lapels of his jacket, seating it firmly on his shoulders.

—But the Coalition is a progressive entity, Pitt. We do not deal in superstition.

He flicks a loose strand of hair into place.

—If it is the *paranormal* that you are concerned with?

I wait.

—You should try talking with Daniel. He is the only one who traffics in such things.

I open my mouth. Hurley taps me with one of his sledge-hammer guns.

—Terry's waitin' on ya, Joe.

I look at Predo. He tilts his head.

—I look forward to seeing you again, Pitt.

I touch my sore jaw.

—Yeah. Do me a favor. Lock up on your way out.

I follow Hurley up the stairs and out onto the street. He tucks his guns into his waistband and buttons his jacket over them. We walk side by side toward Tompkins Square.

—Didn't know you knew Predo, Hurley.

He shrugs.

—Yer around long enough, Joe, ya get ta know everyone.

—Not only is he an agent provocateur, but he's an escapee and I want to know what the fuck has been going on!

—Sure, sure, Tom, we all want to know what's been going on, man. But you don't get knowledge by screaming, you get it by listening. So let's just, you know, try to cool it and listen to the man.

—Fuck that shit. You heard Hurley. Dexter Predo was in his apartment. Fucking Predo! He's their fucking spy master! What more evidence do you want?

—Well, if we're supposed to *execute* a man, as you suggest, then I want a whole lot of evidence, Tom.

It's just like old times.

—Fine. Fucking fine. Then I want to call a tribunal! I want a fucking court of enquiry.

This time I didn't have to be coldcocked by Hurley to get to Society headquarters. But here I am all the same.

—Hey, Tom, if it comes to that, it comes to that. No problem. But let's just get the ball rolling with a few simple questions, OK?

—Fuck questions! I want a full interrogation into this right fucking now.

Terry walks over to Tom, nodding his head.

—Tom. I think I need you to take a walk.

—What? No fucking.

—Hurley.

—Yeah.

—Take Tom for a walk.

Tom stares at him.

—No fucking.

Terry holds up his hand, index and middle fingers spread in a peace sign.

—Cool it, Tom. Take a walk. Now.

—This is fucking.

Terry puts the hand on Tom's shoulder.

—What, Tom? This is fucking what?

He gazes into Tom's eyes, and Tom shuts up.

—That's it, right, man? You're done? You're cool?

Tom nods.

—Yeah. I'm cool, Terry.

—Good. So take a walk.

He pats him on the shoulder and watches as Hurley leads him up the steps.

—Lydia.

Lydia looks up from the cup of coffee she's been staring into since I came in.

—You mind taking a walk with the boys?

—Nope.

She follows them up the stairs without looking at me. Terry waits until they are gone and the door closes. Then he comes over to the old card table and sits down across from me.

—He's a firebrand that one, very passionate in his beliefs.

I play with my Zippo.

—That must help.

—I don't follow, Joe.

—Well, I sometimes get the feeling you're grooming him for my old spot. He'll do a good job. He likes cracking the whip.

Terry shakes his head.

—Nobody will ever do that job as good as you, Joe. You were the best.

—Yeah, well, those days are over.

—They don't have to be. You could always come back.

I don't need to answer that, so I light a smoke instead. Terry holds up his hand.

—I'd rather you didn't.

—Right.

I put the smoke out.

—See you got back OK.

—Yes.

—How'd it go up there?

He sighs.

—It's not like the old days, Joe. Digga is a much different man than Luther was. Luther was from my school, a revolutionary, not a reactionary. He was there in the sixties, saw how change can really happen. Luther made some of that change. It's hard now to explain how big a change that was, getting the Coalition to give up the top of the island. Man, truth be told, I don't know if we could have ever gotten our independence down here if it hadn't been for Luther X. Kid like Grave Digga, history doesn't mean much to him. But I think I got him to see some light. He knows he can't go making war by himself, and he knows we aren't about to join in with his hostilities, even if the Coalition did assassinate Luther. You can't change the world if your motive is revenge. Vibes like that just aren't productive.

—Uh-huh. So how'd you get back down?

—I was able to make an arrangement. You can always make an arrangement if you're patient and flexible.

—That arrangement have anything to do with giving Predo passage down here so he could pop in on me?

Terry shrugs.

—Well, I did grant a transit. But I didn't ask questions about how they would use it.

—That was part of the arrangement?

—One must bend to avoid breaking, Joe.

—Thought you didn't look too concerned about Predo being at my place and all.

—That's not fair. I'm always concerned about you. You're a friend.

—Sure. That why I'm here? Friendship?

He leans forward in his chair.

—I'd like to think that all our arrangements are made on the basis of friendship. But Tom is right. There has been a great deal going on. And I am very interested in hearing your side of it.

—Fair enough.

I take a moment to get my story together.

—So it's like this, Terr, there was some trouble.

I stop. Terry nods encouragingly.

—And I took care of it.

Terry waits. And waits some more. And smiles.

—Is that really the way you want to handle this, Joe?

—Yeah, it really is.

—OK, OK, man. That's fair. But it raises other issues.

—Like?

—Well, you know how I feel about capitalism, no fan of the WTO am I. But there are advantages to doing things on a quid pro quo basis. Like a barter economy. So let's put this on a goods and services level.

—How so?

—Well, like the Dusters. That cost something, asking them to go uptown and pick you up. Not to mention that it aggravated an already sensitive relationship with the Coalition. So that's one, I don't know, call it one unit.

He holds up a finger.

—On a less tangible level, there's just the general bad vibes you've been stirring up around here that last couple days.

He holds up a second finger.

—You're also asking us to kind of, I don't know, take it on faith that whatever's been in the air is cool. That's trust, Joe. That's, and I hate to put it in these terms, but that's an expensive commodity. So that might need a little extra compensation.

Two more fingers.

—And then there's the cleanup I hear Tom did on that Leprosy kid and his dog. Now that's a big service, but I know you liked that kid and whatever went down must have been tough on you. So.

He sticks up his thumb, shows me his open hand.

—I'm not sure how to assign value to all of that. So maybe you have an idea of how to make us even on this deal. Because otherwise, I just don't see any way around it, we're going to have to insist on getting a little more information, a little more than just your say-so that things are gonna be cool. You get me?

—I get you. I come across with something worth something or you're gonna put me in a room with Tom and Hurley.

He puts his hand on the table.

—Don't be like that, Joe. The Society is a collective, man, I have to keep everybody happy. If it was up to me, I'd just take your word, shake hands and maybe ask you to buy me a beer. You know how I work.

—I know how you work, Terry.

He grins.

—Sure you do. So.

The grin goes away.

—What you got, Joe?

I pull the case out of my back pocket and set it on the table.

The hinge creaks open. He looks at the teeth. Looks at me and raises his eyebrows.

—It's a bomb, Terry. Set it off and all hell will break loose.

I don't tell him everything. But I tell him enough.

And he likes it.

—What the fuck?

Tom is standing on the sidewalk with Hurley when Terry brings me out.

—Easy, Tom.

—Where the fuck does he think he's going?

—He's going his own way, Tom, just like all of us have to.

—Fuck his way! You can't just.

—Cool it, OK? You want to be security chief, you have to learn that it sometimes involves some subtlety, some grace.

—Fuck subtlety. You can't make a decision like this on your own. There needs to be a hearing and a vote.

I get out a smoke.

—You know, Tom . . .

I light it.

—You are one lousy anarchist.

His hand goes in his pocket and comes out with the revolver he took off me. Before he can point it at me it's in Terry's hand and Tom is on the ground. Terry looks down at him.

—Joe is gonna take off, Tom. He's walking clean. That's the way it's gonna be and there's not going to be a vote. Hurley, take him back in.

Hurley helps Tom off the sidewalk and they head for the door. Tom stares at the sidewalk the whole way, tears of rage boiling down his cheeks.

I watch till he's inside, then shoot a look at Terry.

—Still got the moves.

He tilts his head and shrugs.

—The tools of the oppressor have to be used sometimes.

—Sure.

I point at his hand.

—That's my gun.

Terry looks at the revolver, then holds it out to me.

—Be careful with it.

I take the gun and drop it in my pocket.

—Always am.

I start down the street, he calls after me.

—By the way, you ever find out who it was that was poking around? The no-scent thing?

—Gonna go look into that.

—Let me know.

I stop and turn around.

—I almost forgot, Predo was asking after you. Didn't know you guys had a personal history.

Terry takes off his glasses and polishes them on his Grateful Dead T-shirt.

—Well, live long enough, and you get to know everyone.
—So I hear.
  He puts his glasses back on, waves and goes inside.

Lydia stops me at the corner.
—She wants to see you.
  I rub my head.
—Later. I have to go somewhere.
—How much later?
—Not much.
  She nods, gives me the address.
—She's a peach, you know.
—Whatever.
—Sure, whatever you say.
  I head west toward A, where I know I can flag a cab.
—Joe.
  I keep walking.
—Yeah?
—No lie, Joe, I don't like men much.
  Still walking, letting her talk at my back as much as she
wants to.
—And I like straight men even less.
  Walking, thinking about what I have to do next.
—But you might be OK with me one of these days.
  Calling back over my shoulder.
—Then I got something to look forward to.
  She laughs.
—If you can keep alive that long, Joe.

—Come in, Simon.
  I do. I sit on the floor of Daniel's cubicle and watch him

eat. He sits cross-legged and holds a tiny bowl between his thumb and index finger. The bowl can't hold more than a generous tablespoon. As we speak he brings it to his lips, wetting them with drops of blood that he then licks away with the tip of a tongue as pale as his skin. He gestures to me with the bowl.

—Would you like some?

I look at the meager brass vessel in his hand.

—Why not, it's probably from my stash anyway.

He puts his nose close to the bowl and inhales.

—Yes, I think it is.

He offers the bowl to me.

—Please, finish it. I've had my fill.

I take the bare thimble of blood, then toss it down my throat. It's good.

—You gonna tell me why, Daniel?

He nods.

—But I would like to ask you a question first.

I run a finger through the gloss of blood left in the cup, lick it clean, and set the bowl on the floor between us.

—Shoot.

—How did it feel?

I watch the empty bowl.

—What?

—Please, Simon. Be coy with others, but not with me. That's not for us. How did it feel?

I think about starving. I think about the cramps and the burning that followed. I think about being helpless. And I think about the shimmering brightness of the world when I was at the naked edge of death.

—It felt good.

—And?

—Dangerous.

His hand spiders over his skull.

—Apt as usual. *Good and dangerous*. You have just summed up the existence of Enclave. Thank you. And your question now. Why?

—Yeah.

—Because you *are* Enclave, Simon.

—No, I'm not.

He shakes his hand in the air.

—We don't need to have this debate again. You are what you are and nothing can change that. You simply need to become aware of it.

—So you decide it's time for me to find out about myself, and you pitch that . . . whatever the fuck it was at me? That *Wraith*? Have that thing come into my place and strip my stash. I almost got killed.

—But you didn't. And tell me, if you hadn't been so close to the Vyrus, so close to your true nature, would you have survived your encounter? Would you have been strong enough to face down your enemies?

I think about the enforcer and his strength, and Horde's bullets ripping into me.

—No. But I don't think I would have been there in the first place.

—But you would have. If you had been fat and well-fed you would have fought events as they happened, and you would have died before you ever reached that room. As it was, you were forced, by what you perceived as weakness, to acquiesce to events. Until you were ready.

—That's just plain crap.

—No, it's truth.

—No such animal, Daniel.

He nods.

—That may be the greatest truth of all.

—Christ. Is there more of this?

He pinches his lower lip.

—Just a little more. Just a small promise from you.

A promise to Daniel. A promise to the man who sent something into my home to starve me. And then sent it again to watch over me. Sent it to kill Horde before Horde could kill me. A promise that will have to be kept.

—What promise?

—Just a promise to think. About your life. How you live your life.

Oh, Jesus.

—You were given the Vyrus how long ago?

—About thirty years.

—Yes. That's quite a good span for most. Many last not even a year. Most, no more than ten. Those who endure find they must dig deeper, burrow into little caves and secret places. They find they need the protection of others who will not question the manner in which they live their lives. The dark hours, the healed wounds, the strange persistence of youth. But you. To live alone, without protection, among those without the Vyrus, for thirty years. That can be seen as an accomplishment. Or a great failure. You, Simon, you are clinging to life as you think it should be led by a man. But you are not a man, not a human man. And you have not been a man for so very long. You have a true nature, all of us who receive the Vyrus have a true nature, but only Enclave see that nature. You see it, and that's why you cling to a life that cannot last, because you are frightened of it. And that's good. The Vyrus is awful. Trying to embrace it, trying to *become* it, is a terrible task. Exhausting. Painful. But to do anything else? Anything else is a lie. And you, Simon, you aren't made for lying. That's a truth.

I stand up.

—That it?

He tilts his head to watch my face.

—Yes, I suppose it is. Just that you keep your promise and think about it.

—I'll keep my promise.

—Of course you will. And what will you do now?

—Now I'm going.

I head for the door.

—You know, Simon.

—What?

—Most of us, we only touch the Vyrus at first under supervision. Even I was watched over when I took my first fast. Few manage it alone. And you did it under extreme circumstances. So I hear.

I stand at the doorway.

—And?

—That could mean something.

—What, Daniel? Can you just tell me what's on your mind and cut the crap?

He laughs.

—What's on my mind.

He wipes a single milky tear from the corner of his eye.

—What's on my mind.

Still he laughs.

—What's on my mind, is that I am failing.

He looks at me, a skeleton smile cracking his face.

—And someone will have to take my place.

And I get the fuck out of there.

Sela's place is on Third Avenue and 13th, above a deli. She buzzes me in.

—She's asleep.

—Wake her.

The apartment is a tiny one-bedroom. The front door opens directly into a living space, doors to the kitchen, bathroom and bedroom open directly off of that. The place is done up in an ultra-feminine Middle Eastern lounge kind of thing. There's lots of pillows and rugs, mandala-printed fabric hanging from the walls, and scarves draped over lamps. Sela leaves me in the living room and passes through a beaded curtain into the bedroom. I hear her talking softly and hear some mumbled replies. She comes out and waves me over.

—Don't keep her up long, she needs her sleep.

—Yeah, tomorrow's a school day.

I start for the bedroom and feel a vise clamp on my shoulder. I turn back to Sela. She takes her hand from my shoulder and puts a finger in my face.

—Whatever she was shot up with is still making her dopey. She needs her sleep.

—Yeah. Got it.

She takes her finger out of my face and I go through the curtain. The bed is a huge futon on the floor, piled with more pillows. There's a little floor space rimming the edge of the mattress, which is fine because all that's in there besides the bed is a hookah and several wicker baskets that look like they stand in for closets.

Amanda is sitting up against a mound of pillows, wearing a tattered and massive Tears for Fears T-shirt that is probably left over from Sela's more conventional youth. However long ago that might have been. She rubs her eyes.

—Hey.

I squat down next to the bed.

—Hey.

She looks around for a clock that isn't there.

—What time is it?

—After two.

—Hn.

My leg starts to throb where the bullet went in. I ease myself down and sit on the edge of the futon.

—You OK?

—Yeah. But I feel tired all the time.

—Sela taking care of you?

—Yeah, she's *fierce*. Says she's gonna show me a great workout so I can get arms like hers.

—Huh.

She scratches at her tangled hair.

—So what happened?

—What's the last thing you remember?

She leans deeper into the pillows and looks up at the ceiling, at the glow-in-the-dark stars stuck up there in a swirl.

—We were getting ready to leave the school.

—That's it?

The air conditioner in the window gurgles and hums.

—Yeah. I think so. But I had all these dreams and it's hard to. What happened?

I open my mouth. The truth sits inside it. And stays there.

—Some guys jumped us.

She sits up again.

—No *way*.

—Yeah.

—Sweet. That's *so* cool. Who were they?

—Some guys your dad had hired. They were following me.

—*No* way.

—Yeah.

—So what happened?

—You got your head bonked, went out. Concussion.

She feels her head.

—There's no bump.

—Happens that way sometimes.
—So what'd you do? Wait. There was a *total* fight. I. One of my dreams was like about a *fight*.
—Yeah.
—You kick ass?
—Not really.
—*Lame*.
—But one of the guys had a gun.
—*No. Way*.
—And I got it from him.
—Dope. That is so *dope*.
—Had to carry you out over my shoulder.

She buried her face in her hands.
—Uhhh. Was I heavy? Did I feel totally *fat*?

I watch her. She looks out from behind her hands.
—Don't be lame, kid.

She smiles.
—So what then?

Once upon a time.
—Then I figured, *fuck this shit*. Your folks want to send out dueling bounty hunters for you that's their business. But it's not mine. So fuck 'em.
—You didn't *call*?
—Fuck them.
—They don't know I'm here?
—Like I said. Fuck them.

She thrusts her arms up in the air.
—*Phat!*

She drops her arms and pushes herself deep into the pillow.
—That is just so *phat*.

I look up at the stars, and back down at her.
—So what ya gonna do?

She shakes her head.

—I. Well, I'm *so* broke. So I'm going to the bank and get some *money*. Then I want to take Sela *shopping* to say, like *thank you*. Then, *I don't know*. She said I can hang for as long as I want. But. I think I'll go home in a couple days. Like *check in* and everything. Get my folks off my *case*. Once they chill I can bail again. But I'll get some real cash together *first*. And if Sela says it's chill, I'll come hang with her some more. For like the rest of the *summer*. That would be so cool. She's *hot*. I just want to like *work out* with her all summer and get *cut* and *hard* before school starts.

—Good plan.

I stand up. She wriggles out of the pillow.

—So, you gonna be around? You hang with Sela much?

—Not really.

—OK.

She drops back into the pillows.

—Cool. What*ever*.

—Yeah.

—Hey. Can I *have* that?

I look. She's pointing at the cuff bracelet still clipped to my wrist. I pull out my wallet and get out a couple picks. Cuff locks are easy, it pops right open. I squat back down.

—Hold out your arm.

She puts it out. I hold the open cuff.

—You have to do something for me.

She nods.

—When you get home. Leave me out. Whatever goes down, don't tell your folks or whoever that I found you.

—*OK*.

—That's a promise I'm asking for.

—*OK*.

—Don't break it.

—As *if*.

—Right.

I snap the cuff onto her wrist. She looks at it.

—*Hot*.

I leave.

Sela holds the front door open for me.

—How much longer do I get to keep her?

I point at the TV.

—Put the news on tomorrow. She'll go home after she sees it.

– Why?

—Because her parents are gonna be dead.

—You have anything to do with that?

I think about killing Marilee, and missing out on killing Horde.

—Not the way I would have liked to.

Sela tosses her head, throwing roped dreads back over her shoulder.

—There gonna be trouble?

—Not for you, she loves you.

She taps one of those ruby-tipped fingers against my chest.

—What about for you?

I walk out the door.

—Sister, she doesn't even know my name.

I stop by Nino's on the way home and get a pie. Large pepperoni, hold the garlic. Then I hit the grocery for a six and a few packs of Luckys. At home I lock myself in and make sure the alarm is on. Not that any of it will keep out Predo's boys if he sends them. Not that anything could keep out Daniel's Wraith. Not that I care much right now. I go downstairs.

I sit up in bed and watch CNN. I eat the whole pie and still I'm hungry so I raid the fridge upstairs and find some leftover Chinese and eat that. That fills my belly. The other hunger, the real hunger, is still there. But it's always gonna be there, and it can wait for another day. I watch more news and drink more beer. When I run out of beer I sit in the dark staring at the TV screen, and smoke.

The story breaks around six A.M. They show some stills of the crumpled, fire-blackened Jaguar sedan. It looks as horrific as Predo promised. They wiped out the car in the early A.M.s, on a lonely stretch of road just off the 27.

The anchor fills me in on how the highway was empty at that time of night and no houses were near enough to hear the crash or see the flames. By the time emergency vehicles arrived the fire had all but burned itself out. Fortunately, the license plate broke off the vehicle in the crash and was spared from the fire. The anchor tells me the car was owned by Dr. Dale Edward Horde and that it is believed that he and his wife were in the car, driving on a late whim to their Hamptons house.

By the time I wake, the Hordes' deaths have been confirmed. So has the fact that their daughter is missing. There's some hyperventilation after that. Some circling of carrion feeders as they sniff a too-good-to-be-true story. Then a report comes in that Amanda walked into a police station and told them she had run away a week ago and had just seen the news on TV. By the time the cameras are there to watch her leaving the police station, she is flanked by a double column of body-guards and lawyers and the TV is already calling her the richest teenager in New York.

I turn off the box and smoke.

*   *   *

The package arrives that evening. It's delivered by a private courier who doesn't ask me to sign for it. I take the box down to the basement room and slide the Styrofoam case out of its cardboard sheath. Inside are several refreezable cold packs surrounding ten pints of blood. A note on top.

> *For services rendered.*
> *Payment in full.*
> D. Predo

I take out one of the pints and think about the dose Horde hit me with at the Cole, the one I thought Predo had him hit me with so they could steal my stash. Now that I know better, I figure Horde did that on his own. Maybe he was trying to kill me, maybe just get me out of the way for awhile while his boy and Predo's enforcer worked the neighborhood. Hell, maybe he just wanted to see how the Vyrus would handle it. I look at the pint and wonder what might be in it other than blood. Then I drink it. Then I drink two more. Then I stop being bothered by anything Predo might be planning, or Terry, or even Daniel. I stop worrying about whether Amanda will tell the cops about the guy who found her. I stop worrying altogether.

I don't have anything to worry about.

For now.

The easiest way for Predo to take care of me would have been to dose the blood. He didn't. He won't bother with anything else. He'll be too busy keeping an eye on the Horde situation, making sure no loose ends come unraveled in front of the press. That will be a full-time job for awhile and he won't want to clutter up his desk with any other projects. Once he empties his in-box, he'll move the teeth to the top of his priority chart. Getting those back or having them destroyed so they don't end up in Terry's hands will be front and center. Too bad for Predo that Terry already has them.

Terry got it right away. I told him what the teeth had inside, and that was all he needed. I didn't have to tell him the story or name any names. I didn't even have to mention Predo. Something like those teeth, Terry could only see one reason for those to be made, and only one Clan who could have had a hand in their making. But he'll hang onto them. For a very long time. He knows it's a one-shot deal. Figure he could try and use 'em for blackmail, but what then? Predo would never do a deal that didn't involve getting the teeth back. And what could be good enough that you'd give up the biggest stick on the block for it?

No, the only way to use the teeth is to show them to the other Clans. Do that and it will mean all-out war, the kind of war that we couldn't keep underground. The kind that would finally rip the lid off the whole thing. The kind of war Terry says he doesn't want. So he'll sit on them for a good long time. Until he's ready to go after whatever it is he really wants.

And I doubt I'll be around long enough to have to worry about that scene. Christ, I hope I'm not.

I heal. The scabs fall from my wounds and the white puckers of scar fade to smooth skin. My stomach fits itself back together and I am whole again. It takes six pints over a couple days to get me there, but I'm whole again. And ready to take care of my last loose ends.

I go out around midnight Sunday.

I make the stop at Niagara first. Billy's behind the bar.

—Joe, whaddaya know?

—Nothing worth the price.

—Good un. Drink?

—Yeah.

He hits me with a double bourbon.

I take a drink.

—Philip?

He jerks a thumb at the back room.

—Saw 'im weasel in past me while I was weeded back here.

—He ever get ya with the rest of what he owes?

—Naw.

Someone down the bar hollers at Billy's back. He flips the bird over his shoulder.

—Fuck ya, ya fucker! Shut up or I'll pound yer fuckin' head.

The guy at the end of the bar shuts up. I toss down the rest of my drink and Billy fills it again and knocks on the bar. I lift the glass to him.

—Thanks. I'll go get the rest of your money.

—Sure, Joe, but you don' gotta.

—Be a pleasure.

I walk to the back room, telling myself I'm gonna do this cool. Keep it easy. This is Billy's shift and I don't need to cause a scene. Then I see him. He's chatting to a girl. She's staring at the wall, trying to ignore him.

I try to keep it cool, but I don't.

I walk up behind him and kick his chair out from under his ass. He goes to the floor. The girl gives a little yelp. I grab the back of Philip's collar and drag him to the bathroom. I kick the door closed behind us, lift the toilet seat and shove him down on the can. His skinny ass slips all the way down into the water and his legs fly up off the floor. He tries to struggle out and I shove him in deeper.

—Want to see if I can fit you down the pipe, Phil?

—No.

—Then stay the fuck put.

—Sure, Joe. Whatever you say, Joe.

—Shut it.

I pick up half a roll of toilet paper that's sitting on the sink.

—You say a fucking word, I will stuff this ass-wipe down your throat.

He nods.

I drop the toilet paper and punch him in the face and his nose breaks.

—I told you to get Billy his money.

I punch him in the face and his jaw cracks.

—Or I was gonna fuck you up.

I punch him in the face and his cheek splits open.

—And now you're fucked up.

I grab his hair and yank his dazed face up so he can see me.

—You do as I tell you from now on, Phil. You go against me again and I will feed you to a fucking shambler. No lie, Phil. I will stick you in a tiny box with a fucking shambler and eat popcorn and watch while it eats your fucking face. Got it?

He jerks his head up and down.

—Now give me your money.

He tries to get in his pockets, but he's too fucked up. I pull him out of the can and rip his pockets open and grab the wad of bills I find inside and shove him back into the pot.

—I'm the badass down here, Phil. I'm the big bad fucking wolf and Predo is all the way up on the Upper East Side. Remember that next time you think about doing a little spying for the Coalition. You be afraid of me from now on. I ever start thinking you're not afraid enough, I'll give you a reason to be.

I walk out and drop the cash on the bar. Billy picks it up.

—Joe, this is more than he owed.

I walk to the door, my heart still pounding.

—Keep it. And there's a clog in the toilet.

She sees me when I come in, but she ignores me. She sees me sit at the bar, but she keeps working the other side. I wait. She lets it go for about twenty minutes. Then someone right next to me orders a beer and she has to come around to this side. She gives the other guy his bottle, then looks at me.

—Yeah?

—Got a beer?

She pulls one out of the ice, pops the top and puts it in front of me. I take a drink.

—Thanks.

She nods.

—Four bucks.

I dig out a five and drop it on the bar. She takes it and goes to the register and brings back a buck and puts it in front of me. Then she stands there and stares at the Sunday night band and pretends that she's listening to the blue-grass.

—Baby.

She stares at the band.

—Baby.

She turns her face to me, keeping her arms folded over her chest.

—Yeah?

—You busy after work?

She looks down into the beer bin.

—Fucking-A, Joe.

—Baby, nothing happened.

Her head snaps back up.

—Did I ask? That's not my busines. I told you, you want to fuck someone, fuck 'em. I shouldn't be surprised if you do.

—I didn't.

—I. Don't. Care.

I take a drink.

—Yeah. Right.

She puts her hands on the bar.

—Joe. I don't care.

She leans closer, not to be heard.

—I can't fuck you. I won't fuck you. So you want to fuck someone? I won't ask you not to. But.

She crosses her arms again and looks back at the band.

—But what, baby?

She doesn't look at me.

—But Tuesday night is date night and you told me you were fucking busy and you were just fucking another fucking girl, a girl with a fucking limo. Fucker!

She yanks her bar rag from her studded leather belt and throws it at me. I let it hit my face and drop to the bar, where it tents over my beer. Someone calls for some margaritas and she goes off to mix them. I pull the towel off my beer and light a smoke. She comes back a minute later and takes up her position staring at the band.

—That was work, baby. I know it sounds like crap, but that woman was the job.

She faces me again.

—And what's that, Joe? I don't even know what the job is. I don't know what keeps you out and why you get beat up and where you get money and why you have guns or what you keep locked in that little fridge. Is it drugs, Joe?

She leans in to whisper.

—Is it drugs? That's fine, you know I don't care. I just want to know. So what is it, what's the fucking job?

I twist the tip of my cigarette against the edge of the tray, lathing away the ash.

—It's hard, baby. The job is hard.

She turns back to the band.

—Great. Thanks. That's a big help.

I keep playing with my smoke.

—The job is hard. But you're harder, baby.

She keeps looking at the band.

—You're the real work.

Still looking at the band.

—And you're worth it.

She tucks a strand of red hair behind her ear.

—Give me that.

She plucks the cigarette from my hand, takes a drag.

—I changed my mind.

She holds the cigarette out to me and I take it.

—Yeah?

—Yeah. It's not OK for you to fuck other women. Or men. Or fucking anybody.

I look at the faint print of her lipstick on the smoke, and put my lips around it.

—No problem.

—And I want to go to dinner.

—No problem.

—Tonight, after work. I want a late dinner. And not diner food. I want to go to Blue Ribbon for oysters.

—No problem.

—And I want to sleep over.

—No problem.

She narrows her eyes.

—You sure you didn't fuck that bitch?

—Yeah.

—OK.

She grabs a beer from the ice and gives it to me.

—I've got to work.

—No problem.

She goes to work, taking care of all her regulars who have been patiently waiting while she fights with her boyfriend.

I drink beer and smoke and use the time until she gets off work. I use it keeping my promise to Daniel. Thinking about my life.

I think about it.

I think about what I do and how much longer I can keep it up. How much longer Predo is gonna let me hang around now that I've finally spat in his face. When Terry's gonna get tired of having me on his turf. How long it might be before Tom slips the leash and lays for me in an alley with a gang of his anarchists. I think about what Daniel said, about digging in.

I could go back to Terry, tell him I'll take my old job back. Tom would have to go. Terry'd make that happen. Kill two birds that way. But then I'd be back where I was twenty-odd years ago, the lash in my hands. And sooner or later Terry is going to get itchy about someone else knowing he has the teeth. No, I've been with the Society, and that hole's not for me.

I could go see Christian. Get my own hog. Bunk out in the Duster clubhouse. Live the Pike Street dream. They'd be happy to have me. The Dusters are always happy to have another good man in a fight. But I'd have to wear the colors, a uniform. And I'd look terrible in a top hat.

I could split the city. Go try my luck in the Outer Boroughs. Maybe find some unclaimed turf. It's out there. Red Hook. Coney Island. There could be good blocks out there. Clear off any other Rogues and start my own Clan. Make a name. Be a boss. But that's a long-odds bet, very long odds. Impossible odds. And I'm not ready to roll those bones yet.

Or I could do as Daniel says, become Enclave. Embrace my nature. Live a life of discipline. Learn how to master the Vyrus. And when the time comes, I could let it take me, and see if I survive. Daniel seems to think I might. But Daniel is crazy. And he's dying. And I'm not anybody's savior.

Amanda Horde knows that.

Besides, none of those lives has Evie in it.

The band plays "Silver Dagger" and I watch Evie open beers. Every now and then she throws me a wink or comes by and leans across the bar and whispers something funny in my ear.

I look at my life, and I find it lacking. But it's my life. I creep a little closer to the edge every day. One day the edge will crumble under my feet and I'll fall.

Fine.

Why should my life be different from anybody else's?

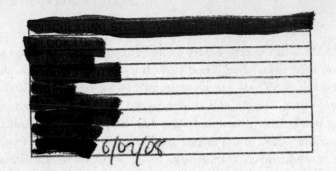

Joe Pitt returns in

NO DOMINION

by

CHARLIE HUSTON